CW00521636

Raincoats & Sunglasses

Caroline Johnston

IC3 Publishing

ISBN: 978-0-9570039-1-0

Scripture quotations [marked NIV] taken from the Holy Bible, New International Version Anglicised Copyright © 1979, 1984, 2011 Biblica
Used by permission of Hodder & Stoughton Ltd, an Hachette UK company
All rights reserved.
'NIV' is a registered trademark of Biblica UK trademark number 1448790.

For more information about Caroline Johnston, please access the author's website at:
www.carolinejohnston.co.uk

Cover design: Tanya Rochat

Published by IC3 Publishing

Dedication

To Innes, Calum, Cameron and Cara

And to my lovely creative friends – Scott Nicol and Ellyn
Oliver – thank you for the music x

KIRSTY

'Jo! Help!' I bashed out the text, squinting through stinging tears. I needed my best friend.

My life was crashing around me. As I looked at my phone, willing Jo to reply, Steven's text was all I could see: '*I don't think we should see each other anymore. It's not you, it's me.*'

Standing at a bus stop was no place to break down in tears. I hugged my raincoat closer, my sunglasses hiding the wayward tears that were spilling over. I had to try to hold it together. But as the number 44 bus approached my resolve crumbled, and the tears started in earnest.

Shuffling to a seat near the back of the bus, I huddled in against the window. I looked at my phone. Still no reply from Jo.

It was sheer relief when my phone pinged with a text a few minutes later. 'What's up?' replied Jo.

'He's dumped me.'

'What?'

'By text!'

'I'll call you.'

'No, don't! I'm on the bus,' I replied. There was no way I wanted anyone else to hear my sorry story.

'What did he say?'

'That we shouldn't see each other anymore. And it was him not me.'

'You mean he's actually taking responsibility for it?'

'No! He's willing to say anything to be rid of me.'

'Stop! Don't start with all that.'

'What else am I supposed to think?' I replied.

I knew Steven was blaming me, despite his clichéd words. He was blaming me for this breakup, just like he blamed me for anything that went wrong; from being late for appointments, regardless of why we were late, to a restaurant not being up to his standard, to the movie having a predictable ending. But now he was trying to make out he was the good guy by taking the blame. Of course he was blaming me.

The ping of my phone alerted me to another text from Jo, 'I need to get ready for my first class. I'll text Lynn and Carol. We'll be round at yours at 7 with ice-cream.'

'Thanks.'

'Don't cry over him. He's a loser.' The directness of Jo's message almost made me laugh. A breakup was bad enough, but on a Monday morning it was brutal. A few texts with Jo would need to suffice until I saw my friends tonight.

'Hugs. And stop crying.'

'Thanks. See you tonight.'

As the bus made its ways towards Glasgow city centre I went through a myriad of emotions: shock; anger; fear; despair. And tears. Countless tears.

Texting Jo had been helpful, but I still couldn't face work. Coffee was required.

The automatic doors of Chocolate & Vanilla welcomed me inside. The warmth of the café, the aroma of the coffee, the familiar setting, all worked their magic at easing my distress.

"How can I assist you this morning?" asked the smiling barista. I was grateful for the sunglasses that hid my red, puffy eyes from this naively happy woman.

"A latte and a croissant, to sit in, please."

To the side of the counter an expansive area of tables and chairs welcome the eat-and-go customers. The first few times I came here I sat at one of those tables. That was before I discovered the haven of comfort and tranquillity that awaited the inquisitive on the mezzanine level. Wander past the functional seating and an almost hidden staircase guided you to an upstairs oasis; a sanctuary of armchairs and settees, cushions and candles, occasion tables and lamps. This made Chocolate & Vanilla my favourite city centre coffee shop, that and the coffee of course.

This morning I had the mezzanine level to myself. After all, who took time on a Monday morning to come to a coffee shop? I made my way to the furthest corner, if anyone came up here I wanted to remain alone, unseen.

The large wing backed armchair provided a safe, isolated spot to enjoy my latte and croissant. I looked at the text message again. Why did I keep looking at it? It wasn't like the text was going to change; looking at it only brought more tears. And now crying-induced hiccups were accompanying the tears. The hiccups would come at random moments and ripple through my body. As I raised the mug to my mouth, a hiccup sent shock waves down through my arm, causing me to mistime my drink and spill the coffee down my front. As the hot coffee spilled down my top, fresh, warm tears ran down my cheeks. Could nothing go right?

Feeling no better, I wrapped myself in my raincoat, thankful it hid the coffee stain. My sunglasses did their part too by concealing my tear-stained eyes.

But raincoats and sunglasses can only hide so much.

Kirsty

The council offices were of the nondescript 1960s concrete design, which seemed to have been commissioned in abundance by councils throughout Scotland. And, like many of their counterparts, were full of leaks, draughty windows and heaters that produced either no heat or far too much heat. The grey exterior matched my mood as I entered the building and walked up the stairs to the third floor, a feeling of dread accompanying each step.

"Where have you been?" said Irene, pouncing on me as soon as I arrived in the department. "There's a meeting going on right now and Gary wants you there. I told him you were always in early, but of course you would come in late today."

I should have made a retort about the flexi system but experience has taught me there is no point in saying anything back to Irene. She has a talent for turning things around to fit her side of the argument, always leaving you the one in the wrong.

My hopes of a quiet, easy day in the office disintegrated.

I don't mind my job, an assistant in the Culture section. As council jobs go it's fairly interesting and varied. My problems with work all centre on Irene, my line manager. She is the bane of my work life. Nothing is ever good enough, she always finds fault with my work. I work harder than a lot of the other admin staff, but she constantly picks on me.

"Come on, stop dawdling! Put your things over at your desk and get your notebook, Gary wants you in the meeting now."

I was exhausted. This brief encounter with Irene had drained my final reserves of energy. How was I supposed to deal with this meeting? A coffee stained top, red puffy eyes, mascara streaks – not the look you wanted when you were called into a meeting. And it wasn't just any meeting, Gary was there too. Gary of the designer suits, perfect hair and intoxicating aftershave. Why on earth would he want me in the meeting? And why did it need to be today of all days?

As I entered the meeting room, everyone looked up and watched me walk to the empty seat at the end of the conference table. I did my best to hide the evidence of my traumatic morning. The notepad, hugged tight against me, hid the coffee stain and, with a tilt of my head, my long hair hid my tear damaged face.

"Thanks for joining us Kirsty," said Gary.

Gary's been the head of department for about six months now. All the girls in the department have been infatuated with him from the moment he walked into our section. In an environment where the juiciest hint of scandal is like gold dust, rumours breed rumours. Whispered tales of womanising within both the office and Glasgow society follow him like shadows. Whatever his story might be, he really isn't the kind of guy you want to be sitting next to with a coffee-stained top and pale face.

The low lighting in the room worked to my advantage. The glances that had come my way as I walked into the room quickly returned to the brightness of the PowerPoint presentation and Gary. I struggled to keep my attention on the presentation, my mind kept wandering to the text. I didn't even notice the presentation had finished until the lights blinked on and Gary was saying, "Kirsty, now we come to the reason I asked you along this morning." All eyes were on me again.

"Laura, my PA, has had to stop early for her maternity leave due to various health issues. A temp will cover her day to day work. However, I need a permanent member of staff to pick up Laura's work on the rebranding launch event."

I had to get my head into work mode and focus on what Gary was telling me. Was he saying he wanted me on this rebranding event? The power of Steven's text began to fade as I turned my attention to this new work challenge.

"Irene, I want you to make this happen. Kirsty's main priority is the event preparation, you can divide her regular duties amongst the rest of the team if she doesn't have time for them."

"Of course," said Irene, "I'll make sure of it." Though her words agreed with Gary, her tone was brittle. I was excited at being chosen to work on the launch event, and to work with Gary, it's never a bad career move to work with management. But I would need to be careful around Irene.

"Great, thanks Irene, I knew I could count on you." Was Gary oblivious to the tension or was this his way of playing the game?

The office gossip suggested major issues and power plays between Gary and Irene; that Irene had applied for the position of department head, but management said no, and brought in Gary. He had a lot less experience than Irene, but a lot more vision. His lack of experience was an affront to 'old school' Irene, but only she would deny that Gary had a lot more drive for the position. The gossip also talked of Gary's fast track career and this posting as a step further up the ladder.

Management had brought Gary in to rejuvenate the section. They expected the Culture department to be the showcase for the council, a prerequisite that had been missing for years. On his first day in the job he told us of his plans to rebrand the department. The rebranding would be unveiled at this launch event.

"Kirsty, if you could wait behind I'll instruct you more fully on what I require and let you know what you need to work on first."

As everyone else left the meeting Gary came over and sat beside me. He opened Laura's folder and explained the work completed to date. Laura's to do list was now my top priority. As he talked, my mind wandered off again. Thoughts of Steven and his text filled my mind, but I had to push them away. Gary was talking, and I was sure it was important.

As he closed the folder, Gary said, "Are you okay, Kirsty?" Before I could reply he continued, "I suppose that's a silly question, because clearly something is upsetting you. Do you need to talk about it, can I help you with anything?" On a morning where words had bruised and cut, his words touched my wounds like a healing balm.

I was speechless at his attentiveness. The intensity of his gaze confused me. I looked away, trying to compose myself and make sense of what was happening. "It's okay, just some personal issues that came up this morning. I won't let it get in the way of my work." I darted from the meeting room before Gary had the opportunity to say anything else. The tears once again threatening.

I hadn't expected such kindness from Gary. Maybe the gossip had him all wrong. Maybe he was a nice guy after all!

KIRSTY

The office toilets were as bland and faulty as the rest of the building. Off-white tiled walls, and grubby grey cubicle doors didn't help the look of the place. At any given time one of the cubicles would be out of use, either due to leaking pipes, or some broken part or another. A constant draught from a faulty window lowered the temperature by a few degrees. The complaint emails to the buildings office never resulted in repairs. I'm convinced management are happy to keep it that way to ensure as little time as possible is wasted on toilet breaks.

Worn out by all the drama and excitement of the morning, I shivered as I entered the toilets. Walking over to the mirror, I checked the facial damage. The reflection from the cheap, hazy mirror confirmed my worst fears – a blotchy face, red-rimmed eyes and mascara stains. "And you've sat through a management meeting looking like this?" I said to the reflection that stared back at me. This day couldn't get any worse. I put my emergency supply of facial wipes, tinted moisturiser and mascara to good use. The reflection still presented signs of tears and upset, but it was a marked improvement.

With the emergency repairs completed, I spent the rest of the morning at my desk, head down and getting up to speed on Laura's comprehensive notes. Laura was a methodical, organised person, I would need to work hard to keep up with this level of professionalism.

By the time midday arrived, I was desperate to escape the confines of the stuffy office. First stop, a new top; it was time to ditch the stain and the non-stop smell of coffee that had been tormenting my nose all morning.

With my new work responsibilities, and to help get over my break-up, I decided to treat myself further and book a hair appointment.

My friend, Jennifer, has been raving about some guy at ByDesign. ByDesign is one of those trendy, city centre hair salons that as a general rule I shy away from. But if Jennifer recommended it, it must be good.

However, as soon as I walked through the door, I knew I had made a mistake. The place was top salon vibe. Protectively I put my hand up to my hair, already feeling sorry for it, it must have looked so lack lustre and limp compared to all the beautiful hair on display around me. The raincoat that hid me in the commuting crowds, now made me stand out like a sore thumb. Designer chic surrounded me, from the footwear to the hairstyles.

Even the receptionist intimidated me. At five foot nine, I'm used to towering over most Scottish women, but the receptionist stood eye to eye with me. Added to that, the extra height of her hair, and I felt uncharacteristically small.

And then there was the makeup. The perfect eye-liner, the fake lashes, the sculpted brows, the dark tan skin tone. It all spoke of hours in front of the mirror, or the beautician's chair. At my regular hairdresser, the receptionist wore jeans and t-shirt and doubled as a junior, but this girl wore a branded ByDesign tunic and designer skinny black jeans.

"Welcome to ByDesign, how can I help you today?" said the receptionist, her monotone voice and raised eyebrow at odds with her greeting. I suspected she really wanted to say, "*Who are you? Do you realise you're in the wrong salon?*"

"Hi, I'd like to make an appointment for a cut and style on Saturday, please."

"Have you been here before?" Again I suspected these were not the words the receptionist wanted to say. She'd probably rather go with something along the lines of, "*Clearly you've never been here before, and we'd like to discourage you from coming back.*"

"No, one of my friends recommended your salon and one of your senior stylists. I'm sorry I can't remember his name."

The receptionist let out a sigh of disdain and said, "We have two senior stylists Paul and Si. What's your friend's name and I can check her file to see who styles her hair."

"Her name is Jennifer Thompson." I forced the words out, trying my hardest to sound coherent.

I looked around the salon as the receptionist turned her attention to her computer. The salon was full of beautiful people in a beautiful setting. Subtle lighting highlighted glossy surfaces. The black and white colour scheme oozed elegance. Everything displayed the ByDesign brand; from the coffee cups, to the stylists' uniforms, to the towels and even a large branded tile in the middle of the floor between the workstations. The sinks were in an alcove at the rear of the salon and workstations took up all the wall space from the sinks to the oval reception desk. It was a world away from my regular hairdressers.

Perhaps this wasn't the right setting to help me feel better about myself. Should I sneak out the door? The receptionist continued to look at her computer; I wasn't sure if she was still serving me or had returned to some social media site.

"Yes. Jennifer Thompson. She's one of Paul's clients. Let me see. You're in luck. We've just had a cancellation that has freed up his 4:30 slot on Saturday. Typically, you need to book weeks in advance for a Saturday appointment with Paul. Would you like me to book you in for a consultation with Paul at 4:30 on Saturday afternoon?"

"Yes, please."

As she entered my details into the computer booking system, she flashed red manicured nails, with diamanté decals on the ring finger nails. I slid my nail-bitten hands into my raincoat pockets.

If I felt this out of place just booking an appointment, how would I cope getting my actual haircut? And what had I booked? Was a consultation a haircut or a discussion about what the stylist would do at my next visit? Did Jennifer really come here? Although Jennifer is pretty cool, so chances are she would fit right in.

In one fluid movement the receptionist handed me an appointment card and turned her back on me. Our interaction over.

I almost ran back to the safety of my desk and immersed myself in the routine of work. My emotions were too raw to deal with anything else today.

JENNIFER

Today is one of those days where experience pays off. Seven years ago it was a very different story. Back then I had no sunglasses or tissues, instead I had tear-streaked cheeks and a runny nose. A few years later I fared slightly better and remembered tissues. But today I nailed it! The sunglasses are on and packs of tissues fill my raincoat pockets. Emotions I'm ready for you!

"Mum! Hurry up! I want to get to school!"

I laughed at Chloe's exuberance. "Just one more photograph then I promise we'll go."

"Mum, you've taken plenty let's go," said Emma, more patience in her voice than Chloe would ever be able to achieve.

As I checked the latest photo on my phone, I noticed the time and realised we were pushing it to get to school on time.

Chloe, full of excitement for her new adventure, darted out the door. She had been counting down the days till she would be a schoolgirl. Desperate to stamp her independence on this brave new world. Quite the contrast to my emotions.

Since my oldest daughter, Amy, came along I'd probably cried at least once a day: whether welling up at an emotional ad on TV, or a distressing image on the news, or over some parenting issue. However, today was set to be a new record in tear volume.

We made it to school as the bell rang, I really had to deal with my awful time keeping. Emma ran off to line up with her class while Chloe and I joined the primary one children and parents.

Chloe sat down at her allotted seat, grabbed some crayons from the middle of the table and began colouring in the picture in front of her. With barely a glance she threw me a "bye mum" and I was dismissed. No longer needed, I left my girls to their schooling.

As I left the infant playground, the tears that had been threatening came full flow.

"I see those tears, Jennifer," said Sarah, with almost a touch of mocking in her voice.

Oops! I had forgotten I'd invited Sarah over for coffee this morning. Now I was glad of those extra minutes I'd spent tidying up the kitchen before we left.

"No tears to see here. I've got the extra-large sunglasses on this morning to hide them."

"I'm only kidding," said Sarah. "I can't see the tears, but I know they're there. You can't fool me."

Why had I invited Sarah over for a cuppa this morning? Out of all my mum friends, she was the most opinionated and the one I had least in common with.

But as I looked around the playground I remembered why Sarah was the clear winner in the coffee invitation. With each passing year less and less of my friends did the school run. As children got older, they wanted the independence of walking to school on their own, freeing their mums to extend their working hours. A child starting primary one offered the possibility of new mum-friendships, but for the time being they were no more than acquaintances to be nurtured.

"I for one am a happy mum this morning," said Sarah, as we walked back to my house. "Great to have the child care taken care of again."

"Is Kevin excited about going into primary four?"

"I've no idea. He doesn't tell me anything."

"Don't you think the summer holidays flew by?" I asked, hoping this new topic would lead to a better conversation.

"Nope. It's the longest six weeks of my year."

My hopes of a more positive conversation disintegrated.

"Well, Jennifer. What are you going to do with yourself now your girls are all at school?"

"To be honest, I don't know. I've been so focussed on Chloe and getting her ready for school I haven't thought about what I'm going to do."

I love being a mum. The pre-school years had been full of activities: gymnastics; toddler groups; painting; story telling; swimming and of course mother and toddler lunch/coffee meet ups. Like most mums I had moments when I longed for the freedom of being child free for a few hours. However, even that was tinged with doubt that maybe I shouldn't be wishing my life away. I loved the parenting input of those pre-school years.

Sarah, on the other hand, never said anything positive about parenthood. We had met shortly after Emma was born, attending the same baby massage class, and for some reason Sarah had attached herself to me. As Emma and Kevin got older a friendship developed between the two children which cemented our connection.

"Your house is far too spotless, Jennifer," said Sarah, as she looked around the kitchen. "Is this how you spend all your free time – housework? You've no reason to stay at home now, it's time to get out there and claim your life back." Every so often Sarah lectures me on the need to be independent and establish my career. My response today was to ignore her and take another sip of tea.

"If you won't respond to me on that. Then let me ask you what you're doing today? I'm going into the city centre for a lovely lunch and to spoil myself with some expensive shopping. Come with me."

"Thanks, but I'm not sure I'd be much company today, wondering how Chloe is getting on at school."

"Are you crazy? Chloe's fine, you know she is, she'll take to school like a duck to water. You need a day out, come with me."

Sarah was right, I didn't need to worry about Chloe. And perhaps spending a few hours in Glasgow would be the perfect way to start the new school year. "Do you know what? You're right! Lunch and shopping sounds like a great way to fill my day."

"That's more like it," said Sarah.

JENNIFER

By the time I collected the girls from school I couldn't wait to hear the news from each of them. Chloe was full of news and excitement at her first day at school: "Mrs Simpson let us colour in snakes," "Mrs Simpson said we were all very well behaved for our first day of school," "Mrs Simpson took us down to the lunch hall and sat with us," "Mrs Simpson wore a beautiful dress," "Mrs Simpson is my favourite teacher." I smiled to myself as Chloe continued to gush out a bunch of sentences about the wonderful Mrs Simpson and how much she was going to enjoy school.

"And how was your first day, Emma?"

"It was good." Emma is the quiet child of the family. If you want information from Emma, you need to ask a lot of questions.

"How was your new teacher?"

"Good. She had to shout at some of the boys, but she was okay."

"Have you got any homework?"

"Not this week, we'll start next week."

"That's not fair," shouted Chloe. "How come I need to do homework and Emma doesn't?"

"Emma had homework on her first day of school too, Chloe. Let me guess. You need to colour in Sammy Snake and write the letter 's'?"

"How did you know?" asked Chloe, in awe I had guessed her homework.

"Because that's the same homework Emma had in primary one, and Amy too."

Amy arrived at the house a few minutes after us. "How was your first day?" I asked her.

"This year is going to be amazing. Now we're top of the school we get extra responsibility and privileges. And we'll soon be learning all about the transition to high school, and then there'll be the leavers dance to look forward to."

"Slow down, Amy. There's a year of learning in amongst all that too."

"Well, of course there is mother. But it's going to be amazing." I smiled at the sudden expansion of Amy's vocabulary. Why are children always in a rush to grow up?

"Have you got any homework?" I asked Amy.

"No, we'll be starting homework next week. Can I go round to Olivia's house?"

"Yes, that's fine. Be back home for six."

With Amy at Olivia's house, Chloe sat and coloured in her snake picture and Emma sat and cuddled in with me. Each of my girls is unique and I love the differences between them. Every day as a mum offers unexpected gems.

"So, how was your first day?" asked Scott, bringing me a mug of tea as we settled down together on the settee.

"All good. The girls were all happy, no school issues for today. Although, I wish you'd come home earlier to see them before bedtime. First day back is a big deal, especially when it was Chloe's first day."

"I got caught up in some client files and lost track of time. I'll catch up with the girls tomorrow."

Scott's reply contained no hint of apology. But I was in no mood to press the point further.

We turned our attention to our latest choice of box set. As the episode progressed, I snuggled into Scott. "Do you ever think back to our university days?"

"Sometimes."

"Like the day you got your motorbike?" I asked. Scott smiled and kissed my forehead.

The day Scott turned up at the Chaplaincy centre with his new bike was the day we started dating. From my first time at the university Christian Union, I had noticed Scott. You couldn't help but notice him. He was the Christian Union president, but whether or not he had been president, every girl there could have told you who Scott Thompson was. As well as being involved with the Christian Union he was also part of the university swim team and had the fabulous build of a champion swimmer. Added to that was the fact he was one of the best looking and friendliest guys around. At that time Scott was dating a girl in his accountancy class. By the time he split up with her, it was my turn to be in a relationship, and so the pattern had continued for the next year.

Then one day Scott had ridden up to the chaplaincy centre on his new bike. The centre was the hangout spot for those attending the various religious groupings at the university. The students lounging around in the common room had seen, and heard, Scott arriving on his new bike. All the guys rushed out to see it, ogling over the machinery in front of them. I wandered out to see what all the fuss was about. As I strolled round the bike Scott asked if I wanted to go for a ride with him. I did.

On that beautiful late spring evening, we drove along Great Western Road, past Clydebank and out to Loch Lomond. I loved it; the exhilaration of the speed, the scenery, and being close enough to Scott that barely a breath of wind could pass between us. It felt like a romantic scene from some American movie. We stopped for ice-cream at the side of the loch and as we finished our ice-creams, Scott put his arms around me and kissed me. The passion and the promise of that kiss had never diminished.

"Don't you miss those days?" I asked.

"I do. It was fun being a student and living a carefree life. But now we're boring responsible parents with a seven seater car instead of a motorbike."

"Don't!" I said, laughing at his goofy expression, but the dread of those words sent a shiver through me. Scott had no sentiment for what had been. I wasn't sure that he realised how much of a struggle my day had been, perhaps some emotions only touch mums.

The memory of the motorbike was wonderful, but as I looked to the days and weeks stretching out ahead there was only uncertainty. Racing along winding country roads on the back of a motorbike was a carefree life; housework and parenting just couldn't compete.

PAUL

"Mick? It's Paul. I'm stuck in traffic. I'll be another ten minutes."

"Don't worry about it. I'm the only one here. Everyone else must be stuck in traffic too."

I hate being late. At least everyone else was late too, but that didn't make me feel much better. Truth be told, I didn't even want to be working the photoshoot today. I used to get a buzz from these assignments; but the thrill of them has gone.

The taxi continued its slow trudge onwards. A journey that should have only taken ten minutes was already half an hour long, and I still hadn't arrived at the warehouse. The only person benefitting from this was the taxi driver.

I looked out the window, trying to distract myself from the growing frustration. Normally I loved the hubbub of the city and the chance to engage in some people watching, but even that was annoying me. We passed a steady parade of office workers making their way to their city centre cubicles. So many women were wearing raincoats and sunglasses. Was this some unofficial uniform that female commuters signed up to if they worked in the city centre? It showed a lack of imagination: Raincoats, mostly beige and tied at the waist; Sunglasses, big, black frames hiding the beauty that lay beneath. Where was the colour?

Finally, we arrived. The photoshoot was taking place in an old warehouse a few miles outside of the city centre. It was a quiet area of the city, so I didn't anticipate too many disruptions or problems once it all got started.

I paid the taxi driver, grateful I had gotten a quiet driver, rather than the ones who complained about the weather, the government or their lot in life. Lugging the cases of hairstyling equipment into the warehouse I saw Mick. "Mick! Thanks for the gig," I said, as I shook hands with him.

"Good to have you working with us again."

"Where will I set up?"

"Over there by that pillar. We've got the generator there for all your power needs."

"Great. What time are the models getting here?" I asked, as I looked around the warehouse.

"Who knows, they should have been here by now, but I've not heard anything from them. Grab yourself a coffee and make yourself at home."

All that pent up frustration for nothing. I shouldn't have let the slow journey get to me. I liked being punctual, but it wasn't like me to get this frustrated.

I set up my workstation with a few basics, plugging in the straighteners and arranging the various styling brushes. The rest of the gear remained in my well-organised cases. I sat down with my coffee and flicked through the call sheet and mood board for the day. It all looked straightforward. Although the irony of it was not lost on me. The photoshoot was for a feature on raincoats and sunglasses.

Eventually the models and makeup artist arrived. I hadn't worked with these women before. Not only was it the first time I'd worked with them, but it was also the first time I'd worked with Dutch models.

Anya was first up for her hairstyle. In my experience the models would either be aloof and keep to themselves, or flirt like mad the whole time. I'd even had the key exchange from some models in the past, or at least the modern equivalent of mobile number and hotel room details. Anya made it crystal clear which camp she was in.

"I'm only in your city for a couple of nights. I did not get the chance to see anything last night as we had to be prepared for the shoot today. But maybe tonight you could show me around?"

"Sorry, can't make it tonight. I already have plans."

"I'm sure you do. But how often do you get to show a Dutch model round your city?"

"Now that is true, but I can't break promises I've already made to other people."

"Maybe the photos will finish early and we can go for a drink."

I acknowledged her comment with a smile, confident that such a situation wouldn't present itself. Photoshoots always run over, and considering the late start for this one, I was certain it would be late finishing. For once that suited me perfectly.

"Mick! That's Anya ready for you." I watch in relief as she walked over to Mick. I turned my attention toward Saskia, hoping it wouldn't be a repeat performance.

Saskia was more beautiful, and quieter, than her counterpart. She exuded confidence; not in a haughty way, but in self-assurance. She was a joy to work with and it didn't take long to have her hair styled for the first of her shots.

Everything was going well, Anya and Saskia worked hard and the weather conditions were favourable for the outside and inside shots. I had to admit the models made raincoats and sunglasses look classy as they paraded up and down the warehouse in their high heels and confident display. The only problem with racing through the shot list was Anya. If we finished early, she would expect me to take her out for a drink. How ironic that I was trying to dodge a date with a tall beautiful model. I smiled to myself; if someone had told me about this six months ago, I wouldn't have believed them.

"We will finish early. Don't you think?" said Anya, the next time she came over for her hairstyling. "Then you can show me all the sights Glasgow has to offer." There was more than just a hint of suggestion in her comment.

"Anya, it's not going to happen. I'm not going to take you out tonight. I've got plans and I'm not breaking them for you."

A weird screeching noise ensued as she proceeded to cry and try the emotional pull on me. Everyone looked over at us. The makeup artist came scurrying over to fix whatever damage Anya's tears would have on her makeup.

"Forget it, it's not going to work with me," I said, walking away from the screeching Anya in search of Mick. I had to do some damage limitation here and make sure Mick got my side before I was struck off the list of photoshoot hairstylists. I might not be loving today's shoot, but I needed to keep my options open. Photoshoot hairstylist always looked good for my portfolio.

As I made my way over to Mick, I noticed Saskia getting up from her seat, ready for her next shot. She didn't look too good, even through all the makeup she looked pale. I stopped walking towards Mick and turned to Saskia, but before I reached her, she collapsed in a heap, all arms and legs.

What had just happened? Between Anya throwing a public meltdown and Saskia quietly fainting, it all felt too surreal. Too much drama for one day. The tantrum throwing Anya was ignored as everyone rushed over to see what had happened to Saskia.

"Let's get her an ambulance," shouted Mick. His assistant grabbed her mobile and called 999. As the first person to get to Saskia, I lifted her head onto my lap. The rest of the crew crowded round wondering what to do next. Anya came crying over. "Saskia, Saskia, can you hear me?"

"Anya, she'll be fine," I said. I had no idea if what I said was true, but the phony concern of Anya grated. Everything about her seemed fake.

Saskia came back round and looked dazed as she tried to focus on my face. "Hey there, how you feeling?" I asked. Saskia tried to sit up, but I put my hand on her shoulder to keep her from moving. "You lie still, we've called for an ambulance. It'll be here soon and we'll get you checked out at the hospital."

"No, no, there's no need, I'll be fine. I only fainted."

"You fainted at our shoot," said Mick. "You're getting checked out at the hospital. I'm not taking any chances, so no arguments, this is my call."

"You want me to go with her?" I asked. I knew Mick would assign an assistant to help, but with Anya lurking around it was worth a try.

"It's okay, thanks Paul," said Mick. "I'll get Carol to go with her. But, as Anya is ready for her next set, can you stay with Saskia till the ambulance comes?" I nodded my agreement.

"Right everyone let's get back to the shoot," Mick shouted out to the crew.

In the end Saskia didn't need to go to the hospital. The paramedics arrived before the ambulance. They completed several checks on her and told her she needed to get back to her hotel and drink plenty of water and rest.

"How are you feeling now?" I asked.

"Okay. A bit light headed and tired. I'm so tired. I need to sleep."

"It shouldn't be too much longer until the taxi is here to take you back to your hotel," I said, handing her another bottle of water. "And here's my card. Call me later and let me know you're okay, I've written my mobile number on the back."

"Thanks, you're very kind."

I looked over to see what Anya was up to. She was getting her makeup touched up, ready for the last few shots. "Do you always work with Anya?"

"I've only worked with her once or twice before, and that's been on shoots including other models. We're with the same agency, but it depends on the job who gets sent out."

"She's very intense."

"She's young and insecure."

"She doesn't come across as insecure."

"I've seen it many times with the new models. They have grown up with adoring families and friends telling them how beautiful they are, how special they are. Then those beautiful girls come and work in a modelling agency, and, suddenly, they are no longer special, just average in a catalogue of beautiful people. It can be hard for many of them to adjust. People learn to use their insecurity as a positive or a negative. Anya covers her's by going over the top, trying to prove that she's still the centre of attention. But that turns people away. She hasn't learned this yet."

I smiled at Saskia. It would be so easy to ask her out on a date. A beautiful woman, only in town for one night, no follow up expectation. The attraction was there, but my resolution stayed intact. I needed to break the serial dating habit.

"Hope you feel better soon," I said, as Carol informed her the taxi had arrived. I stood up and walked back to my workstation. I should get a medal for showing this level of fortitude.

KIRSTY

"Move over," said Jo, as she squished in beside me on the armchair. Surrounded by my three best friends my day finally improved. Friends aren't only a blessing, they are a singleton's lifeline.

When I moved to Glasgow for college one of the first things I wanted to do was connect into a church. I had seen a poster for ChurchX on one of the notice boards at college and decided to try it out. It was much bigger than my home church, just like everything else about Glasgow. But with the size came lots of opportunities and similar aged people to create an exciting new life in the big city.

We connected through various student focussed activities organised by the church. Lynn and Carol grew up in the Glasgow area, but Jo had moved to Glasgow from a village in the Borders. I guess the shared experience of transitioning from small to large brought me and Jo even closer together; kindred spirits in the city.

"So let's see this text that idiot sent you," said Jo.

As my phone passed round the group, the expected comments ensued: "Steven's such an idiot." "Better you know now and move on." "We all said you were too good for him."

"You guys are the best!" I smiled, taking a big spoonful of ice-cream.

"All bias aside, you are too good for Steven, and the guy is an idiot if he can't see it," said Jo. "You need to stop selling yourself short with guys. You keep setting your sights too low and you always end up with these types of muppets." Jo would always tell it as she saw it. It had taken me a bit of time to get used to her directness, but when she had your back, you had a warrior friend.

"The guy is a loser. And he proved it by this text," said Lynn. "Why cry over someone like that?"

"You're right. But it still hurts." I had been determined not to cry tonight; but reliving the text with my friends brought on the tears.

"Stop crying over this guy, Kirsty. He's not worth it." Jo's tone was verging on scolding, but as she passed me a tissue and hugged me I knew her frustration was focussed on Steven.

"I don't know if I'm crying for him, or at the loss of yet another relationship. We were out on Saturday night to celebrate our six-month anniversary, and we even talked about marriage."

"Oh no!" said Lynn. "I suspect we may be getting to the root of the problem. Kirsty, did you bring up the M-word or did he?"

"I can't remember. Me, I think."

"Kirsty! You can't do that. It scares them off," said Jo. "Six months is too soon for that kind of conversation."

"I'm so pathetic," I said, sobbing into the tissue.

"No you're not," said Jo.

"I think you should wait until you find a decent guy who wants to be with you," said Carol. "Don't go straight into another relationship. Give yourself some time. And maybe, give the guy time too?"

"And what is the definition of 'decent guy'? They always seem decent when I start going out with them."

"You need our help!" said Jo. "We'll be your wing women and keep you protected. Before you can say 'yes' to any guy, we need to meet him. We'll be the ones to pass judgement over whether he's good enough for you!"

The room filled with laughter. Doubtless we were all imagining all kinds of strange vetting scenarios. By the time I reached the bottom of the smooth, creamy chocolate chip ice-cream, my mood had brightened.

"One good thing did happen today," I said.

"Do tell," said Jo.

"It's only temporary, but I've been assigned to organise the brand launch night for the department. The department PA, Laura, has done most of the work, but she's off on sick leave then maternity leave. So, I'll be running with it from now till the launch."

"That's exciting," said Carol. "It'll be a great distraction to get over Steven."

"Although I keep waiting for Gary to change his mind. You should have seen the mess of me this morning at the meeting. My face all blotchy from crying, and, my top had a big coffee stain down the front. I was such a mess."

"And in front of gorgeous Gary too," teased Lynn.

"Now, now," said Jo. "We'll not tease her about any men tonight. Our Kirsty is too raw for that. We'll give her a few more days before the Gary teasing starts."

"Ignore them, Kirsty. I think it's great you've got a break at work and sounds like it could be a fun project for you." Carol's the quietest of the group, but she has the gift of saying the right thing at the right time.

"The important thing for tomorrow is to avoid all disasters, Kirsty. And show the gorgeous Gary that you're the right person for the job."

"Lynn! I knew it was a mistake to tell you about Gary. Honestly!"

"It's not Gary we need to be worried about here," said Jo. "The main issue is Kirsty getting through a day with no disasters." Lynn and Carol laughed along with Jo, my penchant for oops moments is always a source of hilarity within the group.

"Enough about me. Did anything exciting happen with any of you today?"

"Our lives are all very quiet and dull compared to yours," said Lynn. "It's why we all love being your friend; it brings us the drama we crave."

"I know. Let's have a night out!" said Jo. "A farewell to Steven, and hello to new possibilities. Let's go out on Saturday night, there's a new restaurant in Merchant City. What time suits everyone?"

"That sounds great, especially as I've booked a hair appointment for Saturday afternoon, I should be done by 5:30. I'm trying out Jennifer's guy at ByDesign."

"I've heard it's fab there," said Carol.

"Good for you," said Jo. "A new hairstyle is perfect for the new, confident, no more losers, Kirsty!"

PAUL

For some people the daily commute is a hassle. Personally, I enjoy my journey to work. There's something about a bus journey I like, even when it's the same route every day. It's a time to sit back, relax and enjoy the scenes that pass by. A buffer zone between work and home: in the morning a time to set my mind to work mode; in the evening time to put work behind me.

As I looked out the window, I noted the array of city workers in raincoats and sunglasses. Funny how, once you notice something, you see it everywhere. Anya and Saskia had transformed the dowdy work uniform into something chic. However, in a sea of commuters it still looked bland.

Walking into ByDesign I was greeted by the smell of hair products and the sight of juniors scurrying around preparing workstations for the day. Until a few months ago I had loved working here, but now I was restless, the job was no longer enough. The restlessness annoyed me. It implied I was ungrateful for my job, one that many hairstylists could only dream of. I wasn't someone who lived by a grand plan for my life, more vague goals, perhaps being a salon manager one day. But now even that didn't seem so alluring.

I hadn't even reached my workstation before Si was on my case. Si is the salon manager. He marched into the salon two years ago, more concerned with spreadsheets and results than his staff. I welcomed him to the salon, as I would have with anyone, but Si made it clear right from the start he wasn't there to make friends: he was on a mission.

Within a few weeks of him being there, we all felt the impact of his management. Everyone came under his scrutiny, getting pulled up if they spent too long on an appointment, if they wasted any products, if they didn't have enough repeat clients, if they didn't have enough new clients. Management had congratulated him on his quick results and promised him a USA posting if he achieved further improvements. Ever since then he had become even more obnoxious. He ordered everyone about, treating all the staff as if they were so far below him he couldn't even see them. The salon became a ticking time bomb, and if Si pressurised things much more the whole thing would blow up in our faces.

"I heard you were causing problems at yesterday's photoshoot," said Si.

"What did you hear?"

"That you distracted the models."

I walked away from him. Si intimidated many of the younger stylists, but I had no respect for someone who treated people the way Si did. While others would take his cutting words personally, I let the words slide away, refusing to give them even a moment's thought.

However, something had Si rattled this morning, and he didn't let me walk away from the conversation. He followed me over to my workstation. "I've told Mick I'll be the one doing the next photoshoot."

"It's not your call to make. It's up to the client."

"Do you think they'll want you back after causing problems with the models? I don't know who you think you are, but the models are far more important than you when it comes to photoshoots, you're just the hairstylist."

"And the role has the same status whether it's you or me at the shoot." My words must have hit the mark. He walked away. As much as Si would like to be on my case a lot more, he won't push me too far. All his number crunching tells him I'm the busiest of the stylists. He needs me here. Si might know numbers, but I know hair.

JENNIFER

"There will be no self-pity today!" I announced as I entered the house after taking the girls to school. The last two days had contained too many tears, and I knew the threat of all those emotions was still lurking. A focussed project would sort me out.

Chloe had been talking all summer about wanting to have her bedroom decorated. She wanted a 'big girl' room, as opposed to the 'little girl' look she declared she currently had. Today seemed like a good day to get started on it. I popped out to the local DIY warehouse and purchased all the supplies I needed.

I opened the tin of pink paint. It was a shade darker, more grown up than the current pink on the walls. Wouldn't it be helpful if paint manufacturers put an age on their pink paint offerings? It would make it easier for parents to pick the right shade to go with the childhood stages.

Before I started painting I fired off a text to Kirsty, 'How you feeling today?'

I wasn't expecting an immediate reply as she was at work, but my phone pinged almost immediately. 'Doing okay, trying not to cry at the photocopier.'

'Try to keep strong. I'll come over early tonight for a chat.' It was small group at Kirsty's tonight, so perfect to team it up with some extra chat time with her.

'That will be lovely. See you later.'

As I painted, my thoughts turned to Kirsty. I was sorry, but not surprised, to hear about Steven. Poor Kirsty. She knew how to pick them! I was frustrated at her attitude to relationships. She constantly needed to be in a relationship, and as far as I could see, there was no discernment from her side. Just as long as she had a boyfriend. And, the aforementioned boyfriends all seemed to pick up on her insecurities and treat her with a complete lack of respect that infuriated me. Like Steven, how dare he breakup with her by text!

Painting Chloe's bedroom was supposed to be cheering me up. I had to regain my positive outlook. Time for some good music. I put on my rock playlist and danced about with the roller as I brought my concentration back to decorating. This new shade of pink was perfect, together with the pale green paint, Chloe's room would be a touch more grown up. Although, the fairy lights, accessories and toys scattered around the floor would signal it was still a little girl's room.

Chloe was doing well at school, so far. I suspected she was coping with the transition better than I was. Decorating her bedroom was a benefit to both of us. It gave me something creative to do and it would further her feeling of being a 'big schoolgirl'.

I prayed as I painted. I prayed for wisdom in parenting. I prayed for wisdom in friendship.

KIRSTY

The next couple of days weren't great. Being involved with the launch event definitely helped, but there were still more tears than I would have liked. Yesterday I had cried at the photocopier, at the toilets, walking up the stairs, reading emails. Basically, anytime I was on my own the tears would come and keep me company, an unwanted friend.

Last night had been a bit of a disaster. Walking in to my empty flat I had never felt so lonely. I didn't even have the energy to make myself a proper coffee, the emergency jar of instant coffee sufficed. I went straight to bed. Slid under the duvet fully dressed and sobbed as I drank my coffee. It was nothing more than a pity party, but I didn't care. I loved Steven, or at least I think I did. My fragile emotions were all over the place. The prevailing emotion was hurt. And the best way to deal with hurt was to hide under my duvet.

Tonight promised a welcome change of focus. It was the start of the new small group season at church. And this year I was in the best small group. The group comprised Jo, Lynn, Carol and myself with Jennifer leading it. Our group was functioning as one of the half-full groups, which meant there was space for people to join a group throughout the year.

As I climbed the stairs to my flat and unlocked the door, my heart sank.

Two days of no housework, discarded tissues, thrown off clothes and unwashed dishes had left their trail of destruction through my little flat. And to make matters worse Jennifer was totally OCD with housework. I'd forgotten all about the mess of the flat when I'd accepted Jennifer's suggestion of coming round early. To get this place in order, dinner would need to be skipped. I threw the dirty laundry under my bed, I stashed the dirty dishes in a cupboard, and I rammed the used tissues into a poly bag. As I switched off the vacuum, the downstairs buzzer sounded. Jennifer was here.

I was enveloped in a great big hug as soon as I opened the door. "Kirsty, I'm so sorry."

"Thanks." I put all my effort into keeping eye contact with Jennifer. I had to make sure her eyes didn't wander the flat and see any evidence of my woeful untidiness.

"How are you feeling?"

"Not brilliant, but I think I'm getting there. Work is helping, I've got a new project to work on."

"That sounds perfect. It's good to have something to take your mind off Steven."

"Definitely! I'll need to get rid of all thoughts of him, to do a good job."

"I know everything seems terrible, but you'll get through this. Steven wasn't right for you. So, whatever you do, don't you dare try to contact him. I hope you've deleted his details from your phone."

"The girls were round on Monday evening and made me delete his number." Strictly speaking that wasn't a lie, they had deleted his number. However, I wouldn't be letting any of them know I had put his number back into my phone under a pseudonym. Despite everything I wasn't ready to give up his number yet.

"And, I bet they agree with me that it's his loss, and his issue."

"Of course, but you lot are all biased!"

"True. But it doesn't mean we're wrong."

"You are all the best. You're always there to help me through. Although, I am getting fed up talking about Steven, so tell me, what have you been doing this week?"

"I'm decorating Chloe's room."

"Oh yeah. Sorry, I didn't even ask. How's her first week at school?"

"No problem at all. You know Chloe, nothing phases her. But anyway, the reason I mention painting her room is because it occurred to me that I could do some decorating for you, cheer your flat up."

"Wow! That would be great. But are you sure? Don't you have lots of things planned now that the girls are at school?"

"To be honest, I don't think it will be long till I'm bored. Working on your living room will give me something to do."

"Well, I won't say no to your artistic eye sorting out this place."

"Okay, I'll have a think about it, and come up with some suggestions, I'll make sure you're happy with my thoughts before I start. I'll come over early next Wednesday, and we can talk through some ideas."

"That would be perfect."

"Great. Now let's get tea and coffee organised for the rest of the group arriving."

Jo, Lynn and Carol all arrived together and came bursting into the flat in one giggling group.

As I went into the kitchen to get the tea and coffee my stomach growled, reminding me I'd been ignoring it all evening. Jennifer and the others were all catching up as I poured out the teas and coffees. I raided the cupboards hoping for some snacks that would appease my stomach. But as usual my cupboards were near empty, and a few chocolate biscuits would need to suffice.

Jennifer started the meeting as I passed out the teas and coffees. "The church leadership have recommended that we follow along with the book of Romans in small groups. That way we'll have time for more in-depth discussions about the passages from the Sunday services."

As we all reached out for our Bibles, Jennifer continued. "But as we're a small, small group I see it as an opportunity to veer off course as needed. Kirsty, you've had a rough few days courtesy of Steven. So, let's use tonight for you."

"Oh no! Please don't change anything on account of me," I said, as the heat of embarrassment spread over my face. "I've already talked way too much about my problems with all of you."

"Nonsense," said Jennifer. "Part of small group is being here for each other?"

"No, really, I would much prefer we keep to the study." But even as the words left my lips I knew my protest was pointless.

"What a great idea," said Jo, with far too much enthusiasm for my liking. Lynn and Carol also expressed their agreement with the plan

I lowered my head and let my hair flop down over my face. If I didn't look at any of them maybe they would get the hint and move on to the bible study.

"I think you need to stop with these one-sided relationships," said Jennifer, getting straight to the heart of the matter.

"I couldn't agree more," replied Jo. "She seems to have this need to always have a boyfriend. She needs to make sure she gets a better guy next time."

"Absolutely," said Carol. "I never liked Steven, I never felt he was right for Kirsty."

"How could someone like him even contemplate breaking up with her," said Lynn. "He wasn't in Kirsty's league."

"I don't think we want to go down the route of running down Steven's character," said Jennifer. "This conversation needs to centre on Kirsty and how she moves on from here."

I'd done too good a job of hiding myself. It seemed the rest of the group had forgotten I was here. Discussing me in third person rather than asking my opinion. Should I laugh or cry?

The conversation continued happily, the other four group members obviously felt they had no end of insight to contribute.

As Jennifer summed up their discussion, I was included in the conversation. "Kirsty, you're too keen to get into any relationship as long as you're able to say you've got a boyfriend. Why not decide what you really want in your next guy, pray about it, and maybe give yourself some time?"

"Couldn't agree more," replied Jo. "We told her as much on Monday night, Jennifer. And we also agreed that she's not to date anyone else until we give the guy our approval."

Jennifer looked as if she was about to add to Jo's comment. I jumped in before she could say anything else, "Thanks everyone, I appreciate your concern for me."

"Then it's agreed," said Jennifer. "Kirsty, you need to learn to love yourself before you get tangled up in another bad relationship."

The girls gathered round, praying for me and hugging me. I was grateful for their concern, but their helpful words only led to more tears. All I wanted was comfort food and sleep.

"Come for lunch on Sunday," said Jennifer as she stood to leave. "The girls would love to see you, and I want to make sure you have at least one healthy meal this week."

"That would be lovely." And I meant it, I loved going to Jennifer's. It was always such a welcoming place. Despite the subject matter of the night, having Jennifer around always helped me feel better.

As I said goodnight to Jennifer, I longed for my bed and a good night's sleep. But, my hopes of an early night were dashed with Jo making another round of teas and coffees.

"How have you been since Monday night?" asked Carol.

"I'll admit I'm struggling. I've cried so much. Will I ever get over him?"

"You'll be fine," said Lynn. "I'm sure you said something similar after your last breakup, then in no time at all you were dating Steven and happy again."

"But if you all think it's best I wait before getting into another relationship my bounce back might take longer."

"What if it does," said Jo. "Perhaps it would be better for you to have a break. Take time to be happy in yourself, without a plus one."

I looked round my friends, "All I want is love. Why is it so hard?"

KIRSTY

"A latte to go, please." It would have been lovely to spend time at Chocolate & Vanilla to enjoy my coffee, but I had too much work to get through. Last night's embarrassing conversations had been helpful. The girls were right; I had to stop pursuing relationships. It was time to put myself first. A fresh coffee on the way to work ticked that box.

The office was quiet when I arrived. There were a few people scattered around the department and Gary was in his office. By the time I got settled and switched on my computer Gary appeared at my desk.

"Morning." I said, I needed to think of something to say about the launch event to show I was on top of it. But my mind was blank. The more frantically I searched my memory for something to say the emptier my brain felt. Perhaps it was all down to my brain being focussed on the cup of coffee sitting on my desk, either that or Gary's captivating aftershave?

"Morning," he replied. "I hope you're not having to come in this early to cover the launch event tasks. I can imagine Irene isn't freeing up any of your regular duties."

"No, it's fine. I like getting up early. It gives me time to get my favourite coffee," I said, holding up my coffee cup as if he needed to see proof. "I prefer to come in and get a start made before the office gets busy and noisy, lets me plan my day efficiently." What was I prattling on about? I sounded like a teacher's pet trying to make a good impression with my work ethics.

"Okay, well don't let me hold you back. We'll chat later once you have your day under control." I sank into my chair and put my head on my desk. I could only imagine Gary's disappointment. He must regret picking me for the launch event team. First I was a complete mess at Monday's meeting and now I had given him empty words, and no update on the event.

Enough of this crazy behaviour. Time to get my head back in the game. No more crying over Steven. Time to take full control of organising the launch night. Work was the perfect opportunity to forget about men for a few weeks and concentrate on something else. Although, when the guy you were working for looked like Gary it might not be as straightforward as it had all sounded last night.

Lists. Organised people work with lists. Look at Jennifer, one of the most efficient people I know, and she always has lists. I would make a list. I opened Excel and created a new file. In the first column I listed the event tasks from Laura's folder. Further columns contained issues outstanding, tasks completed and topics to discuss. I would never be lost for words with Gary again. The spreadsheet would stay with me at all times. It would always be open on my computer and at the end of each day I would print out the latest version and leave it in my desk drawer. As I worked on the spreadsheet, I remembered a couple of issues I needed to discuss with Gary. Now why hadn't I thought of those earlier? Maybe I should go and see him now. I looked over to his office. He was alone and working at his computer.

However, just as I walked towards Gary's office, Irene entered the department. "Have you finished the monthly figures yet?" Unbelievable! Irene hadn't even taken off her jacket, and she was already issuing orders.

"Not yet, I've been getting up to speed on the launch event, and finding out what needs to be done. I'll finish the update once I've spoken with Gary. I'm heading to his office now to go over a few things with him."

"No, your regular work takes priority. Finish the monthly update first, then you can speak with him." Gary had been right about Irene. I would need to add the launch event work over and above my regular tasks.

By the end of the day I still hadn't spoken Gary. Something always seemed to get in the way; Irene continuing to nag me to finish other work, or Gary had been in meetings, on the phone or not at his desk. But at least I had my list now. I would be prepared the next time I saw Gary.

PAUL

After a crazy couple of days I was looking forward to men's group. The group had started up as a men's Alpha group. A kind of faith discovery get together. I hadn't expected much when my flat mate, Matt, had invited me along. But after a couple of meetings I started looking forward to being at the group. Instead of viewing Christians as some weird group who went to church on Sunday and lived by a list of 'thou shalt nots', I realised they were regular guys, trying to navigate through life as best they could. Only unlike me, they had a purpose, they had a faith that seemed to guide them.

Tonight was my favourite format - beer and curry at one of the many Indian restaurants in Glasgow. Scott, the group leader, had discovered the restaurant a few months ago. It was perfect. An alcove at the back of the restaurant provided us with the perfect setting for our varied conversations.

Scott kicked off the discussion for the evening, then it went from man to man, as each person updated the group on what had been happening since our last meeting.

"I'm struggling with work just now. I'm not sure it's what I still want to be doing. On Monday I was at a magazine photoshoot and I ended up having some issues with one of the models during the shoot. Si then suggested there had been a complaint about me distracting the model. I'm trying to get my life in order when it comes to women, but it's not easy." As I tried to find the words to describe my confusion and uncertainty, the rest of the table bonded over laughter and comments aimed at me not knowing how lucky I was.

"Yeah, and you missed out the bit about the second model," Matt added. I glared over at him. Matt raised his bottle of beer in salute. Matt and I started sharing a flat after a mutual friend put us in touch. We hit it off at once. We lived our own lives to a large extent, but also took time to hang out together. Since becoming a Christian, our friendship had deepened further, as we shared Bible studies as well as a flat.

What a difference in my life with these guys. It was a safe place for me to learn and grow in this new faith. The guys laughing at my predicament was the reality check I needed. Sometimes you had to laugh at yourself. As I looked round the table I was amazed at how a Bible study group could bring together such a mish-mash of people. A few of the lads, like me, had no major background issues, just blokes who had made some wrong choices in life.

However, a couple of the men had real baggage; childhood abuse, drug addiction. I marvelled at how Scott directed and helped these guys. What must my problems seem like to them? No wonder they laughed at my model problem. But wasn't non-stop dating a kind of addiction too? Much as I hated to admit it, my lifestyle was potentially more damaging to others, all those women who'd been there for one night. I'd never had any complaints, but then again I'd never hung around long enough to hear any. At least Monday hadn't resulted in another one-night stand. I should be thankful for that.

"Time to wrap things up for this week," said Scott. "I've been reading this verse over and over again this week, so I decided it would be a good idea to share it with you too. It's from the New Testament, the book of Philippians, chapter four, verse seven: *And the peace of God, which transcends all understanding, will guard your hearts and your minds in Christ Jesus.*"

I took notice of those words. I needed that peace.

KIRSTY

It was Friday morning, and I was ready. Ready to update Gary and ask him questions about the launch event. Since Monday morning he had only seen the messed up, unprofessional Kirsty. Now he would find out I was up to the task. And it wasn't only the spreadsheet that signalled my professional mode. My appearance had also been up scaled – I was wearing my smartest skirt and blouse and had added foundation and blusher to my usual work makeup.

This morning there was no coffee stop. I was eager to get to the office early. But, no one was there, not even Gary. Deflated I dropped into my chair and switched on the computer. My professional resolve had disappeared, perhaps a few games of Solitaire were just the thing to settle me.

"I hope you're playing a game because you're up to date with your work and the monthly figures are on my desk."

It would be Irene that caught me out. How on earth had she managed to sneak up on me so quietly?

"Sorry. I got in early this morning." My pale Scottish skin did nothing to hide my blushes.

"All that effort to impress Gary, and he wasn't even here to see you? At least it was me rather than him catching you playing games when you've got so much work to do."

Her words stung. Did she really think I was trying to impress Gary? Okay, so maybe I was, but not in the way she seemed to infer.

"There's a pile of filing over at the archives cupboard. Go and deal with it."

My heart sank as I saw the mountain of filing at the cupboard door. I would be filing for the whole morning. It wasn't a good day to have worn my nice white blouse.

More than ever I needed my Friday lunchtime retreat. Monday to Thursday I took in sandwiches for lunch, but a Friday was Chocolate & Vanilla lunch. The coffee shop was relatively close to work, but with several coffee shops closer to the office, I rarely encountered any colleagues. Chocolate & Vanilla had become my haven of tranquillity, my well-done for getting to Friday. It was my refuge from Irene, a place to escape and lose myself with a delicious coffee and a good book.

I kicked off my shoes, curled up in the chair, drank my coffee, ate my muffin and turned the pages of my latest novel. I drifted a million miles away from my life. It was my chance to read about love, to lose myself in the romance of finding that special someone.

"Is this seat taken?" asked a familiar voice.

"Gary!" The surprise of seeing him there had me bolting upright, feet back down off the seat, shoes on, sitting to attention.

"Well, is it?"

"Sorry. Yes, it's free," I stammered. Great! Another encounter to highlight my ineptitude at conversations.

Gary put down his takeaway mug on the small coffee table between our chairs.

"Did you need to see me about the event? I've got a list of outstanding issues on my desk, I had tried to speak with you yesterday, but never got the chance. If you want, we can go back to the office now and go over the list." What was it about Gary that had me swinging between loss of words to non-stop babbling?

Gary laughed. "It's fine, enjoy your lunch break, Kirsty." Settling back in his chair, he continued, "I noticed your coffee cup yesterday morning, and realised I've never tried this place. So I decided to come for a lunchtime coffee and see if you were here."

Was he just making conversation? My mind was working overtime. Something about his words thrilled me. It was only a sentence or two but his words entered my soul and took root. Gary noticed me. More than that, he had sought me out. Gary! This sophisticated, worldly man. Once again words failed me. What was there to say in response? I tried to get my head back to work subjects. My mind was racing; I didn't know what to think. Before this week we'd only spoken a few times, and now here he was, a presence in my life, and I had no idea how to act or what to say. I racked my memory, trying to remember my spreadsheet to-do list. "When do we need to confirm the dinner menus?"

"Kirsty, relax, we're not in the office."

What should we talk about? Why was he here? I willed him to say something, anything.

"I hope you don't mind me asking, Kirsty. But you seemed upset on Monday. How are things now?"

Really? Why was he taking me back to that? I had spent too much time this week talking and moping about Steven. I was trying to move on, but people kept dragging me back to it. But then again that wasn't Gary's fault, and I couldn't be rude, he was trying to be nice. "Yeah, I'm getting there," I said. "My boyfriend sent me a text Monday morning breaking up with me, I didn't see it coming."

"Wait a minute you mean to say he split up with you by text?"

I nodded. How pathetic did I sound right now? Gary reached over and put his hand on my arm.

"Kirsty, look at me." A thrill ran through me as I looked into his eyes, the warmth of his touch coursing through my arm. "The guy's an idiot!"

"Pardon?"

"He's an idiot. He split up with you and he did it by text."

"Thanks." If you had told me a week ago that I'd be sitting having coffee with Gary I would not have believed you. And even more far-fetched would have been the notion of him comforting me over the breakup with Steven. "You've no idea how much that helps. My friends all said the same, but they're my friends, they're supposed to say that. You didn't need to say anything."

Gary's smile of response melted my heart. I needed to get this conversation to safer ground. I picked up my cup from the table, freeing my arm from his touch. A sip of latte gave me the time I needed to think of a neutral topic.

"Do you like Chocolate & Vanilla?"

"I can see why you come here. This part of it's great. The rest of it could be any coffee shop, but they've got the 'stay and rest awhile' section nailed."

"They really do. It's my Friday lunchtime oasis." Now why had I told him that? This conversation was too strange.

If we were going to be working together for the next few weeks I needed to learn how to talk to this man.

"What are your plans for the weekend?" asked Gary. It was an innocent enough question, the kind of question that would be innocuously used amongst friends. But Gary wasn't my friend. He was my manager, and this was only the second or third time we'd spoken.

I decided it was best to play it cool and respond the way I would with any other colleague. "Nothing too exciting. Going to the hairdressers tomorrow then going out for dinner with my friends."

"Well, enjoy. I need to return to the office. I've got back-to-back meetings all afternoon. I hope I've not spoiled your sanctuary." Without giving me any time to respond, Gary stood up, placed his hand on my shoulder and walked away from our secluded corner of anonymity. As he walked towards the stairs, I noticed the way he caused female heads to turn, everything from quick, hidden glances to the more obvious lingering stares. Gary was a man who got noticed.

JENNIFER

I travelled into the city centre as soon as I dropped the girls off at school. Looking forward to the prospect of a morning of coffee stops and window shopping. Activities I had been unable to enjoy with pre-school children in tow. Perhaps I needed to focus on the positives of this new life stage rather than mourning those irretrievable days.

Strolling down Buchanan Street, I relished the vibrancy of the autumnal colours in the shop window displays. I loved the energy of the city centre. People rushing around. The sea of colours. The ever changing aromas as I walked past cafes, restaurants and shops. Suburban life was conducive to raising a family, but with my new found freedom I had time to enjoy city centre excursions, including lunches with Scott.

"How was your morning?" asked Scott, as we settled down at our table. The restaurant was in one of Glasgow's smart shopping centres, the kind of place you couldn't fully enjoy if you had the kids with you. This was grown-up lunching; white table covers, glasses of iced water with lemon slices and waitresses who had a chic trendiness to their uniforms.

"It was lovely and relaxing. I came into town as soon I dropped the girls off at school, to enjoy some leisurely window shopping."

"What, no housework or painting?"

"Nope, taking a break from all that today."

"What's Chloe saying about her new décor?"

"She's very excited about it all. We'll look through some websites after school and she can choose the finishing touches."

"She'll love that. And, what are your plans for next week?"

"I said to Kirsty I'd come up with some ideas for decorating her living room. She needs brightness around her. As I was wandering around town earlier, I was taking note of the latest colours in the shop windows. I might incorporate some trend colours into Kirsty's living room."

"Next thing I know you'll be starting a home décor business."

I took a sip of water and considered Scott's comment. He was only making a flippant, passing comment, but it had been a strange week for me with Chloe starting school.

"Do you think I should go back to work?"

"I was joking."

"I know, but I guess Sarah's comments on Monday got to me more than I realised. And I'm wondering if she's right. Should I be out there working?"

"Only if you want to. What do you want to do?"

"I'm not sure. I guess moving into this new phase of life I'm questioning and wondering about a few things."

I paused as the waiter placed our lunches in front of us. My mind raced through my thoughts desperately trying to put words to them and make sense of what I was feeling.

"On the one hand, I'm surprised by how quickly the school day can go past, and then, once the girls are home, it's a frenzy of activity. But there's been an emptiness I wasn't expecting. I knew I would miss Chloe, but there's more to the emptiness than just a few Chloe free hours. Perhaps I'm feeling a sense of dread at the unscheduled weeks that lie before me. Should I be looking for something to occupy those child free hours? Painting Chloe's room has helped, but what lies beyond?"

"It's a big change for you. It'll take time to adjust."

"I'm beginning to realise that."

"Just don't use up all your energy on housework."

I laughed. "I know, but I like to have the house tidy and ordered for us all. But enough about me. How are things with you? How's the latest work project?"

"Good, should have the paperwork all sorted by the end of next week, then it's full on focus of starting work with our new big client."

"I'm so proud of you," I said. I was amazed at the way Scott had built up the accountancy firm. He'd started there straight from university, taking his professional exams in his stride as he gained practical experience, and when the opportunity presented itself, taking over the business from the previous owner. With free reign to follow through on his ideas, the business had grown and seemed to be constantly taking on new clients. Although the flip side of all that was the long hours he put in and the time he missed with the girls and myself.

"How are the new recruits working out for you?"

"They're doing well. As usual with these graduate trainees, what they lack in experience they make up for in enthusiasm. It's good for the company to inject fresh energy levels from time to time."

"And, how about Peter, is he stepping up to his new role as partner?"

"So far so good. He's already taken over as lead accountant for one of my clients. So that's another bit of pressure off me."

"Glad to hear it. Don't fill that new space with other work things."

"Trying not to, boss," replied Scott. "What will we do this weekend?"

"Let's keep it fairly quiet for this weekend. Wait and see how the girls are doing after their first week back at school."

"Works for me. I think we could both do with a nice quiet evening on the couch," said Scott, and winked.

My heart fluttered. The guy still had it!

KIRSTY

The dream had been so real. So intense. I wanted to stay in bed and let it sink deeper, to relive those intoxicating moments again and again.

I had dreamt of Gary.

We were alone in his office. No one else in the department. The only light was the low lighting in his office. Darkness shrouded the rest of the floor. The atmosphere full of tension. Both knowing where things were headed. He had told me what a great job I was doing. Then he took me in his arms and kissed me. The intensity of that kiss held me breathless.

I wasn't happy waking up and leaving the kiss in the dream realm. I longed to know more. It was a moment to savour as long as possible. I lay in bed playing out the scenario again and again. Smiling, I imagined I could be the one to tame Gary, that with me the tales of his philandering would cease. My subconscious had made it clear, I was attracted to Gary, and now my conscious agreed.

A twang of guilt ran through me as I lay in bed thinking of him. But I was only enjoying a dream, it wasn't something that would happen in real life. There was no way Gary would ever be attracted to me. And I would never go there if he wasn't a Christian, not that my recent spate of Christian boyfriends had proven themselves to be a brilliant choice.

Rumbles of hunger eventually persuaded me to get up and go in search of a late morning breakfast. As I opened the fridge door and looked at the sparse contents, I made a note that part of my day's chores would be grocery shopping. The final slice of bread in the cupboard would need to keep me going until I got to the shops.

An afternoon of mundane chores lay ahead of me: food shopping, vacuuming, cleaning the kitchen and bathroom. On the way to the supermarket I grabbed a limp looking sandwich from the newsagents at the corner of my street. Best not to go hungry to a supermarket or I'd buy too much food. The rest of the afternoon sped by as I tackled the housework; the memory of the dream took me through it all with a smile. I was being silly; it was only a dream, but I had allowed the vividness of it to sink deep inside.

By late afternoon it was time to head into the centre of town for my hair appointment. My stomach felt strange as I left my flat, but I put it down to the nerves of going to ByDesign for the first time.

Sitting in the reception area at the salon, my stomach still felt queasy. Why was I so nervous about trying out a new salon? I distracted myself by checking my phone for a few minutes before flicking through one of the glossy hair magazines. My thoughts returned to my dream of Gary. What would he think if I got one of these trendy hairstyles?

PAUL

Saturday was always a jam-packed day in the salon, especially with Si's precise timings. Despite my preference for the laid back vibe of the start of the week, there was something exciting about a busy Saturday. Working non-stop the whole day, grabbing food and drink where you could, then realising you had reached the end of your shift. I looked through my client list for the day. As usual, I had a full rota, mostly regulars, but the last appointment of the day was a new client. The chat with regulars was always easy. But I liked getting to meet someone new, and with any luck I would get that person converted to become another one of my regulars. Despite the recent restlessness, winning a new client still gave me a buzz.

"You checking to see if you have time to eat today?" asked Trish, as she joined me at the reception area to look at her schedule for the day. Trish was one of the newest stylists at the salon. She was fun, and you knew where you stood with her, which was refreshing in this place.

"Looks like the usual eat and style Saturday. How's your schedule?"

"Not as busy as yours, but quite full."

The other stylists always joked about my full rotas.

"Great, that means you can grab me some lunch when you go out for yours."

"Isn't that the job of the delightful Chantelle?"

"You're kidding, right? I've never seen her consume anything other than water."

"Don't look now, she's coming right for you. I'm off." And true to her word, Trish disappeared seconds before Chantelle entered the reception area.

As with the other senior stylists, I had my own assistant to help me speed through my client list from Thursday to Saturday. Chantelle had been at the salon for about six months. From her first day I was aware of a cattiness about her. She seemed to get on well with Si, which did nothing to dispel my distrust of her. I wasn't usually so judgemental, but somehow she brought it out in me.

Chantelle would greet the clients, bring them to my station, and then wash their hair. Although, she was always on the lookout for an unsuspecting junior to deal with the menial task of hair washing, hopeful I would give her the opportunity to style a client's hair. I didn't like her attitude to the clients. Part of me wondered if Si paired her up with me to try to reduce my return bookings.

With my full schedule the day flew past. The chat was flowing with the regulars. For forty-five minutes I was a part of someone else's life. Some days I felt like a counsellor, listening to people's problems, but Saturdays were all about nights out and parties. There was a buzz: the salon full of people, the noise of hairdryers and chatter filled the place.

It was near the end of the day when I noticed her. It was hard not to. A salon like ByDesign has three main client types. First of all, those who want to be seen here. They demand attention and recognition. Next up, are the majority of clients. They come here because of the quality service and the styling reputation of the salon. They want to be seen here too, but are much more subtle about it. And third, are the people like this woman. Chewing on her bottom lip, she looked out of her comfort zone. She was trying her best to deflect attention. We don't get many of this type of client but, they are my favourites. They are a different kind of challenge.

The appointment would start with small talk and jokes to put her at ease. History told me I had a high chance of converting this woman to my regulars list. And I wanted to. She belonged here. She was tall and gorgeous. *Please let her be my final appointment of the day.*

Finishing up with my current client, I used the mirror to look over to the reception area where the stranger was sitting. Her hair looked okay. But either she hadn't been to a hairdresser in a while, or she had been going somewhere that was too basic to understand how to cut a style to a client's face shape. I hoped she would let me advise her on what style to go for. I knew the perfect cut for her. But, that all depended on whether she would even be coming to my station.

I watched her as she concentrated on her phone. With any luck, she was checking her phone to fill her waiting time. It bugs me when a client loves the cachet of 'checking in' at ByDesign on their social media, but then misses out on the experience by spending the rest of the appointment on said phone.

"You're next client is at the reception," announced Chantelle, pointing over to the girl I had been watching. "Shall I bring her over now?"

"Yes." The end of my day was looking good.

KIRSTY

From the outset I should have known it was a disaster waiting to happen.

The aloof receptionist from Monday directed me to the waiting area and informed me Paul and herself would be over to speak to me as soon as he was finished with his current client. Strike one: this intimidating, perfect receptionist would somehow be a part of my salon experience. Strike two: the insanely hot guy she indicated would be cutting my hair! There was only one way this scenario would end – disaster! But nothing could have prepared me for the catastrophe about to unfold.

When I first sat down in the waiting area I had glanced around the salon to try to guess which of the male stylists would be cutting my hair. In my dream world state, I had hoped it would be this man who was now sitting beside me discussing what I wanted from my visit. I was glad it wasn't the short, officious looking guy, who was strutting around the salon as if he owned the place, checking his reflection in each mirror he passed.

The earlier confidence drained from my system. I was Cinderella without the glass slippers and all the other magical trappings. I was back to plain, raggedy, tongue-tied Kirsty. I realised I didn't have a clue what I wanted done to my hair. How could I possibly know? Everywhere I looked there were perfect, confident people. As I tried to say something of worth, I noticed the perfect receptionist roll her eyes. My last drop of confidence evaporated.

But just when it all seemed hopeless, Paul gave me a heart-warming smile that empowered me to convey the simplest of instructions. "A tidy up of the length and layers. Or if you have any suggestions that would be great too." I could only hope my words came out with some kind of sense and didn't make me sound like a complete idiot.

"I agree. This time we'll go with what you've been used to, and next time you come we can get more adventurous. This is my assistant Chantelle, she'll take you over to the sinks and get your hair washed and treat you to a head massage."

Chantelle - really? It certainly was Hollywood glamour here. With her blonde hair extensions, fake lashes and fake tan she definitely had the right look for working in this place. I felt a flash of reproach for being so judgemental about someone I didn't know.

"Let me know if the water temperature is okay for you," said Chantelle, as I settled in at the sink.

The unsettled feeling in my stomach seemed to be getting worse. Was it the stress of trying to express myself in this foreign place, or perhaps the heat from the spotlights shining right into my face? It was probably a combination of both. I needed to calm myself down and relax.

After the hair wash, Chantelle started my head massage. Under normal circumstances I love a head massage, but I was feeling more ill with each passing minute. This was more than just nerves.

"You're so lucky to be getting Paul to cut your hair," said Chantelle. "He's one of our best stylists. During the week he was working on a photoshoot for a magazine. I like to help him out when I can, but I had to stay here. I was devastated to miss out. The photoshoots are so glamorous; getting to hang out with the models and the photography crew. Most of the time we all go out afterwards and party together. It's so much fun." Chantelle's words continued to pour out, gushing about how great it was to be working at ByDesign and all the extra assignments they got to take part in. I knew it was just another way for her to communicate how little my custom meant to the establishment. But I could not have cared less. I focussed all my energy on working out what was wrong with me.

Chantelle led me over to Paul's workstation and combed through my hair. "Paul will be with you in a few minutes."

The reflection looking back at me from the gleaming salon mirror was not a healthy sight. Salon mirrors are never the most flattering, and with all the beautiful people in ByDesign my chances of looking okay were never going to be great, but the face that looked back at me was a strange shade of grey, and the glazed eyes were lifeless. My stomach was flipping and making the strangest gurgling sounds.

"And how was that head massage?" asked Paul, as he came over. His expression changed as he looked at my reflection. Before I could reply to his first question he had moved on to his next. "Are you okay?"

My only response was to put my hand over my mouth and run for the toilets at the back of the salon. I didn't make it to them. At least I made it as far as the hair washing sinks, they would need to do.

Paul was beside me in a flash. "What can I get you? Do you want some water? I'll get you some paper towels." And he was off dashing about to get me the necessary supplies. As the bout of sickness ended I let go of the sink and slid down onto the tiled floor, finding relief in the coolness of the tiles. My stomach was in agony, I was fairly certain there was more to come.

I wanted to be back in the safety of my little flat, away from the all the bright lights and glamour. The sickness was strike three; I could never come back to ByDesign.

PAUL

Walking over to the water cooler, I realised this was the second time in a week I'd brought water to an ill, beautiful woman. Matt would get a laugh out of this latest tale of heroism.

I'd watched the colour drain from her face and the fear fill her eyes as she realised what was about to happen. It was the first time I'd ever witnessed a client throwing up in the sinks. There'd been plenty of times I'd heard the retching of stylists or juniors in the toilets after a particularly heavy night out, but never a client.

By this time in the afternoon the salon was quiet. But the staff and clients who were still around looked over at Kirsty in disgust. Grabbing a couple of seats I blocked off the sink area, hoping to protect Kirsty from the prying eyes of the remaining clients and stylists. Best to give her a few minutes to gather herself together. I'd barely turned my back to her than she was up and running, this time making it to the ladies' toilet.

With Kirsty out of the way I ran water around the offending sink, clearing away the worst of the mess. Cleaning up wasn't my thing, but I wanted to get rid of the pervading smell as quickly as possible. A can of hair spray from my workstation served as an air freshener.

Si came steaming over. "What have you done now?"

I laughed at the absurdity of his comment and expression. The guy wasn't real!

"Come on Si, even you can't blame me for this one. I don't know what's going on, this is the first time the client's been here. I'm assuming she's got a bug or food poisoning or something. It's not going to help with you standing here, so I suggest you go back to your perch and leave me to deal with this."

Kirsty came out of the toilet a whole new shade of grey. She was shaking like a leaf. Taking hold of her arm I led her over to a seat by the sinks. "Are you in town with anyone? Can I phone someone to tell them you're ill?"

"No, it's okay, I'll just go home."

"How are you planning on getting home?"

"I don't know. Bus probably?"

"You can't get the bus when you're sick. Let me phone for a taxi for you." I walked over to the reception desk to phone the taxi company. But as soon as I mentioned to the dispatcher that Kirsty wasn't well they refused the fare. The only other option I could think of was to phone Matt and ask him if he could help.

"Sorry, the taxi company won't come. I shouldn't have mentioned you were sick. But my flat mate will come and get you."

"Oh no, you can't. Please don't. I've caused you enough problems already. I'll call one of my friends. Please don't."

"Kirsty, look at me." Her pitiful eyes looked into mine. "It's fine. You were my last client today and Matt was going to come in and meet me anyway." Which was true, only we had planned to meet later than this. Kirsty needed to get home as soon as possible, and this was the only thing I could think of.

"Will you be okay for a few minutes? I'll finish cleaning up and get ready to leave."

"I'm so sorry," said Kirsty. Apologising yet again. But the effort of talking was telling on her, she leaned over the sink and rested her head on her arms. While she rested, I finished cleaning up.

However, it wasn't long before Kirsty had to dive into the toilets again. This time she didn't come straight back out. She must be mortified. I couldn't blame her for wanting to hide.

Matt sent me a text to say he was outside but would wait in the car as he was on double yellow lines.

"Kirsty? Kirsty? Can you hear me? That's my friend Matt here now. We need to go." My calls were met with silence.

"Please God, don't let me have to deal with another passed out woman!" Was there some kind of record for how many fainting women you assisted in a week? How strange for this working week to begin and end in such similar fashion.

"Kirsty?"

There was nothing else for it, I needed to go into the ladies' toilet. One cubicle was locked. "Kirsty? Can you hear me?"

She still didn't reply. But the gentle sobbing from behind the door reassured me she hadn't passed out.

"Kirsty, I'm sorry we need to go. Matt's waiting outside, and he's on double yellow lines. I've got poly bags and paper towels just in case you need them for the car journey home."

She unlocked the door and shuffled out. She looked absolutely awful. The smell of sick followed her out of the cubicle and left me feeling nauseous myself.

"Come on, let me help you." Taking her by the arm I led her out of the toilets. "Do you want us to take you to the hospital, you look really ill?"

"No, home. Please, just take me home."

"Where do you live?"

"Moss Street."

"Okay, let's get you in the car and get you home." As I led Kirsty out of the salon, Matt got out the car and opened the back door for us.

"Thanks mate," I said to Matt as we got into the car.

We made it back to Kirsty's flat without her being sick in Matt's car. However, as we helped her out the car she was sick again, this time all down my trouser leg and shoe. How could she have anything left to bring up? I tried not to think about the mess on my trousers or shoes.

"Kirsty, give me your keys and we'll get you up to your flat." Without fuss or argument, she handed her keys to Matt, and I supported her up the stairs to her flat.

"I'm not happy about leaving you on your own. Is there anyone we can call for you? Do you want us to stay for a bit to make sure you're okay?" But even as I spoke Kirsty was already trying to shoo us out of her flat.

"I need to sleep. I'll be fine. Thanks. I just need to sleep."

There was nothing else for us to do but guide her to the settee, get her duvet through from the bed and set her up with a glass of water and tissues. Matt put the TV remote and her mobile phone beside her. I wanted to stay. She needed looking after. I wanted to make sure she was okay. What was wrong with me? Why would I want to stay in the company of someone who was being sick? This no-dating thing must have me desperate.

I paused at the doorway as we left. I didn't want to leave her like this.

KIRSTY

What was wrong with me? Who else could go to an expensive salon and cause so much commotion? No one! If I didn't feel so awful I would be mortified.

I shivered as the door closed behind the two chivalrous heroes. Should I be concerned at how easily I had allowed two perfect strangers to bring me home? Two unknown men had taken my house keys from my bag and opened the door to my private domain. They had led me to the sofa and lowered me down. They had fetched my duvet from my bed, a glass of water from my kitchen, a wet towel from my bathroom. They had been in every room in my flat while I lay helpless and half comatose on the settee. Perhaps it should bother me. But right now I didn't care.

As I waited for sleep, my mind was racing. Torturing me with the memories of the salon and the journey home. Had I been sick down Paul as I got out of Matt's car? I had caused so much trouble. Disaster and good-looking men seemed to go hand in hand in my life. As the memories continued to torment me, I was left with the certainty that Paul would never want to see me again.

Pulling the duvet over my head, I longed for oblivion, hoping that sleep would not bear any reference to Gary or hairdressers.

I wanted to sleep. I wanted to forget.

PAUL

As Matt drove back to our flat, I could sense him looking at me. "You okay?" he asked.

"Yeah, sure."

"No, you're not. Talk to me."

"I'm worried about Kirsty."

"Let it go. You only met her today. She'll be fine. It's a bug or something. Like the girl said she needs sleep, then she'll be fine."

"Didn't you think she looked fragile?"

"I'm certain everyone looks like that when they are that sick."

"I suppose you're right, but something about her makes me want to look out for her. Make sure she's okay."

Matt laughed. "I see what's going on here. The mighty Paul has met his match. At the start of the week you were fighting off models, now you're longing after someone you've just met. Someone, I may add, who has barfed all down your leg."

Matt was right! If I allowed myself, I would admit there was a humour to my attraction to Kirsty. She wasn't my 'usual type'. My previous track record was one of dating models, or model-like women. Women who were all show and confidence. Kirsty seemed nothing like them. She didn't come with the paraphernalia of bags of makeup and bling. There was no flaunting of showy good looks that required hours of prepping and preening. Of course I was attracted to her looks, she was beautiful, but there was something else, something unique that drew me. I couldn't put my finger on what it was. I had to see her again. I wanted to know more. At least I knew her address. I would send her flowers on Monday.

"Why not pray for her?" said Matt, interrupting my thoughts. "At least that way you're doing something positive for her, rather than sitting here pining."

"Thanks, mate. Great idea." I still had a lot to learn about this new faith. Maybe my prayers would extend to more than just her health!

JENNIFER

My week had been a strange mixture of change and introspection. If I hoped church would be a break from that, I was wrong.

We started coming to ChurchX as newlyweds. Reaching out to 'GenX', the church was fresh and appealing, and attracted other young singles and couples. We established a great social life with our new church friends, hanging out together several times during the week and at weekends.

Within a year we went from small group attendees to small group leaders to leaders of the young adult ministry. We thrived on it: the speed of life; setting up something new; being in the centre of things and doing life together. For both of us, it filled the gap left by our student days. It was a place that fanned our dreams of changing the world.

But parenthood changed all that. Our lives transformed from fresh young couple to tired, struggling parents. For the first time in our married lives we no longer served together at church; Scott took on a role in the management team and I went on to the kids rota.

As I looked around the church, all I could see were the ghosts of friendships past. The friends who had moved on elsewhere: moves to pursue careers; moves to get that dream house.

I felt the loss of those friendships and that spirit of adventure. It didn't help that I was sitting on my own. Scott was busy with church announcements and business, he was up and down and in and out from the meeting room. Loneliness wasn't an emotion I was used to. I looked round to find Kirsty. Jo, Lynn and Carol were together near the back of the room, but there was no sign of Kirsty.

At the end of the service I got my phone out to call her. There was a message waiting, "Sorry, can't make it today, was sick yesterday, Kx".

Our afternoon was now clear. Normally on a free Sunday afternoon I would get the family mobilised to go out for lunch somewhere, or embark on a family outing. But for today a quiet afternoon on the sofa sounded perfect.

KIRSTY

Monday mornings never seem to get any easier. Last Monday I was dealing with the whole breakup trauma and today I'm still feeling a bit queasy. Thank goodness for my raincoat and sunglasses. I hugged my raincoat around me like a protective shield, keeping me safe in my own little space. The sunglasses hid my sensitive eyes from the beautiful morning sunshine. At least there were no tears this Monday morning. Despite my weakened body, my mind was working overtime processing all the things that had happened over the past week: Steven's text; the Gary dream; Paul's attentiveness. That was a lot of guy activity for one week. I was beginning to suspect taking a break from relationships might not be as straightforward as it sounded. Plus, that was Jo, Lynn and Carol's suggestion. I still wasn't convinced by their reasoning.

I needed coffee. I got off the bus a stop early and popped into Chocolate & Vanilla. However, walking into the coffee shop reminded me of Gary; the time we'd spent here Friday lunchtime and my dream. As I waited for the staff to prepare my order, my thoughts latched on to my dream and the memory of that kiss. The barista calling out my order brought me back to Monday morning reality. Unlike last week I took my latte to go, I still wanted to get into the office early and ease myself into the week's workload.

On Friday I had hoped Gary would be in the office, this morning I was hoping to get the place to myself. I wanted the luxury of time and peace to settle and get started with my work before anyone else arrived. But my hopes of a quiet start were shattered from the moment I walked into the department and almost bumped into Gary. "You trying to make me the coffee stained one this week?" he said, laughing at the near accident.

"I'm so sorry Gary." My face flashed a bright shade of red. I had to turn this round before once again I looked inept and tongue tied. "Can we grab some time together to go over the latest updates on the launch event?"

"I'd love to grab some time with you," he said, struggling to hide the smile tugging at the corner of his lips. "But I've got non-stop meetings today. Can you come in tomorrow morning for eight and we can go through it then?"

"No problem."

I walked over to my desk hoping for a day clear of Irene. I needed today to be only about work; no more dramas or issues, and definitely no more thoughts of Gary, or hairdressers.

PAUL

From the moment I entered the salon Si was on my case about Kirsty.

"She was sick, Paul! Right here in my salon. Your client vomited! Thank goodness it was at the end of the day and the salon was quieter. But let me tell you I had unhappy cleaners to deal with this morning, complaining about the smell in the place and the clean-up required around the sinks."

"Si, don't be such a jerk. She couldn't help being sick. And she didn't make that much of a mess. What did you expect her to do? At least she got to the sinks and didn't throw up all over a workstation, or equipment." I walked away before he had the chance to say anything else. Si wasn't a people person, he only cared about himself and his precious profit rating for the salon.

The confrontation with Si bothered me. What was going on? Hairdressing is great, but right now everything about it annoyed me. Maybe after the events of last week, Saskia fainting and Kirsty being sick, I should retrain as a nurse and look after people. Wasn't that a higher calling than a hairdresser? Was this the reason for the restlessness? Was it time to be something more useful to the world?

Hairdressing had seemed an obvious choice when I was introduced to the idea. Mum and dad divorced when I was six, and when dad moved out, I was left to the nurturing of mum and my older sister. Being the only male in the house I'd adapted and become an expert in the unspoken female cues. Picking up on their moods and feelings through the way they spoke to me and each other, the way they reacted to situations, even how they dressed.

By the time I got to high school I excelled at knowing how to speak to girls. I turned the experiences of home to my advantage and, while other boys were terrified of speaking to the girls at school, I had no such inhibitions. I started dating the first week of high school and, for most of my time at high school, there was a girlfriend by my side.

When we reached the stage of career chats at school, I had no idea what I wanted to do. The careers advisor wasn't all that helpful, suggesting I consider apprenticeships in building companies. Building wasn't the career path for me. The other boys appeared to have received much the same advice, so I asked some girls what the advisor had suggested to them. There were a variety of options from joining the police to university and college courses. A couple of the girls were excited about the prospect of becoming hairdressers. I sat with them as they read about the hairdressing course at the local college.

The idea of becoming a hairdresser took hold that day. I was desperate to get out of school and make my mark on the world. Hairdressing appealed, it was a career choice I could find no negatives with.

Now I could find plenty of negatives with it!

JENNIFER

Last week I had kept myself busy with housework and painting Chloe's bedroom. This week I would turn my attention to Kirsty's flat. But what lay beyond decorating Kirsty's living room? How was I going to fill my days between school drop-off and pick-up? When the girls were out of school my time was jam-packed, but what was my purpose for those six hours in-between? Last week's chats with Sarah and Scott had me questioning the future. Should I be looking for a job, finding a purpose for the empty hours?

However, even the idea of introspection bores me. So, for today I would choose my fall back; great music and housework. I selected Scott Nicol on my playlist, and rocked about the house as I cleaned, polished and scrubbed. By the afternoon I was on a major clear out in the kitchen, emptying cupboards and cleaning every nook and cranny. A text message from Sarah interrupted my activity, 'Can you collect Kevin from school and take him to gymnastics, thanks'. It was fortunate that Sarah had texted me: I had five minutes to get to the school and get the girls, and Kevin. I grabbed my raincoat from the hallway coat rack and ran along to the school, just making it through the school gates as the bell rang.

I collected Chloe from the infant playground then rushed round to the main playground to ensure I got Kevin as well as Emma. But there was no need for any panic. Kevin came sauntering out with Emma. "Hi Kevin," I said. "Your mum just sent me a text asking if I could take you to gymnastics with Emma tonight. I guess you'll just need to do gymnastics in your school uniform tonight."

"It's okay. Mum said I would be coming back to yours, so I've got my kit in my bag," said Kevin, tapping his bag to confirm his story.

I tried not to let my frustration show. The situation wasn't Kevin's fault. I was annoyed at Sarah. She had decided before school I could deal with her son's homework, dinner and club drop off, and yet I was only let in on the plan five minutes before school pick-up! What would she have done if I wasn't available? Sarah had left herself no time for alternative arrangements.

Back at the house I put out bowls of fruit for snacks and told the kids to do their homework. Kevin objected to being given fruit rather than crisps, but I ignored him, in no mood to put up with his whimsical notions or his mother's assumptions of other people.

First night at gymnastics after a holiday break was always a lengthy process with payments being set up and forms being completed.

"Where's Kevin's mum or dad?" asked the instructor.

"They're both stuck at work, so they asked me to bring Kevin."

"Will one of them be picking him up?"

"Do you know, I didn't even think to ask? I'm not sure." But even as I gave the reply, I knew who would be collecting both children and taking Kevin home.

"I need them to fill in Kevin's forms and set up payment earlier than they did last year," continued the instructor.

"If I'm taking Kevin home, I'll take the forms and give them to Sarah."

"Thanks," she replied. The tone of her voice communicating how frustrated she was interacting with parents and financial details rather than teaching the team how to perform their moves.

As suspected, I got a text from Sarah asking if I could drop Kevin at home as she was still at work, and would only just make it home before Kevin was due in. With all these last minute texts there was no opportunity to push back. I would need to find an appropriate time to talk to Sarah about it later.

When I went to collect Emma and Kevin, the gymnastics were still in full flow. I made the most of the delay by giving Kirsty a quick call to see how she was doing.

"I'm doing so much better, thanks," said Kirsty.

"What happened? Were you not feeling great, or catch a bug or something?"

"I think I got food poisoning. But of course it's never that straightforward with me!"

"Oh no! What happened?"

"It's a long story, I'll tell you Wednesday night at small group. May as well give you all a laugh."

"You have got my curiosity raised. Were you back at work today or still off?"

"No, managed back to the office today, still felt a wee bit queasy, but not too bad. How are you?"

"Okay, just waiting for Emma and her friend to get out of gymnastics. It's non-stop glamour as a mum."

"It's not much better down here in the twenties," said Kirsty. I was relieved to hear the laughter in her voice. I was looking forward to catching up with her and the others on Wednesday night and hearing more about her latest disaster. And, there was the added bonus of turning my attention to decorating Kirsty's living room.

As I was hanging up, Emma and Kevin were getting their shoes on ready to leave the hall. "Have you had fun back at gymnastics?" They both seemed hyper enough from it; weren't they supposed to have worked off some of that energy?

"We played warm up games," said Kevin. "And I won all of them."

"No you didn't," said Emma.

"I did! The instructor didn't have a clear view of me all the time that's all."

"Did not, Julie beat you at least twice."

"No she didn't. Boys always beat girls."

Before Emma could say another word, I instructed them to gather their drinks bottles and hoodies and leave.

I drove Kevin back to his house, waiting to make sure he got into the house before I drove off. Kevin rang his doorbell and after a minute or two Sarah finally appeared at the door, clothed in her dressing gown. A green face mask covered her face and a glass of wine was in her hand! This was not the appearance of someone who had just arrived home from work. I didn't wait to wave goodbye. I drove off without looking back.

As Emma waved goodbye to Kevin, I prayed for grace to deal with Sarah.

KIRSTY

The following morning I arrived at work at 8am, hopeful of making a good impression. Glancing over to Gary's office I saw he was already there. I tossed my raincoat on my chair, grabbed the launch event file and rushed to his office.

"Let's sit at my meeting table," said Gary, standing up from his desk and directing me to the other side of his office. He had two coffee cups in his hand from Chocolate & Vanilla. "Your reward for coming in so early."

And just like that my willpower was gone. Goodbye best of intentions; hello silly, unrealistic daydreams of love. My life was conspiring against me. And it wasn't all down to this coffee cup sitting in front of me. Last night when I got home my neighbour came over with a stunning bouquet of flowers. The card explained they were a gift from Paul, expressing his hopes for a speedy recovery and that I would come back to the salon soon.

And now, here was Gary offering me a cup of coffee. Steven probably didn't even know I liked coffee, never mind my favourite type. But Gary, just a week after our first conversation, already knew.

"Thanks. This is so kind of you."

I expected Gary to sit across the table, but instead he sat in the chair next to me. I was keenly aware of how close we were to each other. My thoughts returned to my dream. The fantasy was touching reality. Would someone like Gary be interested in me? The office gossip proclaimed his reputation, but if he was a serial womaniser would he bother with such small details as a person's favourite coffee? Surely such small details would be beneath that type of person. Maybe all the gossip about Gary was nothing more than gossip. Perhaps he had been misrepresented.

The memory of the dream lingered, but that was all it was; a dream. I needed to get my head back to reality. There was no attraction from his side, there was no kiss; it was only a meaningless dream. All Gary needed was a competent member of staff he could rely on for the event planning. I was that person. This was office work, manager and subordinate, nothing more.

"I've got a list of updates and questions since last Monday's handover," I said, moving the conversation, and my thoughts, to the safer subject of work. With my spreadsheet in hand I tried to regain control, working through my list of questions.

Despite my best efforts to focus on work, the dream was edging ever closer as we sat alone, no one else in the department, right next to each other, heads close together in discussion. As he discussed various aspects of the event I was captivated by his deep blue eyes, the colour further intensified by his blue shirt. The cut of his expensive suit highlighted his physique. And the scent of his aftershave played havoc with my senses. Did he realise the effect he was having on me? There was nowhere to hide my emotions, the dream was teasing me now, weaving its fiction into reality.

"That's been a good meeting," said Gary, breaking the spell with words of work. "We should do this each week. Let's meet again next Tuesday morning at 8am."

"Yes, that should be fine." In an almost dazed state, I collected my notes and folder from the meeting table.

"And Kirsty," said Gary, drawing me back into the office just as I was about to leave. "It's your turn to bring the coffee next week." The familiarity in the tone of his voice had me in flux again.

How was I supposed to deal with all these emotions? From the work point of view it was all exciting and fresh. I'd paid my dues with the mindless, boring work; I was ready for this challenge and I wanted to enjoy it all without my emotions messing it up. It was time to be professional and do the best job I could, no emotion allowed. This was my chance to prove my worth in the department. It could even be my opportunity to step up to the next pay grade. But even as I tried to rationalise it all I wasn't fooling myself, the biggest thrill was getting to spend time with Gary.

JENNIFER

I earmarked Tuesday as a day to sit and dream and plan Kirsty's living room. The only items being kept were the settee and armchair. The rest of the furniture comprised odds and ends Kirsty had picked up at thrift shops or street recycling. I had learned early in our friendship that Kirsty needed the softly softly approach to change, so I was pleasantly surprised when she agreed to the redecorating. The break-up with Steven must have been the catalyst she needed for change.

I fetched an old noticeboard out of the garage to serve as my mood board. I had taken several photos of Kirsty's living room when I was there last week; I pinned a couple of these to the board. The starting point for the room would be the settee. It was covered in beautiful cream material with an array of scatter cushions. It lost its WOW factor by having cushions the same colour as the settee. That would be easy to change.

Sitting in my kitchen, I enjoyed the glow of sunlight streaming in on me. The morning drifted by in beautiful colours and creativity as I surrounded myself with interior design magazines and online searches for the latest colours, trends and styles. As I immersed myself in the world of interior style, I considered various colour schemes and themes that would transform Kirsty's drab living room into a place of modern chic. A place to suit a young woman in the city. I spent the afternoon developing the ideas further. Grey was the perfect on-trend colour for the walls, and this year's autumnal colour palette would be perfect for the soft finishes. I looked through some of my favourite home furnishing websites in a quest for additional pieces of furniture and accessories. I made up a list with suggestions and attached it to the board. The front of the board was covered in photos, magazine cuttings and internet print outs.

The creative day had invigorated me. I was thrilled at the prospect of bringing colour and style to my friend's flat. For the next two weeks I had purpose.

Perhaps this project held potential for both Kirsty and myself.

KIRSTY

"Kirsty, we need to know, what happened at the weekend," said Lynn. It was Wednesday night, small group night at my flat. Although it was feeling more like 'Kirsty's self-help group'. "Your text on Saturday didn't tell us much, but hinted there was a story."

The flat was full of laughter as I recounted my drama from Saturday's hair appointment.

"Only you," said Carol, as she tried to compose herself. "Have you been okay since then?"

"I felt washed out on Sunday, but I was more or less okay by Monday."

"And what's with this gorgeous big bunch of flowers?" said Jo, as she pointed to the bouquet sitting on my coffee table.

"I got them from the hairdressers."

"From Paul?" Jennifer asked.

"Yes, wasn't that nice of him, after me being the cause of the disaster?"

"Interesting," said Jennifer. Followed by 'oohs' and 'aahs' then giggles from the others. "Didn't I tell you he was great?"

"Yes, he was great. In fact, he was an absolute hero. But, Jennifer, how can I go back there again after embarrassing myself that much. Everyone there will remember me as vomit girl."

"Don't be silly. I'm sure they are used to lots of unusual happenings at the salon."

"I doubt it! And besides I'm just not sure it's my kind of place."

"What are you talking about?" said Jo.

"It's all glitz and glamour there. Even the receptionists are mega glam."

"Stop downing yourself," said Carol. "You're like a model with your height and build. You can totally pull off a visit to ByDesign."

"I agree," said Jennifer, before I could get a word in. "All this not fitting in nonsense is all in your head. I love it there. Go back, treat yourself."

"Yes, we want to hear more about Paul." At Jo's words they were all back to their 'oohs' and 'aahs' again.

"Honestly, you lot are the worst." But despite all the laughter at my expense, I knew they were sympathetic to my plight. After the disaster of last week, I was excited to be with my favourite people. Plus, I had missed seeing everyone at church after the sickness episode.

"So, as we missed our night out last Saturday, I've got a new proposal for this weekend," said Lynn. "There's a deal online today for wall climbing at my climbing centre; who's up for it Saturday night?"

Lynn's question was met with silence.

"Oh, come on, it'll be fun. Jennifer, you going to come with us for this one?"

"I'll give it a miss, but you girls have a fun time!"

"I'm ordering four tickets now," said Lynn, as she picked up her phone. "I'm not accepting any refusals from the rest of you, climbing is lots of fun. Jennifer's only excused because she has a family and can't be hanging out with us all the time."

There still wasn't much enthusiasm, but no one dared say no to Lynn. She had made it clear she expected us all to join in.

Saturday night arranged, we turned our attention to the Bible study for the night.

JENNIFER

Last night, at Kirsty's, had been rejuvenating. She was excited and enthusiastic about my ideas for her living room. Then, once the rest of the group had arrived, we had laughed together in helpless astonishment at Kirsty's tale of being sick at ByDesign. You shouldn't laugh so much at someone being ill. But the circumstances were so unusual and Kirsty had a way of expressing herself that demanded a response of laughter and not just sympathy. When her tales of woe didn't revolve around male complications, she was able to see the funny side of things.

As I lay in bed, in the empty moments between Scott leaving for work and the girls waking up, I realised I hadn't laughed much over the last few weeks. Where had the joy of life gone? I had so much to be grateful for; a beautiful family, good friends and a lovely home. But somewhere along the years joy had slipped away.

A horror thought gripped me. Was I becoming a bored housewife? No! I couldn't be. Was I? No, I would not be cast in a stereotype role. My life was more than that. It had to be!

When I collected the girls from school that afternoon Emma was particularly quiet. She was always the quietest one, but something about her demeanour alerted me to all not being well in her little eight-year-old world.

With Amy and Chloe settled with snacks and drinks in the kitchen, I directed Emma to the living room. "Are you okay, Emma?" I knew the answer to this one, but with Emma it was always best to start off slowly and give her time to open up. The only reply was a shrug of the shoulders.

"Did something happen at school today?" I asked, continuing the one-sided conversation. I would get there eventually. Sometimes it was like playing the twenty questions game, you had to keep asking till you hit the answer-giving question.

There was no verbal answer, but Emma looked up and then away. "Did you get into trouble at school today?" This time tears answered the question; big, heavy, end-of-the-world sobbing.

"Emma, tell me what happened. I can see you're upset but I can't help you if you don't talk to me."

"But you'll shout at me. And I'll be in trouble all over again," said Emma, struggling to get the words out through her crying breath.

"Take a deep breath. Calm down and tell me what happened." Emma would tell me everything, with a truthfulness that only a child was capable of. She would leave nothing out once I got her started on the tale of woe from school.

"Me and Kevin got into trouble today. Kevin was talking to me when Miss Robertson was talking and she put us on probationary warning. But then Kevin spilled his juice all over the table and blamed it on me, and Miss Robertson believed him and I got put on official warning. But honestly it wasn't me, mum. It was Kevin's juice, and he spilled it." As Emma got to the end of her explanation, she cried again.

Scooping her up in my arms I snuggled into her. There were two sides to every tale, and you couldn't always take your child's word as the total truth. But I know my children, it would be uncharacteristic for Emma to lie about something like this.

"I'm so sorry, Emma." I kept her wrapped in my arms for several minutes. Letting her know the bond of parent and child was stronger than any issue from the school day. It was one of those incidents to soothe over, nothing more said.

With Emma consoled, it was time for the Chloe homework battle. After being restrained by classroom decorum all day, sitting down to homework was a challenge. An hour later, Chloe's homework was finally completed and back in her school bag. As Chloe charged upstairs to play with her dolls, Emma wandered through to the kitchen table to start her homework. Although Emma didn't need any help with her homework, she liked to work through it while I made dinner. Scott was working late, again, so I would keep dinner quick and simple. I was in the middle of putting the food in the oven when the phone rang. "Jennifer, this is Sarah." Oh great! I knew what was coming. "I've just got home and Kevin told me he got into trouble at school today because of Emma."

"Yes, I've had Emma in tears about it too."

"It's not a question of tears," said Sarah, intent on protecting her son's innocence. "I want Emma to apologise to Kevin. He's not happy at someone getting him into trouble."

"That's not going to happen."

"What do you mean?"

"It would appear our children have told each of us very different versions of the same story."

"Well, I know who I'm believing!"

"Yes, Sarah, and I know who I'm believing too. The school dealt with it, I'm leaving it at that." I slammed the phone down. As I released the handset, my hands were shaking. It wasn't like me to get so heat up. I have different ways of reacting to confrontations with other mums. My first option is to find an element of humour in the situation. If that doesn't work my next step will be to work to a neutral solution. If pushed I would go to confrontation. Until today I'd never had to go that far!

I needed to have a proper chat with Sarah. I knew through my friendships with other mums at the school that I was the only one still on speaking terms with her. The other mums had given up on her by the time their children ended primary one. I had either ignored the other mums' comments about Sarah, or defended her, but I wasn't so naïve that I couldn't see where the comments came from. Sarah was hard work at times and, on days like this, it all felt too much.

By midnight I crawled upstairs to bed. I considered forgoing the routine of face cleansing and tooth brushing in favour of an extra few minutes of sleep, but I knew I would regret that decision in the morning. With my final strands of energy I nestled into bed. Despite my exhaustion, sleep didn't come immediately. It didn't help that Scott was sound asleep and snoring beside me. Since three o'clock my time had been consumed with the girls, Scott and household duties. How could I even consider a job when evenings took this much emotional energy? Normally I loved the pace of family life, but today had me completely exhausted and worn out. This was a day for the 'to be forgotten' pile.

PAUL

"I'm confused," I said to Scott and Matt. It was our monthly catch up, something that Matt and Scott had instigated for the men's group. "I'm not sure whether to stay with hairdressing, or look into something more worthwhile. Maybe something in the healthcare profession, or working at the church in some capacity?"

"Why?" asked Scott. There was no further explanation to his question, no indication as to the level of response he expected.

"Is hairdressing an appropriate profession for a Christian? Shouldn't I be doing something nobler or life affirming?"

"Why would you think that?" said Matt.

"A bunch of reasons. Si is taking all the fun out of the salon; the coincidence of having a couple of sick clients last week; and generally feeling restless every time I walk in the salon. Are things coming to a head because it's time for a change?"

"If it's a change you're looking for it, then explore your options," said Scott. "But don't be misled into thinking there is a holy hierarchy of job titles. Over the years, I've met a lot of people who think pursuing a career in the church is the ultimate job title. It's not. It's never a wrong thing to ask God if you're in the place he wants you to be, but don't assume your spirituality is defined by your job."

"Think of your client list," Matt added. "You have the most repeat clients. They're not coming back just because you're a great hairdresser. They're coming back because you listen, really listen to what they have to say. You provide a unique service for a lot of people."

I liked their feedback, but I still wasn't convinced it was as simple as all that. Matt's comment about repeat clients got me thinking about the range of clients I get to meet day-in day-out. From there my thoughts drifted back to Kirsty. I wondered what she thought of the flowers, and if I'd ever get the chance to see her again. I hoped so.

"You okay?" asked Matt.

"I don't know. When I became a Christian I felt whole, probably for the first time ever. And part of that was a sense of peace. But now, suddenly, I'm restless? I miss the peace. Have I done something wrong? Should I be changing something?"

"Maybe something does need to change. But don't rush into anything. If God's got a different plan for you, he'll make it clear, you don't need to force it. This is just a period of restlessness to get you ready to move when the time comes," replied Matt.

I looked at them both, "I've got so much to learn."

Matt nodded. "We all have, mate. We all have!"

JENNIFER

"Did you lose yourself in housework again?" asked Scott, as I rushed into the restaurant.

"I know. I know. I'm sorry. I'm such a terrible person," I replied, as he stood up to kiss me. He was right. I had completely lost track of the time as I worked my way through my Friday housework routine. I'd left myself so short of time I'd had to grab my brush and makeup bag on the way out the door so I could spruce myself up during the train journey to the city centre.

"Although, I would like to say it wasn't all down to my bad time keeping. I had a stressful start to the day."

The waiter brought over our drinks. "I've already ordered for us. I need to get back to the office for a one o'clock meeting."

"Sorry. Thanks."

"What was this stressful morning then? Something to do with Emma?"

"As suspected, she didn't want to go to school today and was quite emotional and clingy. But while I was in the living room speaking quietly and calmly with Emma, I was also issuing instructions to Amy and Chloe to keep…"

I was interrupted by Scott's phone pinging with a new text message. Immediately Scott's attention was diverted to the device as he picked it up and replied.

"Sorry, honey, what were you saying?"

"Just that I had to spend my pre-school time shouting instructions to the girls to get them ready for…"

The phone pinged again. And again, Scott picked it up and replied. This time he didn't even apologise. "Poor kid, let's hope she has a good day today. Did you see Sarah?"

"I did. But she was keeping her distance, and I must confess I was happy with that. I'm feeling too raw…" This time the interruption was Scott's phone ringing.

"Peter. No problem, I'll be back in a few minutes." Scott hung up the phone and turned his attention back to me, "Sorry, honey. I need to go back to the office now to deal with some issues before our meeting."

"Fine. Go." It wasn't the first time Scott had left me halfway through a meal for work.

"I'll be home late tonight. I've got that leadership meeting at church."

Sometimes I felt like a single parent.

When I collected the girls from school, I noticed Sarah in the main playground. By the time I got Chloe and walked round for Emma, she was gone. But all thoughts of Sarah and Kevin disappeared at the excited screams from the girls when I told them I was going to take them out for dinner.

At dinner Emma picked at her food while Amy and Chloe scoffed theirs. When they finished their food, Amy volunteered to take Chloe over to the restaurant's soft play section. I could have kissed Amy for her sensitivity to the situation.

"How did things go today?" Again my question was met with the shrug.

"What happened?"

Emma looked up with big, sad eyes, "Kevin spilled paint during our free play afternoon. And he ruined my painting."

"Did you get into trouble?"

"No, this time Miss Robertson saw him do it."

I hugged Emma. My heart broke for my sensitive child, I wanted to take the pain away from her. This weekend would be about reassuring Emma. As I sat hugging her, I wondered again what was going on with Sarah and Kevin. Something was off somewhere. Whatever was going on there, my priority was to protect Emma. If there were any further issues next week, I would phone the school.

"Let's head home now," I said. "We'll make up a bowl of popcorn and get a fun movie on." Emma smiled. That one smile was all I needed.

JENNIFER

Hill walking was the perfect activity for a family day out. For once we had a Saturday void of any arrangements. I needed a break from the house. Emma needed activity to get her thoughts off the problems at school with Kevin. And, as for the other three, exercise and fresh air would do them the world of good.

But a sunny day in Glasgow doesn't necessarily equate to a sunny day in the hills. As we got to Loch Lomond, the rain started. The car became full of complaints. It was up to me to get them enthused, out the car and started on our way.

"Why do we need to go walking?" said Amy. "Why can't we be like a normal family and stay at home or go out shopping?"

"Because this is a better way to spend our day. And it's fun. Isn't this fun?"

My reply was four grunts. Still no enthusiasm then! It was refreshing to be outdoors, the colours on the hillside were beautiful. But the grumpiness from the rest of the family was wearing me down.

By the time we got part way up the hill, Chloe at least was showing signs of enthusiasm for the walk. It was always the same with Chloe. She would complain non-stop at the start of an activity, and then, at some point along the way, she would get into it, and end up being the most enthusiastic, leading the rest of us, gushing with enthusiasm for what had previously been an ordeal to her.

A wide, shallow stream interrupted the path; boulders in the stream provided the natural path through. Chloe, now in full adventure mode, was looking at the stones to determine the best way across. "Mum, look at me! I bet I can get across here using only two of the stones rather than four."

Before I had time to respond I heard the splash. The unusually dry summer meant the streams were slow and shallow. But for Chloe, the drama expert, depth wasn't the issue. "Dad! Get me out of here!" she screamed.

"Take my hand," said Scott. It took all my effort not to laugh at the absurdity of the situation. The water wasn't deep, Chloe could easily get herself out, but five-year-old drama demanded parental action. Scott put his hand down to pull her out, but in doing so his foot slipped off one of the stepping stones. Now there were two wet walkers. It looked like this walk was being prematurely curtailed.

The walk down the hill was even grumpier than the walk up. Scott and Chloe kept glaring at each other, both blaming the other for their wetness. Amy and Emma were still complained about having to be outside walking in the soggy hills. And me? Despite seeing the humour in the stand-off between Scott and Chloe, I felt deflated and drained. I had needed energy giving time today, but instead I was the one holding the family together and trying to make everyone else happy.

And, on that grumpy hillside, it hit me once again. When had I last been truly happy? I gave so much to the family, and I loved to do that. But right now I was the one needing their support. When had the joy slipped away? Did happiness change its face with the differing seasons of life? Or had it evaporated somewhere along the years while my attention had been distracted by demanding pre-schoolers?

KIRSTY

From the outside the climbing centre resembled a warehouse and was only slightly more appealing on the inside. All around the interior were climbing walls; a myriad display of multi-coloured walls further brightened by different coloured hand and foot holds. Below each of the climbing walls were crash mats. The sight of the mats filled me with dread. Had they been put out especially for me?

We were taken to an instructor for our safety talk. Nerves were kicking in and we couldn't stop ourselves giggling through the talk. The height of the surrounding walls had our nerves on high alert, and when you're with your friends that somehow translates into uncontrollable giggles. The instructor told us which wall we would be attempting, and how to assist each other in the climb and descent. He went through the safety equipment and importance of making sure it was all fitted correctly. More giggles followed as we clambered into the safety harnesses.

"Does my butt look big in this?" said Jo, laughing at the sight of us all in the most unflattering accessory any of us had ever worn.

The instructor looked at us with a bored, 'I've heard it all before' expression. "Safety is no laughing matter ladies."

Jo's expression told me she was fighting to keep her face straight and not offend the instructor with any more hilarity. She even managed a quiet, little, "sorry" to the instructor. If he heard it, he didn't acknowledge it.

"Would you mind taking a photo of us?" said Jo to the instructor. I was in awe of her confidence. After seeing how much we had annoyed him, there's no way I could have asked him anything, much less such a favour.

We all hugged together for a funny-faced picture, posing in our hard hats and harnesses and laughing at ourselves and each other.

However, once the climbing started we all focussed our attention on where to put our feet and hands; dress code and unflattering harnesses forgotten. After a couple of times of going up and down the wall, the instructor left us to it. We were so taken up with our own climbing achievements we didn't notice the group of male students who were gearing up at the wall next to ours.

"Hey," shouted over one student. "This your first time here?"

"No! We come here all the time," said Jo.

"How about a race then?" replied the student.

"What's in it for us?" I asked. With the fun and adventure of the night, and the adrenaline of the climb pulsing through my body, my challenge hungry trait came to the fore.

"If you win, we'll give you our phone numbers," said the student.

"And what if you win?"

"Then you give us your numbers."

"That seems like the same outcome no matter who wins," I said, laughing at this barter game we had entered. "But you're on!"

"What are you like," said Lynn. "You never can resist a challenge."

"I say Kirsty should climb for our team," said Jo. There was an unmistakable twinkle in her eye as she looked at me. "After all, this is your night out."

"Is it your birthday?" asked the student.

"No, it's her get over a breakup night," said Lynn, before I could stop her.

"Interesting. The stakes just got higher," said the student, winking at me.

We stood next to each other. Ready for the climb. I was shaking with anticipation.

"Ready, set, go!" shouted Lynn. We scrambled up the wall as if our lives depended on it. The student was getting ahead of me. I would not let him win.

"Come on Kirsty!"

"Come on Adam!"

Between the two groups at the bottom of the wall, the hall was getting noisy. I was determined to beat this student. Girl power demanded that I win. I pushed myself on further, the last few holds just a few reaches away. Our height from the ground no longer concerned me. It was all about winning. I stretched myself out as far as I could and got a hand hold ahead of Adam. His feet slipped from the hold he was standing on, and he needed to use every ounce of arm muscle to keep himself where he was. There was no room for niceties during a challenge. I took full advantage of his mistake and grabbed for the final hold.

"Woo hoo!" I shouted down to Jo. "I did it. I won! I'm coming down."

With Jo holding my support ropes I launched off from the top, enjoying the feeling of victory and free fall as Jo supported me back down. It was high fives and hugs all round.

"I need a rematch," said Adam. Who, in contrast, was getting a hard time from his friends for letting a girl beat him.

"No chance," I said. "I won."

To rub it in, just that bit more, we started a victory dance, jumping about and cheering. But in all the enthusiasm I failed to notice the discarded safety helmet at my feet. As I jumped up in a victory celebration, my foot landed on the helmet, then slipped off it, twisting as it went.

"Ouch, ouch, ouch." I grabbed my ankle as I flopped onto the ground in pain.

"Can you stand?" asked Lynn.

"No, it's too sore."

"I'll get a member of staff," said Adam. "They should have something to help with the pain."

A member of staff came over with an ice pack. The freezing cold pack brought instant relief. But I still couldn't put any weight on my ankle.

"Let's get you to A&E," said Jo.

"No, it'll be fine, I'm sure it's not that bad," I said, not at all happy at the thought of spending a Saturday night at A&E.

"That wasn't a question Kirsty," said Jo. "I'm taking you to A&E now!" With the help of the others I freed myself from the safety equipment and we gathered our things together.

"We're sorry she's hurt," said Adam. The group of students stood to the side, giving us space to get ourselves collected and leave. They made no further mention of swapping telephone numbers.

"I'm sorry everyone," I said, as we made our way to the hospital.

"Life's never dull," said Jo.

"And we wouldn't have it any other way," said Lynn.

"On the plus side, you were having lots of fun till the accident. And you totally beat that guy," said Carol.

As expected, A&E was busy. It was too early for the influx of drunk party people, but busy enough. The next few hours were split between triage, assessment, x-ray and then my ankle being encased in a protective support. The doctor instructed me to keep it elevated and rest.

"Come and stay with me tonight," said Jo.

"I won't argue with that." I was grateful for Jo's offer and for the pain medication that was already kicking in.

"Sorry I don't have anything for breakfast," said Jo, coming through to the bedroom the following morning. Not only had Jo invited me to spend the night at her flat, but she also gave me her bed while she slept on her settee. "So, let's have ice-cream!"

Jo sat down beside me on the bed and set the tray with an ice-cream tub and two teaspoons between us. "Remember that personal trainer guy you dated for a while," said Jo. "He would never approve of you eating ice-cream for breakfast."

"Can you imagine his reaction? Too funny! Yep, he was dumped when I realised all his training schedules for me were targeting my bum. Don't be shaping me up for your own pleasure, mister!"

"So is that why you ended up opting for the overly sensitive guy the next time? What self-respecting guy cries at puppy adverts? Come on!"

"Okay, okay. I admit I have picked a few clangers. At least with those guys I got to dump them rather than it always being me getting jilted."

"I reckon I still win at being ditched for the most insane reason. Who breaks up with someone just because they take some chips off your plate? Come on! Just tell me 'no'. Don't be Mr OTT and go berserk!"

"Jo, don't be so unhygienic!" I said, attempting to mimic Michael, Jo's ex.

"I don't know if it was better or worse having Steven end things with no explanation. He's the first guy to split up with me and not give any reason. What do I take from that?"

"Sometimes things just end, Kirsty. It doesn't mean it was something you did or didn't do. Maybe it had just run its course."

"You know what Jo?"

"What's that?"

"I think you are right about me not dating for a while. When I was a wee girl, I expected to grow up, meet someone, fall in love and get married. The reality is so much harder. All I want is love."

"Awww honey, you know we love you. You're an amazing person, and somewhere out there is the right man for you. A man who will love you as much as you love him. And preferably someone who won't try to make you do a million squats or cry through the puppy adverts on TV."

Jo grabbed a pillow and hit me with it. "Now come on, enough of the self-pity! Time to get ready for church. Let's hope Ben's got a great sermon lined up for us today. Maybe you need a bit of outward focus to distract you from all this man chat."

Everyone should have a best friend like Jo. Someone to eat ice-cream with on a Sunday morning. A friend who loves you despite your confused heart.

KIRSTY

Despite the ankle incident, I had enjoyed the weekend. It had been what I needed, lots of laughter, and great times with my friends. But now I faced the problem of how to get to work. Yesterday had been easy, Jo had taxied me around in her car, ensuring I got from place to place with as little inconvenience as possible. Although, despite her assistance, I had struggled to walk up the stairs to my flat. With my ankle still throbbing I decided the bus wasn't a viable option; it involved too much walking from my flat to the bus stop and then from the bus stop to the office. Booking a taxi was the only solution.

I wasn't sure how long it would take me to hobble downstairs, so I made my way down and waited in the street. And that was the moment the rain started. I looked in my bag for my umbrella, but then remembered I'd transferred it to another bag for the weekend. At least my raincoat would protect my clothes. I put my sunglasses on in the hope they would protect my mascara clad eyelashes from the rain. If they failed in that task, they would at least hide the panda look from anyone who saw me. I made a mental note to invest in waterproof mascara; this was becoming a habit.

The taxi turned up twenty minutes later. Wet and frustrated I clambered in, my ankle desperate for a rest. The arrival of the taxi, however, did not bring an end to the stress of the morning. The journey to work was marred with roadworks at one of the main junctions into town. Temporary traffic lights were doing their best to control the situation, but the hold-ups aggravated my already hassled emotions. By the time I got to the office I was stressed, soaked through and miserable. Things didn't improve at the office as I stepped out of the elevator and met Irene.

"You're late."

"Sorry, I called for a taxi, but it came late."

"Why on earth are you getting a taxi to work?"

"I hurt my ankle at the weekend and can barely walk on it." I pointed down to my strapped ankle, hoping that it would help my cause.

"Do you think I've got time to stand here and listen to your weekend shenanigans? And you don't have time for it either. I suggest you sit yourself down and get some work done."

The woman did not have a sympathetic bone in her body. The happiness from the weekend evaporated bit by bit as I hobbled through the department. Gary was waiting for me at my desk.

"What's happened to you?" he said, a touch of amusement in his voice.

"Don't ask!" For once I didn't care it was Gary standing before me, he would need to deal with my grumpiness; I was in no mood to disguise it. The journey to work plus the encounter with Irene had depleted my weekend joy.

He walked away from my desk laughing.

By mid-morning I was stiff from sitting, plus I was desperate for the loo and needed something to drink. I eased myself up from the chair, but as soon as I put any weight on my ankle the shooting pains started. Walking to the toilet then over to the water cooler helped ease the pain.

As I was filling a cup of water, Gary came over. "So what happened to you, hoppy?"

"I had a small incident at the climbing-wall centre on Saturday night."

"What happened? Give me the details."

"I went climbing with my friends, a group of students challenged us to a race to the top of the wall. I won, but then twisted my ankle when I fell over a safety helmet."

Gary laughed. A big out loud laugh that attracted the attention of those sitting close to the water cooler.

"Shh! I'm already in Irene's bad books for being late this morning. Don't draw attention to me."

He laughed more quietly. "Let me guess. It was a group of male students who challenged you."

I gave him my best huffy, raised eyebrow stare and hobbled back to my desk. There was no point talking to some people at times!

However, Gary followed me back to my desk. "You're not getting away from me that easily. Tell me all the details or I'll laugh so loudly Irene will come over." He leaned against my desk, arms folded, an expectant look on his face.

"Fine!" Best to get it over with and get back to peace and quiet. "I beat the student, and yes it was a guy, to the top of the climbing wall. But then as I was jumping about celebrating with my friends I landed on a safety helmet and twisted my ankle. I then spent hours in A&E waiting to get it checked and bandaged. Satisfied?"

"That's all very interesting," said Gary, with more laughter in his voice than I liked. "But why did they challenge you? And why accept the challenge?"

"I guess they wanted more fun in their night than only competing against each other."

"And what was the reward for the challenge winner? A date?"

"No!"

"Come on, what was the reward?"

I stood up. And, with as much defiance as I could muster, replied, "The reward was swapping phone numbers."

"I knew it!" As he walked away, I heard him laughing. Why had I told him so much? Probably because he seemed to know already. And come to think about it, why was the department manager having this conversation with me, chatting with me as if we were best buddies? On any other day I would be all girly and happy at this attention from Gary, but between the pain in my ankle and the morning grumpiness, it annoyed me more than anything else.

I glanced around and noticed Irene watching Gary walking away from my desk. Before I looked away, she looked at me. I couldn't read the expression in her eyes, but I'm pretty sure it wasn't anger.

The next time I hobbled to the water cooler Gary appeared at my side again. "So did you call him yet?"

"Who?"

"The boy you beat on the climbing wall?"

"No."

"Why not?"

"What is with all these questions? Let it go, please!"

"Okay." Why was he being so insistent? I wanted to forget about Saturday night. No, that wasn't true. Saturday night had been brilliant, laughter and dares were the therapy I had needed. But all these questions from Gary made me feel like I was back in high school. Back then if I ever admitted I liked a boy, everyone seemed to hear about it and would tease me about it for weeks. Whereas if any other girl said she liked someone her comments would be met with positive responses. Why did my life get so complicated whenever men were in the equation?

"Nope, still can't let it go. I'm surprised at this side of you. I wouldn't have pegged you as the challenge hungry kind. You always seem so quiet, sitting alone at your desk, working harder than anyone else in the department."

I looked up into Gary's eyes. All this time he had noticed me? He recognised how hard I worked. It was more than Irene ever acknowledged. But I wasn't sure I liked this serious turn in the conversation. Time to lighten it again.

"If you must know I have three brothers, who I could never keep up with, so to make up for it I would accept any challenge cast at me, whether from my brothers or classmates at school. And yes, it got me into lots of bother as a kid, but the result is I still can't resist a challenge. Saturday night had nothing to do with getting a random guy's telephone number!"

"I better watch myself round you then. Don't want your reckless behaviour rubbing off on me." And with that he walked off, leaving me to get my water. Again, I was annoyed at myself for giving him so much ammunition. Why was he so interested?

"You still okay for our early meeting tomorrow?" said Gary, when he came over to my desk later on to drop off some information for the launch event.

"Should be okay, I'll phone the taxi company tonight in the hope a taxi comes on time in the morning."

"Did you get a taxi today?"

"Yes, my ankle is too sore to walk to and from the bus stops."

"We can't have you spending all your hard earned salary on taxis just to get to work. I'll pick you up in the morning."

"Pardon?" I was sure my jaw dropped in shock. It was kind of him and it would make life a lot easier, and save money, but was it okay to get a lift with the boss?

"I'll get you at 7:45," said Gary. Without waiting for a reply, he turned and walked back to his office, my reply assumed.

Wow! Gary driving me to work! What was going on?

Jennifer

Over the years I've come to the realisation I have a couple of traits not considered normal by the majority of the population. First of all, I like Mondays. I enjoy the newness of each week and the anticipation of the new possibilities that could lie ahead of me. Second, I like housework. I realise this may be down to some control issues on my side, but; I like having my house in order.

However, when the week starts with: "Mum, my stomach is really sore. I think I might be sick.", your Monday is no longer so promising. Now I had to guess if my child really was sick or trying to avoid school.

"You're okay, Emma. Its worry and nerves; you'll do great. You have nothing to worry about. The incidents at school were not your fault."

"But what if Kevin does something else to me today?"

I pulled her into a hug. Sometimes a hug was all there was to say.

"Mum, where are my school socks?" shouted Amy from upstairs. No matter how many times I told the girls not to shout through the house they always did it.

"Mum!" screamed Chloe, as she knocked over her bowl of cereal and spilled milk on the kitchen table.

"Chloe!"

"It was an accident."

Instructing Emma to go upstairs and get ready for school, I mopped up the spilled cereal, then went upstairs to help Amy find her missing articles of school uniform. Some days I was well and truly outnumbered!

"Amy, I need you to walk with Chloe this morning, please."

"But I was going to walk with Olivia!"

"Amy, I need you to do this for me this morning. Emma's nervous about going to school today, so I want to be free to concentrate on helping her. And maybe look out for her at playtime and lunchtime and make sure she's okay."

"Being the oldest sucks!" said Amy. The teenage attitude was getting ever closer.

"I know it's not fair to ask you to help with your siblings, but you also know I don't do it very often, so when I do I expect you to help. You have perks from being the oldest too."

Amy gave a non-committal reply, but I knew I could rely on her to come through and help. Underneath the huffiness was a good and helpful heart.

"Emma, how are you getting on?" I asked, walking into Emma's room. She was still sitting in her pyjamas.

"Come on Emma. We need to get you ready for school. I don't want us all to be late." Emma was more than capable of getting herself ready for school, but for this morning it was about doing whatever it took to get out the door on time. My heart broke at the sadness in her eyes.

"This will all blow over, Emma. Just wait and see. In a day or two it will all be forgotten and you and Kevin will be friends again."

"No it won't. I'm never playing with Kevin again!"

To be fair, I didn't blame her. I would feel the same if I was in her place.

"Well, try to stay away from him and play with your other friends."

"But we sit at the same table. I can't get away from him all the time."

"Okay. Then, at least at play times and lunch you can play with your other friends, and avoid him. But, if he follows you around and gives you a hard time tell the playtime assistants. And if he does anything to you in class, tell Miss Robertson." I didn't want to create a tell-tale, but right now it was a question of self-preservation. "And if anything else happens, I'll phone the school about it."

Those final words seemed to reach through to Emma, enough to help her cope with getting ready for school and making the journey to the school gates.

For me, it was another morning of doing the school run in my raincoat and sunglasses. The girls had consumed all my time. Thank goodness for the props that hid the impact of my morning dramas.

JENNIFER

It was so difficult to walk away from school knowing Emma was struggling. As I walked home, I prayed that her day would go well.

I wandered round the house. Like the house, I felt empty. Under normal circumstances I would be full of enthusiasm and have a list of things to tackle, but today lethargy controlled me. Part of it was down to Emma's situation, but a larger part of it was down to my own feelings of disquiet.

"What is wrong with me?" I asked the empty house. Fighting through my dull emotions was becoming a habit. A habit I didn't like. I had plenty to keep me occupied this week. Saturday was Scott's birthday, and we were celebrating with a party here at the house.

I strolled round the house, assessing what needed done in each of the rooms. I love my house. As with most couples we had started off with our little flat, then moved to a small terrace house when I was pregnant with Amy. Once Scott gained all his professional qualifications and achieved his first major promotion we moved to his house. It was perfect. A beautiful old sandstone villa, on a quiet, leafy street.

Downstairs was full of wonderful old features: the wooden floors, the fireplace, the cornicing and the detailing round the windows.

I made a list on what needed done in the kitchen-diner, the living room and the family room. As these would be the main rooms used for the party, I would leave them till nearer the end of the week. I began the big clean and tidy with the bedrooms, not that I expected anyone to be upstairs, but house-proud tendencies demanded that the whole house be cleaned, scrubbed and polished.

I sang and danced along to my playlist as I went from bedroom to bedroom picking up discarded pyjamas, socks, pants and tops. Then there was the washing and ironing; putting the myriad toys in the appropriate toy boxes; vacuuming; dusting; cleaning the windows; stripping their beds and letting the mattresses air before putting on the clean sets.

By the time I walked along to get the girls from school I felt invigorated and equipped to help them in whatever way I could.

Chloe came out with her usual complaint, "Mum! I've got homework."

"Chloe, you always have homework."

"But doesn't it end soon?"

"I'm afraid not. You've got years of homework ahead of you."

"Ugh! I hate school."

The arrival of a skipping, happy Emma silenced further complaining.

"And, how was school for you today?"

"No problem at all," she replied, skipping round me. Emma was smiling. That was one less stress to deal with.

"Right, let's get you pair back home. We'll leave Amy to walk back with her friends. It's early dinner tonight as I need to get back to school for a PTA meeting."

"Who will look after us?" asked Chloe.

"Dad will be home in time for dinner. Do you want to do your homework with him or me?"

"You!" said Chloe. "Daddy slows me down."

"I'm pretty sure you're the one who slows yourself down," I said, laughing at her huffy expression.

"Thank you so much for coming out to the first PTA meeting of the new academic year," said Mrs Evans, the head teacher. "We are excited about the year ahead of us and look forward to all that we can achieve together.

"As some of you may be aware, most of our committee from last year have stepped down, either due to children moving on to high school or increased work commitments. I'm happy to see Jennifer Thompson has returned for another year.

"Jennifer, can we count on you to remain on the committee this year?"

"Yes. No problem." I've been active in the PTA since Amy started school. In the first year I helped wherever I could. My willingness to be involved led to a committee post the following year. I've been contributing more and more to the group with each passing year. I suspected this year I would be promoted to chair of the PTA.

"Excellent. Who else would like to be on the committee?" I find it amusing when Mrs Evans asks for volunteers for committee posts. People always react the same way – heads down looking at the floor. It's the adult equivalent of the toddler covering their eyes with their hands to hide whilst playing hide and seek.

"Jennifer, would you be willing to be PTA chair this year?"

"Yes. No problem."

"There you go everyone, our experienced member is taking the lead. You can now volunteer in the knowledge that post is now filled."

There was more shoe staring then gradually a couple of the other mums volunteered for committee posts.

"Excellent. Jennifer, can I suggest you connect with Mrs Blake, Mrs Brady and Mrs McLaughlan to discuss potential fund-raising activities for the year?"

Mrs Evans then continued with the rest of the meeting. Updating us on staffing and general information for the coming year.

"Let me guess," said Scott, as I got home after the meeting. "You're the new head of the PTA?"

"How did you know?" I asked, laughing at how predictable the situation was.

"Did you get a choice, or was it assumed?"

"No, Mrs Evans asked me. I'm looking forward to it. It gives me a new challenge for this year."

"So, have you decided yet how you'll transform the school?"

"You flatter me," I said, and laughed. "I've invited the rest of the committee here on Friday morning so we can discuss ideas for the year."

"The usual school discos and Christmas Fayre?"

"They are a good starting point. They work well and raise a good level of money. But it will be fun to think of something new this year."

"I can almost see those creative wheels whirring around your brain."

Scott was right. The creativeness of it excited me. I was beginning to think this year was about finding new creative outlets.

KIRSTY

As promised, the following morning at 7:45am prompt, Gary drew up outside my flat and beeped his car horn. Grabbing my raincoat and bag, I made my way down the stairs. My ankle was better than it had been yesterday, an evening of elevating it on a cushion had helped, but I still had to take my time. As I walked towards his car, I couldn't shake the feeling that Gary was used to beeping his car horn and having women come running. Although, if that were the case, the women in question would all be models, or at the very least, exceptionally glamorous.

His car was gorgeous. I know nothing about cars, but even I could tell it was top of the range of whatever model it was. It oozed luxury and fine craftsmanship. It probably cost more than my modest little one-bedroom flat. I was so enthralled with the luxury of the car I almost forgot I was sitting next to Gary.

"How are things coming along for the launch event?" asked Gary, bringing my attention back to him. "What do you want to discuss with me this morning?"

With a twinge of disappointment I reached into my bag to get out my notes. I was thankful I'd put the spreadsheet and notes in my bag at the end of the day yesterday. Gary was too confusing. Yesterday at the water cooler he'd been all social chat about the climbing wall incident. And now he only wanted to discuss work.

As he drove, Gary asked lots of questions. I was amazed at his focus on the details. I hadn't expected him to be so knowledgeable on every little aspect of the event. It was a pleasant change to have a manager who was so focussed and aware. Although, on the flip side it meant I would need to be on top of every little detail.

Working with Gary had its issues, but as we continued our journey to work, the realisation that I had the opportunity to learn so much from him inspired me. He was unique amongst his management peers. He was the youngest manager in the city council as far as I was aware. However, he carried himself with an air of importance and purpose that made it clear to everyone he was still climbing his career ladder, and wasn't interested in slowing down his ascent until he reached the top. That mind-set kept him apart from both staff and other managers, something he barely seemed to notice.

My thoughts were interrupted by Gary pulling up outside Chocolate & Vanilla. "I'm tight for time this morning, but there's always time for a decent coffee. You able to hobble up to the counter and get us our coffees?"

"I'm sure I can manage that."

"We'll have a look at the delegate list once we're in my office," said Gary, as his car purred into his management parking space in the office car park. "I want to see who we've got on board so far and have one final check through my contact lists to make sure I've got everyone I need on the invitation list."

Seated in Gary's office we spent another half-hour going over the guest list for the event. Gary worked his way through his various contact lists, doing the final check that everyone he wanted included had been invited. "We'll get the delegate list finalised next week and see if anyone still needs chased up by then. Send these additional five invites today."

I wrote down the to-dos for the invitation list. We had covered a lot of ground this morning; I needed to make sure I didn't miss anything.

"There is one more thing we need to work on together this week. Are you free tomorrow night?"

"I can be." But as I gave my semi-committal I realised I should have waited to hear what he wanted. What could require working in the evening?

"I want to check out the hotel's suggested menus."

"Don't they have set menus?"

"They do for most events. But I'm an important client for them, so I'll be choosing the menus, and I want to know what to expect from my choices. I'd like you to come with me to sample the menu options. It's always good to have a second opinion. And, it will give you the chance to meet Samantha, the hotel event planner, face to face. There are still a few things to finalise with her.

"So you want the two of us to have dinner, at the hotel, tomorrow night?"

"Is that a problem?"

"No, no it's fine. I can be there."

"Great, I'll leave you to set that up with the hotel."

I was dismissed from the meeting. I was so confused. What was the deal with Gary? The whole morning had been all work; but now I was arranging for us to have dinner together. Was that also just work? I would need to cancel small group. It seemed I was missing a lot of church at the moment between one disaster and another.

I needed to get my life under control.

PAUL

"Good to see you again, Paul," said Iain, as I sat down across from him. Iain is the Scottish director of ByDesign. He had called me yesterday to set up this meeting. The fact we were meeting in a restaurant rather than the salon had me curious.

During my time at ByDesign, I had met Iain several times at the salon as well as at company functions. I liked him; he was direct and to the point. Over the years I made sure he knew who I was. Iain was in a position to make or break your career.

"Thanks for the invite. You've got my curiosity aroused."

"We'll come to that later. Right now I'm starving. Let's order and eat, and then we'll get to business."

I would rather have started with business, but he was the boss. Over dinner we talked about the latest results from the Premier League and the usual small talk. As the waiter cleared away our empty dinner plates, Iain turned the conversation to the reason for our meeting. "At your last appraisal you talked about your long-term goal to be a manager of your own salon."

"Yes, that's right." I was intrigued.

"A vacancy is coming up for the role of manager at our Edinburgh salon."

"The Edinburgh salon?" I was shocked Iain was offering me Edinburgh, it was the flagship salon for ByDesign in Scotland. When Iain asked to meet I hadn't expected anything like this.

"We've been keeping an eye on the weekly reports we get from Si, and you're by far the most consistent stylist. That's the kind of person we want to promote."

I nodded, trying to take in all that was being said. Iain continued his monologue, informing me of the promotion benefits and what it would mean for my career. But throughout his discourse, I was quiet.

"I'm surprised you're not saying anything, Paul. We want you to step up to this role. It's about recognising that you're one of our best stylists, and we want to use that to keep the Edinburgh salon at the top of the performance tables for ByDesign."

"You've taken me by surprise. Can I have time to think this through?" It was a risk to voice my uncertainties. ByDesign had been a great employer to me, they didn't praise their stylists easily, and to be offered the Edinburgh salon as my first management post was unheard of. But the restlessness was still there. Six months ago I would have said yes with no hesitation. But that certainty had been replaced by a floundering unrest that kept me from pouncing on this offer.

"Vacancies like this don't come along all that often. But we want you in the post, so I'll give you a week to consider it. We'll have coffee after your last client next Tuesday."

"Thanks Iain, I appreciate the offer." And I did. But appreciation wasn't a big enough motivation to make the wrong decision.

I walked home to give myself some time to think about all that this conversation meant. Being a hairdresser was all I knew. I was good at it. At the start of my career I'd thrived on the creativeness and freshness of it all, not to mention all the dates it led to. I had to figure out what was nagging me about Iain's offer, and in fact my current attitude towards ByDesign. But if I wasn't a hairdresser what else would I do?

As I walked through Kelvingrove Park, I passed a couple kissing. And without meaning to, my thoughts turned to Kirsty. I wondered how she was. I wanted to see her again. What was it about her that had gripped me and wouldn't let me go? I needed answers. But to get any kind of resolution I needed to see her again. I had no idea how to make that happen.

KIRSTY

"Hey, Jennifer," I said, as I made my first excuse call of the evening. "I can't host small group tomorrow night. I have a work thing I need to go to."

"Is this anything to do with your new project?"

"Yes, we need to go to the hotel to check a few things."

"Well enjoy your evening, don't worry about us. We'll cope without you for one night. I'll phone round the others and decide what to do."

"Thanks Jennifer."

"How's that ankle?"

"It comes and goes. It's pretty sore just now. I've got a pile of dishes needing done, but I think I might ignore them and soak in a big bubble bath instead."

"Quite right. You need to get your rest. Speak to you soon."

Jennifer's friendliness added to my crankiness. I felt guilty at bailing out of small group. Dealing with my ankle was tiring. I hobbled through to my bathroom and ran the bath.

I eased myself in amongst the bubbles. The scented candles cast a cosy glow and enriched the ambiance. I leaned back with a satisfied sigh and turned my attention to my latest novel; chick lit and bubble baths were the perfect combination. After a luxurious half-hour in the bath my ankle felt much better and calm had returned.

The important thing now was to keep the calm, relaxed vibe going. I made myself a cup of soothing camomile tea and took it through to the bedroom. I snuggled down under the duvet, carefully positioning my ankle on a pile of cushions. It was time for some much-needed Bible study - but perhaps I'd quickly check my phone before I got into my reading. A text message was flashing at me from Gary, demanding my attention. 'I'll pick you up at 7:45'. I smiled at the text. All these rides to work meant more time with him, and that was something I was looking forward to increasingly. Thoughts of Gary were threatening to consume me. I needed to stop making more of it than it was. I picked up my Bible, determined to forget about him.

The following morning I spent longer than usual choosing my work clothes and applying my makeup. I was excited about the dinner with Gary. I needed to wear something that fitted the requirements of work and an evening out. In the end I opted for a black skirt and a colourful blouse.

"How's that ankle this morning?" said Gary, as I got into the car.

"Definitely not as bad in the mornings, thanks for asking."

"You're looking very presentable this morning," he said, as he looked over at me. "Mmm, and you smell nice too." My face flushed with the compliments. He didn't seem to notice my discomfort. He was probably used to being around women and passing out compliments without it being a big heart stopping deal.

The rest of the journey returned to the safer topic of the launch event. We discussed the tasks I would work on that day, and what Gary would be looking for from the menu samples.

By the time we walked into the office I was enthused and motivated for the day ahead. Rounding it all off with dinner with Gary was a huge bonus.

But my bubble was well and truly burst when Irene called me into one of the meeting rooms. "I thought it was best to give you a friendly word of advice," said Irene, by way of introduction. A jolt of panic put me on high alert. Irene had never shared an amiable word with me, let alone a friendly one. Why start now?

"I've noticed Gary is spending a lot of time with you, early morning meetings, driving you to work, coming back to the office with the same coffee cups." I tried to interrupt her, to explain it was because of the launch event, but Irene held up her hand.

"I've seen Gary do this before. He uses work to spend time with the young girls in the office. Don't be fooled by the expensive clothes and luxury car, it's nothing more than a façade. When it comes to his treatment of women, there's nothing classy about him."

"We're only spending time together because of the launch event, talking over what's been done and what still needs to be put in place."

"Be careful," said Irene, with more compassion in her voice than I had ever heard before. "Be careful of what you tell yourself. And be careful of the time you spend together. I see the way you look at him now, and he'll see it too. Don't be taken in by him." And with that Irene walked out of the meeting room.

I remained in the room for a few minutes, dealing with my warring emotions. My immediate impulse was to rage at Irene, she was nothing more than a grumpy old woman. And why would she talk to me about this? It made me wonder what her story was. In an environment where rumours run rife, little was said about her. Why was that? No one seemed to like her very much, but then again, did anyone even know anything about her? After all the time she'd spent nagging me about my work, why this sudden interest in my wellbeing? But what if she was right? Did Gary know I liked him from the way I looked at him? Do I like him that way?

Full of confusion and questions I made my way back to my desk. I checked my mobile and saw a text from Gary: 'Sorry. I can't make tonight you'll need to decide menus on your own.'

That was it! No explanation? Just a 'can't make it'. First Irene's warning and now this! What was it with men and text messages? The disappointment consuming me was merely another confirmation I was attracted to Gary. Who was I fooling?

The dinner loomed ahead of me. Now more punishment than treat.

KIRSTY

The hotel for the launch event occupied a prestigious position in the city centre, in prime location between Central Station and the M8 motorway. I had never been to the hotel before; it was way above my pay grade. The foyer was palatial. The floor tiles shone and sparkled. The reception desk had a black, glittering façade, which spoke of an expensive establishment that kept the staff at a distance from the clientele. The high ceiling housed four chandeliers, which cast myriad shards of light around the reception area, their opulence complimenting the subtle floor lighting.

Samantha, the event planner, exited from a door to the side of the reception desk and walked over to me, demonstrating perfect poise as she navigated her way across the shiny floor tiles in her four-inch heels. She extended a manicured hand in welcome and took me through to her office. It was a small room, functional and smart. With efficient precision Samantha worked through the arrangements that were still pending.

"Why don't I give you a tour round the areas you'll be using, and then I can take you to the bar area to sample the menus," said Samantha. I would have been much happier to have stayed in the little office to try the menus, but I had the feeling the efficient Samantha was dismissing me from the meeting.

"That would be lovely, thanks."

Back at the public side of the hotel, it was every bit as stunning as the reception area promised. The banquet hall, where the event would take place, was large and airy. The walls were a non-descript cream colour, but again large, beautiful chandeliers adorned the ceiling. The cornicing, intricate and decorative, suggested a room of character, rather than the large, modern function room that it was.

"A platform will be constructed here," said Samantha, indicating an area at one end of the hall. "During the meal and speeches the top table will be on it. After the speeches the delegates will be ushered to the bar area, this will allow the staff time to clear all the tables and the entertainment will set up on the stage."

I wasn't sure how much I liked the efficient Samantha. But, she knew what she was doing, and would operate the night with military like precision.

"Out here we have the function suite bar," said Samantha, as we moved on from the hall. The bar area took up a mezzanine level over the reception, the chandeliers I had admired earlier almost at touching distance from the balcony. The area was sparsely furnished, merely a staging area for the main room, a waiting-time area where drinks would be ordered and delegates would mingle. The toilets and cloakroom were situated to the side of the bar. Everything perfect and set up to cater for large functions.

"I'll take you down to the bar area now and arrange with the kitchen to serve you the various dishes Gary has requested." It surprised me that she referred to Gary by his Christian name. How well did they know each other?

As soon as we walked into the downstairs bar, I knew this would be my favourite part of the hotel. It was more intimate and comfortable than the other areas of the hotel. High-backed, narrow leather seats were arranged in twos or fours, around linen-covered tables. I sat on one of the chairs arranged in a 'two people' set up.

Armed with my phone, I captured images of each of the dishes and wrote up notes on what I thought of each one. I was halfway through the process when I realised that I probably looked like some sad woman taking pictures of her food to post on social media sites.

As I moved onto the dessert samples I received a text from Gary, 'Sorry not there with you, how's the food? Won't be in the office tomorrow so you'll need to go back to public transport'.

Despite sampling an array of fantastic desserts, my lonely mood dipped even further.

"Would you like a coffee?" asked the bartender as he cleared away the dessert dishes. I was inclined to say no. I wanted to go home.

"We have a lovely coffee area just over there," he said, pointing to the far end of the bar. "It's got comfy chairs and a fire." I appreciated his friendly, comforting smile. I wanted to explain that I was here on corporate business, tasked with making the menu choices for a large event. I dreaded the idea that he thought I had been stood up for a date.

"That sounds lovely. I'll have a cappuccino, thanks." He didn't need to hear my story. He was nothing more than a friendly stranger and I didn't need to justify myself to him.

I walked over to the area the bartender had indicated. He was right. It was lovely. A comfortable extension to the bar. On this quiet midweek evening, I had my choice of seats. I opted for a large armchair that faced the fire. It wasn't cold in the hotel, but I was drawn to the mesmerising, magical swirling of the flames, even if it they were fake.

While I sipped my coffee, the feelings of loneliness drifted away. I was able to enjoy a relaxed half-hour, letting my mind drift over the events of the last few weeks, specifically the encounters with Gary. I was drawn to him, I could no longer deny it. But I suspected Gary was like a dancing flame - pleasing to look at, but get too close and you'd get burned.

KIRSTY

"Chinese delivery," sang Jo, as I opened my front door to her.

Eating alone last night had been dreary; plus all the weird Gary thoughts were messing with my brain. I had called Jo earlier in the day, badly in need of takeaway and best friend chat.

Over chow mein and beer, I filled Jo in on the previous evening at the hotel.

"Sounds amazing," said Jo. "This new project seems good for you. A fresh challenge."

"Eating along last night was not my idea of fun, but I am enjoying working on the event. Although I've not done that much as I took it over from someone else, and the event planner made it very clear last night that she's got it all in hand."

"Don't be putting yourself down. You still need to take it forward and manage it to its brilliant conclusion." I laughed at Jo's enthusiasm, she was the perfect best friend.

"And how are things going with Gary?"

"Okay." I tried to be nonchalant about it, but my blush gave me away. "To be honest, I'm still confused with what's going on. Sometimes he hangs out and chats with me like I'm the only person in the room. Then other times it's all work and nothing personal is mentioned."

"Watch out for him, Kirsty. I bet he knows just how to play you."

"Funnily enough, Irene said something similar yesterday. I'm sure it's not like that at all, it's probably just me reading it all wrong. Like I said he's way out of my league."

"There you go, running yourself down again. Why do you think you always end up with guy trouble?"

I shrugged and looked away.

"It's because you're gorgeous, and loads of guys want to be with you. While us mere mortals must look on from the side-lines hoping for just one chance of a decent guy. But you're so down on yourself that guys pick up on it and they always end up making you feel you need them rather than the other way round."

I wasn't enjoying the direction this conversation was taking. Time to change the subject. "All Gary stuff aside, I am enjoying the change of role with my job. The one downside is that I still need to endure Irene's disapproving stare over me all day."

"What will happen after the launch event? Will you be back to regular duties?"

"I expect so, which is kind of sad. Maybe I should speak to Gary about it during one of our meetings, ask if there are new opportunities about. He's keen to shake things up more in the department, probably one of the many reasons that Irene dislikes him. I guess it is a good time to ask for a change of role, or even a wee promotion."

"Go for it! You've got to take the opportunities as they come, it's not as if Irene is one to sing your praises, or do anything to encourage you."

Perhaps it was time to take a step forward in my career. Why not take advantage of my time with Gary?

JENNIFER

This morning the parents from the PTA were meeting at my house. I love hosting. I also get a thrill from starting something new. Not that the PTA is new, it's been going for many years. But leading it was a new challenge for me.

In the morning glow in my kitchen I offered the other mums teas and coffees, scones and cookies. As we ate, we chatted happily together, using the time to get to know each other, ascertaining whose child was whose, talking careers, etc. In between the clouds the sun shone its bright rays into the kitchen, warming my soul with the promise of a new challenge and new friendships.

"I'd love us to come up with some fresh ideas for PTA fundraising this year," I said, turning to the work at hand. "I'm sure we've all taken our turn at the fetes and discos, and they are all good at bringing in money for the school. But wouldn't it be fun to do something different this year?"

"It would. But what? I can't think of what else we could try," said Sandra, who had accepted the position of secretary for the group.

"We don't need to come up with lots of ideas right now," I said. "I want to use this morning's meeting to encourage us all to think of new things." My words were met with enthusiastic smiles and nods, but the silence that followed suggested the group was struggling to think of anything different.

"For examples, at the next parents' night we could set up a coffee/tea bar. We could sell decent tea and coffee for the parents to take into the hall with them as they wait to speak to the teachers. I'm not sure how successful it will be, but we won't know if we don't try."

"I like the sound of that. We could get the school to advertise it for us when they put out the information letters," said Sandra.

"Great idea. It will take a team of volunteers to run it, but it shouldn't be much work. We can ask around and see if we can get additional volunteers beyond the PTA." I was relieved to see that one simple idea was encouraging the rest of the group. They were moving on from merely interested listeners. The idea for the tea and coffee wasn't ground-breaking, nor would it be a huge money maker, but hopefully it would encourage the rest of the group to suggest new things too.

For the remainder of the meeting we planned out the regular events for the school year. I was pleased with how the first meeting had gone. The committee seemed like a good bunch. I was confident we would excel at making this the best fund raising year of the PTA yet. They were all smiling and enthusiastic as I waved them off. I took that as a good sign.

Before moving on to the party to-do list, I checked my emails and Facebook, just in case there were any last-minute party replies. I deleted through the usual array of sales emails, but then I saw an email from Scott's best friend from university days. I hadn't heard from John since I emailed him about Scott's party several weeks ago.

The email conveyed a message of disappointment. He regretted to inform us he was unable to make the party as he had a work event on Saturday evening. My elation from the PTA meeting began to wither away. At university Scott and John were almost inseparable. They had so many shared memories from those days; the pranks they instigated at the swimming club, their popularity in the chaplaincy centre, the wilderness camping weekends they enjoyed together.

My thoughts drifted to a weekend of camping together. Eight of us, all friends from the university Christian Union, had driven up north for a weekend of wild camping and hiking. We set up camp in a beautiful glen, surrounded by hills on three sides. The days were filled with hiking the Munros, the beauty and ruggedness of the scenery breath-taking. John had taken his guitar and, in the evenings, we would sit round the camp fire, leg weary but content, singing our favourite worship songs and dreaming about our futures. We discussed our aspirations, how we were going to make a difference. We pledged to stay friends forever, to do life together. Our futures lay ahead of us, so much raw potential just waiting to be let loose. It was the autumn before Scott and I became a couple, the autumn of Scott's final year at university. The last times we had been away together as a group.

I could see each of the faces sitting round the campfire, but to my horror I realised I couldn't even remember everyone's name. John was the only one we still had any contact with, but that was patchy at best. And now here he was, letting us know he could not come to Scott's party because work now controls our lives.

From a morning that started with so much potential and excitement, my mood came crashing down. I missed the Jennifer of those student days.

KIRSTY

After what felt like an everlasting week at work, it was sheer bliss to get to Chocolate & Vanilla for my Friday lunchtime haven. The damp August weather was doing nothing to help my mood. I could wrap my raincoat round to protect me from the rain, but the humidity of the day seemed to penetrate all barriers. I was tired and worn out. My ankle was feeling better, but it was still painful by the end of each day, adding to my current mood. I snuggled into one of the armchairs, hot steamy latte beside me and a good book in hand. Today, more than ever I needed my wee piece of aloneness, the sanity in my working week.

I hadn't even finished reading a page when once again he was there, interrupting the peace and setting my heart racing. "Is this seat taken?" he asked, putting his hand on my shoulder. Why did he even ask, he knew I came here to be on my own?

"I didn't think you were around today," I said, as Gary sat down across from me with his coffee. It was in a takeaway cup, I hoped that meant he wouldn't be staying long. I needed peace, not more confusion. How was he capable of setting my emotions in overdrive with just one short question? Was he playing with me?

"A day full of meetings, as usual. So I thought I'd pop in and check on my favourite girl while I was in the area."

I refused to let myself rise to his comments. It was time to show him our meetings were only for work. "The sample menus went well on Wednesday night. I've taken photographs of the various dishes, and written up my thoughts and recommendations, but it's all back at the office. Maybe we can go over it this afternoon or early next week."

"I love your attention to detail, I can't believe you took photographs and wrote a report on it. With you involved the launch will be a great success. I'm so glad I've got you on my team."

Despite my resolve I giggled and blushed at his compliment. I looked up just in time to see the hint of a smile playing on his face. He was toying with me. And I could do nothing but play along with his game.

"I need to rush out on you now, I've got meetings all afternoon. But, Kirsty," as he said my name my eyes flicked up to meet his, "I'm counting on having more time with you soon."

How was I supposed to decipher these words he spoke so effortlessly? I sat my book down on the table. My mind was too focussed on reality to take any notice of fiction.

As I left Chocolate & Vanilla to return to the office, I wrapped my raincoat around my body, wishing I had a raincoat that could protect me from the storm of my emotions.

JENNIFER

It was party day!

My week had sped by in a flurry of housework and party preparations. The only tasks that remained for today were putting up decorations and the party food delivery. I am not talented in the culinary side of domestic life, so, to protect everyone's sanity I had placed an order with the local delicatessens.

I had a raft of gifts for Scott. The presentation of each one would be spread throughout the day. First up was his appointment with Paul at ByDesign. It wasn't the kind of place Scott would consider going, but I wanted to treat him to a bit of pampering and style; Paul was just the person for that job.

Plus, I needed him out of the house to give the girls and myself the space and freedom to go to town decorating the house for his party. We had decided the girls would go over to my mum and dad's for the night. It would have been lovely to have the girls at the party, but, a child free party allowed my full attention to be on Scott and the guests, plus they would be 'bored' by all the adult conversations. However, there was no way I would decorate the house without their input. With Scott gone, we set about unleashing our creative styles.

I have instilled my love of music on the girls; party decorating called for party music. Amie Aitken was on the playlist, inspiring us with her catchy tunes to sing along to. With the music at full volume we sang and danced as we decorated the house, transforming it from suburban modesty to party ready. Balloons and bunting adorned the downstairs rooms. Fairy lights and photos of Scott, from his baby pictures all the way through to a photo taken of him that morning, covered the hallway walls.

Chloe pointed and laughed at a boyhood photo of Scott. "Look at daddy's silly hair!"

"You think that one's bad?" asked Amy. "Look at his outfit in this picture." Amy held up a photo of Scott in his teenage years.

"We've told you before, the 80s weren't always the best decade for fashion. But you know what? We all thought we looked great at the time and I can guarantee you'll wear things as teenagers that you'll be embarrassed about in later life."

I left the girls giggling over Scott's hairstyles and fashion choices and walked through to the living room. My gaze was drawn to the framed photograph of Scott and myself on his motorbike. I picked up the picture and ran my fingers over our smiling faces. The noise from the music and the girls drifting to the background as my thoughts returned to that first kiss. I had known right from that moment I wanted to spend my life with Scott. It was a happy picture, a wonderful memory, and yet a sadness touched me and some tears spilled down my cheeks. What was wrong with me? It was a day to celebrate Scott. A day to celebrate our life together. But the dreams of youth haunted me. Was I sad because those days were gone, or was I mourning that I no longer had dreams to reach for?

What did you aspire to once your dreams were safely in place?

PAUL

As we ate our way through a pizza before heading out to Scott's birthday party, I brought Matt up to speed on my current job reflections. I appreciated having a level-headed flat mate, and friend, someone I could discuss anything with. As a high school computing teacher, Matt was used to advising pupils through their career hopes and aspirations. It was time to draw on that wealth of experience.

"What do you think is causing your restlessness?" Matt asked.

"I don't know. I don't even know when it started. It crept up on me and it's showing no signs of leaving any time soon."

"Do you still enjoy being a hairdresser?"

"I do. It's the peripherals I'm more hassled with. Like last week, I couldn't be bothered with doing the photoshoot; I used to love those assignments. In the salon I still get a buzz from spending my day talking to people and getting to be creative with hairstyles as much as people will let me. But the salon politics are frustrating; who is saying what about who and whether I'm meeting Si's targets or not."

"So, what are your options?"

"I'm not qualified for anything else, so that question is difficult to answer."

"Okay, assume things stay as they are. How would you feel?"

"Dissatisfied, like it was time for something else."

"Now consider how you would feel about the Edinburgh position."

"Funny, my initial reaction was still dissatisfaction."

"What if you moved to a different chain?"

"That wouldn't help. They've all got a lot of the same issues."

"What if you started your own salon?"

"My own salon?" It was something I had considered when I first took up hairdressing. What fresh new hairdresser didn't dream of the possibility of opening his own salon, then a chain, then becoming a world famous stylist? But I had become comfortable, hidden within a big chain of salons. The business risk was with others, not on my shoulders. I was able to turn up each morning and do my job, stress-free. And yet...

"You've gone quiet on me. Does that mean you're thinking about it?"

"Do you know what? I think you might just have hit on something. I used to imagine setting up my own place. But it's been so long since I even considered it I'd forgotten all about it." Was this an option? Could I start my own salon?

KIRSTY

"How about some pre-party ice-cream?" said Jo, as she stood at the mirror applying her makeup.

"Excellent idea. Chocolate or vanilla?"

"Both of course! How's the rest of your week been?"

"Much the same," I replied. "Which means I'm extra glad it's Scott's birthday party tonight. I'm looking forward to hanging out with my best friends and having a laugh. No sickness, no twisted ankles. And, most importantly, no guys."

"You do realise there will be men at this party? After all it is a man's birthday."

I threw a cushion at Jo as I walked through to the kitchen to get ice-cream. It was always fun starting off a night out with Jo, invariably it involved a lot of giggling and carrying on.

Jennifer and Scott always put on the best parties. Jennifer is a great hostess; she is a complete neat freak, and yet her house is always welcoming and relaxing. Anytime I come to Jennifer and Scott's for a party I know I'm in for a fun night. They excel at bringing together a divergent group of people for an entertaining evening.

As we entered, the house was in full party mode: music playing, food and drink in abundance, party lighting and decorations complimenting the atmosphere. Lynn and Carol were speaking to Jennifer, who turned round and greeted me with a great big hug, "I've missed you this week, glad to see you're hobbling well."

"I've missed you too. Where's the birthday boy?"

"He's around here somewhere. Probably showing off his latest gadgets to his friends."

The door opened and a new group of party guests entered. "I'll catch up with you later once everyone's here and catered for." She handed me a drink and set off to greet the latest arrivals.

We wandered round the downstairs, hoping to find seating for the four of us so I could rest my ankle as much as possible. We hugged and chatted with friends from church as we made our way around. The family room was quiet, so we took full advantage of the large, comfy corner sofa.

"I know this is a party and we're supposed to be socialising, but let's hide here for the rest of the night," I said, as we all nestled into the sofa.

"That's a great idea," agreed Carol.

"Well, I'm happy enough to start off here, but it won't hurt to explore later and see who is about," said Lynn.

"I don't want to hang out with anyone else but you lot tonight, so I'm going to stay right here."

"You have a good excuse," said Carol. "You need to keep that ankle up."

We spent the next half-hour catching up on each other's week and other general chit chat. Despite my earlier proclamation, I decided it would do me good to move around, plus I hadn't seen Scott yet to wish him happy birthday. "I'm off to find the birthday boy and get another drink. Does anyone want anything?" They all shook their heads, and I left them to their chat.

Scott was in the kitchen with a group of his friends, I didn't recognise them, so I assumed they were work colleagues. "Happy birthday, Scott," I said, and gave him a hug.

"Thanks Kirsty. Great to see you. How's that ankle doing?"

"It's getting there. Have you had a good day?"

"Mostly getting ready for tonight, but now it's party time! Let me introduce you to the work gang." And with that I was being introduced to his colleagues. It was nice to meet new people and chat in the safety of Jennifer's kitchen.

"Can I get you a drink?" said Scott, realising that I was standing empty-handed.

"Don't worry I'll help myself." I looked at the array of bottles on the kitchen table. I abused my familiarity with the hosts and opted for a bottle of wine to take back to the girls. However, as I reached for the bottle, I glanced up and saw a face that spelled disaster to all my hopes of a relaxing evening.

KIRSTY

I needed an escape route. I looked around frantically for a way to disappear. Escaping to the loo would be an easy way out, but after our last encounter I didn't want to be seen as always dashing to the loo.

There was no way to avoid him. I hoped he wouldn't notice me, or remember me.

"Kirsty! It's great to see you again," said Paul, as he enveloped me in a hug. I didn't know how to react. The last time we had seen each other he had been the perfect gentleman and treated me so kindly. I was grateful for his care that day, but seeing him now only reminded me of yet another embarrassing incident in my life. All I wanted was a stress-free night out with my friends.

"Hey Paul." I didn't know what to say. And then I remembered the beautiful flowers he had sent me. I hadn't even acknowledged them, let alone thanked him for them.

The thought brought a blush to my face. What must he think of me?

"Sorry, I never got in touch to say thank you for the flowers. Thanks, it was kind of you, especially after I was the one who gave you hassle. I hope I didn't cause any problems at the salon. Did the place get cleaned up okay? Sorry, maybe I should have paid for the extra cleaning that would have been needed." I was talking at a hundred miles an hour. Was I even making any sense? Just what I needed, another guy I couldn't talk to coherently.

"Don't worry about it."

Embarrassed and awkward, I had no idea what to say to him. "Scott is just over there if you want to say happy birthday to him."

"No, it's fine. Scott was in the salon earlier today for his birthday haircut, so I've already done the birthday thing." Paul leant against the wall, an air of easy confidence about him while my entire world was out of control? I needed to get back to my friends, but just as I was trying to figure out how to make my excuses, Jennifer appeared.

"Kirsty, I think you need to sit down. You don't want to spend too long putting your weight on that ankle," said Jennifer. Oh great! Now Paul would need to know the whole story of the injured ankle.

"You two go on through to the lounge and I'll bring you some food."

The obviousness of Jennifer's ploy made me blush. Again! I shot her a look as Paul placed his hand on my elbow and directed me through to the dining room. Her reply was an endearing smile.

My feelings were spiralling out of control. I was out of my depth. What was expected? What should I do? How long should I sit with Paul before I could re-join my friends?

Jennifer appeared with two plates full of yummy-looking food from the buffet spread and a couple of glasses of wine. I shifted nervously in my chair, curling up as best I could on my good leg.

Before Paul had time to ask me about my ankle, I came up with a neutral train of conversation. "How do you know Scott? Is he a regular at the salon? It was Jennifer who suggested I book an appointment with you."

"No, today was his first time there. And I must remember to thank Jennifer for recommending my services."

"His hair looks great tonight," I said, steering the conversation away from the embarrassing subject of my visit to the salon, and keeping things focussed on Scott and Paul.

"Thanks."

"So, if not from the salon, how do you know Scott?"

"I met him through my flat-mate, Matt. Do you remember Matt from the other week?"

Of course I remembered Matt, or more accurately I remembered he came to my rescue. Although, I wasn't sure I would recognise him if I met him again.

"Anyway, Matt asked me along to his church a few times, but I always found excuses not to go. Then one day he told me about a new thing he was starting up with a guy called Scott from another church. It was going to be a men's Bible group, called Alpha, and they'd be chatting about God and stuff over beer and curry. It sounded pretty cool, and I'm always up for a free curry, so I tagged along. And that's how I got to know Scott. Both he and Matt have been game changers for me. Don't know what I'd do without either of them."

"Wow, that's great. I've known Scott and Jennifer for a few years, since I moved here from Argyll. Like you, they've been a lifeline for me. I met Jennifer at church my first

Sunday there, and we've been friends ever since. She helped me to acclimatise to city life."

"Here's to Scott and Jennifer then," said Paul, as he clinked my glass in a toast. He looked over his glass at me as he took a sip of wine, his gaze capturing me.

"Are you still going to the group?" I asked, diverting the conversation back to safer ground.

"The course ended a couple of months ago. But we still get together. Sometimes we go out for curry and talk about God for hours."

"Sounds great. And are you going to church with Matt now?"

"Yep, but I've been thinking of trying out ChurchX sometime. And now I know you're there too, I'll definitely need to get along."

I never know how to interpret these kinds of comments. Was he being friendly? Was he flirting? I don't know. Now, more than ever, I wanted to get back to my friends. I wanted to hide in the corner.

"So are you going to tell me what happened to your ankle?" asked Paul.

"It was silly really, I was at the climbing centre with my friends last weekend and had a small accident." The shortened version was easier to explain.

"If you don't mind, I need to excuse myself," I said. Enough was enough I had to get out of this situation. However, I hadn't noticed that as we chatted my good leg had 'gone to sleep'. As I stood up to walk away my leg, numb with pins and needles, collapsed under my weight. I stumbled and fell onto Paul! Caught in his arms, I was only a whisper away from his face.

There was no way to retrieve the situation gracefully.

"I'm so sorry, my leg... I'm sorry."

"Kirsty," said Paul, looking right at me and forcing my attention to his eyes. "It's fine. Trust me no guy will ever be upset at having you fall for him. Let me help you."

I was mortified. We were so close. I could feel the warmth of his breath on my cheek. His eyes locked onto mine; my discomfort levels were going through the roof.

"Are you okay?" asked Paul.

Time for honesty. "I'm sorry. I'm so embarrassed. Please excuse me." Now that the feeling was back in my leg, I was able to hobble away without falling. Both times I'd met Paul he'd come to my rescue. A knight in shining armour might sound charming. But I was fed up being the damsel in distress.

PAUL

This was a great party! Life was good. I couldn't believe it when I walked into Scott's kitchen and there she was standing in front of me. She was even prettier than I remembered. Which to be fair probably wasn't hard, given that the last time I had seen her she was throwing up all over the place.

I couldn't have planned it better. Jennifer's clumsy attempts at match-making confirmed my own thoughts that there was relationship potential for Kirsty and myself. We'd been having a great time chatting and getting to know one another. And then she'd fallen into my lap. She had been so embarrassed, but I had loved every minute. But with her embarrassment the easy going Kirsty had disappeared back to her fortress of shyness.

I took our plates and glasses back through to the kitchen, not because I'm a good guest, rather it gave me something to do. Picking up a bottle of beer from a cool box in the kitchen, I meandered through the downstairs rooms, waiting for Kirsty to reappear. I considered the no-dating pact I was in. It was a self-imposed thing I'd worked through with Scott and Matt, a means to breaking my non-stop dating lifestyle. Was it time to bring the embargo to an end?

As I walked into the family room, I noticed three women occupying the settee. Didn't Kirsty say she had come to the party with her friends? Only one way to find out. "Hi, I'm Paul. Are you Kirsty's friends?"

"Yes, we are. Hi, I'm Jo," said the petite woman, as she held out her hand. "And this is Lynn and Carol."

"Hi, great to meet you. Would you mind if I joined you?"

"Please do," said the one introduced as Lynn. "Are you Paul? As in hairdresser Paul?"

"Guilty as charged."

"Interesting," said Lynn.

I wanted to bombard them with questions about Kirsty. But that would be rude. So, instead, I opted for small talk, getting to know them rather than the one I was really interested in. They were a fun group. In no time at all we were joking and chatting like lifelong friends. The contrast was painfully obvious; this group of women, with whom I had only a platonic interest, were easy going and engaging. While the woman I wanted to spend time with was reserved and hesitant and nowhere in sight.

Getting to know her friends was probably one of my best chances of spending more time with Kirsty. Get a girl's friends on your side, and you were setting yourself up for success. It was my old way of working, but with the depth of attraction I felt towards her I was willing to do whatever it took.

KIRSTY

Jennifer's upstairs bathroom was beautiful. The tiles were a shiny beige, which glowed in the warmth of the candles placed around the bath and on the windowsill. The fluffy floor mat and towels completed the feeling of luxury and gave me a comfy seat as I composed myself.

I needed to get back to Jo, Lynn and Carol, but I was enjoying the peace and tranquillity the bathroom provided. The knock on the door, as another party goer needed to use the facilities, brought me out of my reverie. I made my way back downstairs to the family room. I heard Jo's laughter before I saw them. They were still sitting where I had left them earlier, but now Paul was there too, sitting in their midst, looking like he had settled for the evening.

"Kirsty, are you okay?" asked Paul.

"I'm fine, thank you." He stood up and let me have the seat he had been sitting in. The seat was warm from his body heat, and the scent of his aftershave lingered in the fabric. Part of me hoped that he would leave, but another part longed for him to stay.

With the group established in my absence, I felt like an outsider. But, as the outsider, I was free to take on the role of observer. I watched Paul as he worked the group, regaling them with his stories of hairdressing. His stories were full of animation and laughter, he had the group in the palm of his hand, captivated by his every word.

"And then," he continued, "there are all the women who walk about town in their raincoats and sunglass. What's that all about? It's like one continuous sea of beige."

"Better watch what you say about raincoats and sunglasses," said Jo. "That's pretty much Kirsty's look."

"No, Kirsty! Please tell me it's not so." Paul's comment was met with laughter from the group.

"I don't see why you think it so strange," I said, in defence of my uniform. "We live in the West of Scotland, you know, four seasons in one day and all that. No matter what the weather you've got what you need, and your work clothes are always protected."

"Well I guess, when you put it that way, there is a practical reason, but still, it's boring to look at."

Before I could say anything more on the subject, he turned the conversation back to funny stories of life in the salon.

As I listened, I realised that in a different grouping I would be one of his stories, "and then there was this girl who came in and before I even cut her hair, she threw up all over the salon sinks." Paul had a willing audience in my friends, but I didn't want to hear any more.

"Excuse me a moment," I said. "I've just remembered I need to see Jennifer." Paul offered his hand to help me up. I accepted his help without looking at him and walked off in search of Jennifer.

She was in the kitchen chatting with some of her neighbours. I recognised a few of them from previous visits to her house. That little recognition was enough to welcome me into the group conversation.

After a while the party thinned out. The men congregated in the living room playing with the games console. And the women were split between the kitchen and family room. Now that Paul was with Scott I went back over to my friends.

"Paul seems very nice, Kirsty," said Jo.

"And, very pleasing to the eye," said Lynn.

"Why are you directing your comments at me?" I asked. Jo, Lynn and Carol laughed.

"Come on! You were the ones telling me to take a break from dating. Don't start with the knowing nudges and winks now!"

"We're sorry, Kirsty," said Carol.

"You're right," said Jo. "Why don't we head on through to the kitchen and get coffee and cake?"

I looked over at Paul as we made our way to the kitchen; he was engrossed in the game and didn't notice us. Maybe it was best to forget about him.

JENNIFER

As the last of the party guests left, Scott and I collapsed onto the sofa. It had been a great night, all former gloominess vanquished by a fun party.

"You looked so happy and beautiful tonight," said Scott.

I love this guy, and not just because he comes out with such great lines. "I really enjoyed myself. It was wonderful having the house full of friends."

"And you're always happy when you do a bit of match-making."

"I can't think what you mean!" I said, pretending to be offended by Scott's remarks. When Kirsty arrived at the party, I had noticed how much she was still hobbling on her sore ankle. My heart went out to my accident prone friend. She needed protecting.

"Kirsty and Paul needed time to talk, that's all," I said in my defence. Scott didn't understand. Kirsty needed someone who would love her and look after her. I had a sneaking suspicion Paul was that guy! I confess, I enjoy match-making. I'm good at spotting compatible couples and getting them together with an ease that ensures the unsuspecting couple have no idea I've even manipulated the situation.

"Don't push too much though, honey, let them find their own way with it," said Scott, taking my thoughts away from my self-congratulation.

"Of course, but sometimes people need a little push in the right direction, the encouragement to explore possibilities," I said. Fun though it was to do a bit of match-making, I didn't want to discuss Kirsty and Paul anymore. Tonight was about Scott, it was time to put the attention back on him. "So what presents did you get?"

"I got the usual suspects: some wine, some whisky, some gift vouchers. But my favourite gift was a great party. Thanks so much." He leaned over to show how much he appreciated my efforts. It was always a good night when the girls were at my parents.

Kirsty

Despite my misgivings about meeting Paul at the party, I woke up thinking about him. He had the whole 'tall, dark and handsome' vibe going on. Combined with a great hairstyle and strong features, you couldn't help but notice him. The dark jeans and checked shirt he'd worn to Scott's party accentuated his height and lean frame. More than just great looks, he came across as a nice guy, although maybe a bit showy at times. But reading guys wasn't my strong point. Could I ever trust myself to get it right? Would I ever fall for the guy that was right for me?

As I got ready for church, I continued to think about Paul. The stories he told, the way he looked, the confidence that exuded from him. Everything about him drew me to him, and I couldn't help but smile as I recalled some of his stories, told with such detail and relish.

When would I see him again? I battled with the thoughts of whether I should try another appointment at ByDesign or stick with the safe option. I was still thinking of him as I walked to church. So it was quite the shock when the first person I saw in church was Paul!

"Paul, what are you doing here?"

"Probably the same as everyone else," he said, greeting me with an all-enveloping hug. "Doing the Sunday morning church thing."

"I thought you went to another church."

"Remember last night I said I was thinking about coming here to check things out? And I decided why not today?"

"Well then, welcome and great to see you."

"How about after church I take you out for lunch?"

"That would be lovely, but I've already arranged to go out with the girls for lunch after church. Or did you mean all of us?"

"Yep, that would be great. I'm off to sit with Scott, see you after the service."

I was so confused. At that moment Jo came over beside me. I dragged her off to the side. "Jo, help! I've no idea what is going on with Paul. Last night I got annoyed with him, this morning I woke up thinking about him. And now he's here! He asked me out to lunch, but when I said we were all going out, he invited himself along. I don't even know if it was just me he was inviting to lunch or all of us."

"Slow down. You're doing it again. You're getting yourself in a flap when you don't even know what's going on."

"But after all our conversations about me being more careful about dating I've got all these thoughts going round and round my head about Paul. And Gary."

"Okay, stop now! This is the problem. You are over-thinking everything. You're trying to solve all these issues in your head before a question has even been asked. Take a deep breath."

I took a deep breath. She was right; I was getting ahead of myself. Why did I always do this?

"Let's just work through the next few hours. We're going to sit down and enjoy the service. Then we're going to go out for lunch, which includes Paul. And all we're doing is hanging out as friends. There are no further agendas. You got that?"

Another deep breath. "Yep. I can do that."

As we sat down I took more deep breaths. I could do this. For the next ninety minutes I would direct all my focus on the service and nothing else. But try as I might, my mind kept wandering to thoughts of Paul and Gary. What did I want? In my daydreams they both wanted to date me. Paul had the edge over Gary in terms of faith. But, Gary... Gary's reputation screamed danger from every angle. The kind of guy I shouldn't be attracted to. And yet, to be noticed by him sent a thrill through my body every time he looked at me or spent time with me. But then again, neither Paul nor Gary had done or said anything that made it clear how they felt. Plus, they were both way out of my league. Jo was right, I was running ahead of myself and chasing fantasies? I had to force my thinking back to the real world.

Now... what was Ben preaching on?

KIRSTY

"Thanks for a great lunch," said Paul, as he hugged us all before we headed off in our separate directions. Jo, Lynn and Carol giggled and laughed together about how much fun it had been hanging out with Paul. They had all engaged in the lunchtime conversation while I merely sat back and left them to it.

"Come on, Kirsty," said Jo, as we waved off Lynn and Carol. "I'll walk you home."

We were barely out of earshot when Jo started her questioning. "Okay, Miss Insecure, what's the deal?"

"What are you talking about?" I was dreading where this conversation was going.

"You know exactly what I'm talking about. Paul came to have lunch with us today, with the sole purpose of hanging out with you. He spent the whole lunch glancing over to you. And you ignored him."

"He wasn't there for me, it was you lot he was talking to."

"Only because you refused to engage in any of the conversations. I know I told you earlier not to get ahead of yourself. But now it's as if you've swung to the opposite extreme. Give the guy a chance, Kirsty."

I stopped walking and faced Jo. "What if I don't know how to? What if I don't know how to be friends with men, or how to work with them? Anytime I'm near a good-looking man I start dreaming of the possibilities." My whole body slumped at my confession.

For once Jo had nothing to say. She didn't appear to have an immediate answer to my predicament.

"Now do you see how hopeless I am?"

"You're not hopeless, Kirsty. Like the rest of us you're a work in progress."

Unsure of what else to say, we parted company. Jo has my back. She's my best friend. But after a weekend full of people and emotion I needed the solitude of my little flat.

That night as I snuggled down on the settee my phone pinged with two messages.

One was a text from Paul saying how much he'd enjoyed hanging out with me over the weekend and that he expected a call at the salon to book a hair appointment.

The second text was from Gary, asking if 'limpy' would like a lift to work again in the morning, or had I been successful in actually breaking something this weekend?

Both messages made me smile. Oh how quickly my fickle heart was swayed. I decided to leave Paul's message for the time being. Perhaps, I would phone ByDesign tomorrow and book an appointment with him.

As for Gary, why not take advantage of his offer? It was only a lift to work...

KIRSTY

Monday mornings are easier to deal with when your weekend has ended well. I was re-energised for the week ahead. Added to all that, there was the lift to work in Gary's luxurious car. It was more than just the early morning sky that was looking bright and sunny.

In general, I'm fine with getting out of bed as soon as the alarm clock sounds. For me the struggle comes in getting out of the shower. It's too easy to lose myself in the hot, steaming water, thoughts meandering over whatever subject grabs my attention. Over the last few weeks thoughts of Gary had distracted me, now thoughts of Paul were vying for my attention. I needed to sort myself out; I didn't have time for this in the morning. Eventually, I forced myself to turn off the shower. I checked my phone before drying my hair. A text message was waiting from Gary, announcing that he would pick me up earlier than arranged as he had a busy day ahead of him.

Panic set in as I realised I only had fifteen minutes to dry my hair, dress, put on my makeup and have my breakfast. I spent a few minutes roughly drying my hair, just enough to take away the dripping. Thankfully, I had decided on my wardrobe last night. My makeup was restricted to eyeliner, mascara and lip gloss. Breakfast would have to be missed. I amazed myself at achieving the fifteen minute deadline and was even standing outside waiting for Gary when he arrived. With a feeling of confidence from the weekend, and a beautiful blue sky, I had taken the brave decision to forgo my raincoat defence, relying on my navy blue cardigan to fend off the early morning chill.

"No raincoat today?" Gary asked, as I stepped into the car.

"No, I'm trusting the weather forecast today."

"How's your ankle this morning? You don't seem to be hobbling as badly."

"It's getting better, thanks. I should be fine to get the bus again tomorrow."

"That's good, because I'm not in the office tomorrow, so now I can go to my meeting in the knowledge that my taxi services are no longer required."

I laughed at Gary's joke. He was in a fun mood this morning, the tone of his voice and the choice of his words drew me in. He had a knack of making me feel incredibly special. It was intoxicating to receive his exclusive attention. I melted into the comfort of his car and smiled as Gary navigated his way through the busying streets of Glasgow. With the morning spark of sunlight it was the most beautiful city in the world.

We chatted the whole journey, catching up on each other's weekend. There was no mention of work. As we got closer to the office, Gary pulled over at Chocolate & Vanilla and bought our coffees. "Our Monday morning dose of caffeine," he said, as he passed the cups over to me. "We can enjoy these while we have our weekly catch up meeting."

As Gary pulled into his underground parking bay, I noticed there weren't any other cars. It was too quiet. The contrast from the bright sunny morning to the cold, dark underground set my senses on edge. I shivered in the darkness and cool air of the parking bays. Gary must have noticed my shiver and came beside me, wrapping me in his arm. "Oh no! I'll never get you out of that raincoat again. One morning without it and you're shivering." I tried to laugh it off, but my laugh was hollow. It wasn't just the surroundings that had changed from bright to dark, something in the interplay between us had shifted. I couldn't quite put my finger on it.

The ride in the elevator only heightened my tension. The lift was like the setting from some 1970s disaster movie; stainless steel on two sides and a full-length mirror facing the doors, with fluorescent lighting above. Gary released me from his hold to check his appearance in the mirror. I hate these unflattering mirrors, but even the scratched mirrors couldn't hide Gary's sharp looks. And he knew it.

"Wouldn't it be funny if the lift broke down," said Gary to my reflection. "Imagine being all alone together, no one here to come and rescue us. What would we do to pass the time?"

Why would he say that? There was nothing funny in such a scenario. His words did nothing to dispel my unease.

We were the first to arrive in the department. "Great, it's nice and quiet," said Gary. "Let's get started and then we'll be up to date on things before the day gets inundated with interruptions." He led the way through to his office. I sat at the meeting table while Gary switched on his computer. As I waited for him to join me I looked out through the window of his office. The only lights illuminating the floor were the lights in Gary's office, the rest of the department was, as yet, unlit. Some rays of early morning sunshine forced their brightness upon the gloomy office, the brightness at odds with the shadows. The last time I had been in Gary's office I had enjoyed the suggestion of the dream. Now it was a haunting memory.

Gary seemed oblivious to my discomfort and sat down beside me. "What updates do you have for me since our last meeting?"

With barely a hair's breadth between us it took all of my willpower to focus on work. I took a sip of coffee to give myself some time. But even in that pause I was all too aware of the pleasing aroma of his expensive aftershave.

"When I saw you on Friday, I started telling you about the sample menus. Here's the list of dishes I tried, what I thought of them and what I would recommend."

"You are organised, aren't you?" said Gary, as he took the list and read through my notes. "I agree with your suggestions. Get in touch with the hotel today and confirm the menu."

"No problem, I'll get that taken care of." As Gary passed the menu list back to me, his hand grazed against mine. I looked up to see him staring at me. The narrative of my dream was becoming far too real. As it etched closer to reality, it seemed to morph from a dream of romance to a predatory nightmare. Fear pulsed through me, but at the same time everything about him captivated me. I was powerless to flee to a place of safety.

A surge of light broke the spell. I looked out from the office and saw Irene at the light switches. As she walked to her desk, she glared at us. Who would have thought I would be so happy to see Irene, especially when she bore her usual cantankerous expression.

The entrance of a third person broke the intensity that had been building up with Gary. The power of the dream released me and my focus was back to the event planning.

"Here is the updated list of replies. So far we've only had three 'not comings', and we're still waiting to hear back from about thirty people." This time as I passed the document to Gary, I slid it along the table to avoid any contact.

As Gary looked through the list, he nodded his approval at how many key business leaders would be attending his event. He circled the names of a few of the people on the pending list. "Contact these people this week. They are key influencers, I need them at the launch. Text me as soon as you find out if any of these are 'no's' or 'uncertain' and I'll give them a follow-up call."

"What about the other names on the list?"

"You can leave those for now, there's still time to confirm numbers with the hotel. But we want these delegates to attend." He sat back in his chair and considered the list further. "In fact, when you chase up on these delegates, make sure you only go as far as their assistants to see if they know what their bosses are planning. If they are still undecided or leaning towards not coming, I'll speak to them myself."

Since Irene's arrival things had cooled dramatically. Even the way he looked at me seemed to have changed. He was in manager-only mode now, rather than the familiar approach of just a few moments ago. I was sure it wasn't just my imagination, or was it? Was I being silly?

"Okay, that's fine for this morning. Follow up on the points we've discussed, and next time we'll sort out the seating plan." I picked up my notes and coffee cup and walked back to my desk.

"More early morning coffee then?" said Irene, as I walked past her desk. I couldn't decide if her comment was friendly or sarcastic. My relief at seeing her was short lived.

JENNIFER

The week that follows a great weekend can be difficult. Once again my Monday morning enthusiasm had deserted me. At the first alarm my arm stretched out from the security of my duvet and whacked it. Just another five minutes, but I had to make sure I didn't go back to sleep. The five minutes turned into half an hour and once again it was a race around morning.

The girls were tired too. Mum and dad had kept them entertained with non-stop activities and now they were struggling with the demands of a new morning. Even Chloe was quiet and sluggish; not the usual force of energy I was used to having to deal with.

We made it out the door and got to school just as the bell rang. But at the school gates Emma clung onto my hand just that bit longer than usual. There had been no Kevin issues for her last week, but the new week seemed to bring back some of the worry. I bent down to give her a reassuring kiss. A mother's heart always holds worries and concerns; some days more than others.

Despite the sluggishness of its beginning, I was enthusiastic for the week ahead. When I got back home, I made myself a cuppa then set about tackling the housework.

I'm a great believer in multi-tasking; with good music on I can combine a dance workout with housework. As I danced round the house, enjoying the familiar routine of housework, and having the place to myself, I had space to remember. Space to remember the fun I used to have; the laughter that used to fill our little flat and lives; the conversations Scott and I shared, dreaming and hoping together.

I pulled Amy's baby album from the bookcase in the living room. The first picture was her scan image. As I traced round the outline of the little alien-like form, I remembered the day we'd gone for the scan. After seeing our baby for the first time we treated ourselves to dinner at our favourite restaurant. The morning sickness was subsiding and my appetite was returning.

"I think I'd like to give up working and stay at home with the baby," I had suggested to Scott.

"Really?" replied Scott.

"Seeing this little person makes me realise how much I already love it. I want to stay at home and be with it. To see our baby take its first steps. To be there for every accomplishment, big or small."

"Are you sure you want to give up the challenge of work for the challenge of nappies? Won't you miss your colleagues?"

"It will be a big change for me. For us. But it's a good change. It's going to be a new adventure for us. The adventure of becoming three."

Swapping (paid) working life for parenting had been full of anticipation and excitement. At times it was difficult, tiring and scary, but having a new little person around made it fun and exciting. What a contrast to entering this new stage in my parenting journey where I was struggling to find the joy.

Perhaps there was some kind of inverted graph that would show joy and responsibility at odds with each other. In your twenties with all of life's adventures ahead of you it was easy to feel joy, but by the time you hit forty the pressures and responsibilities of adult life conspired to squeeze out that joy. The thought terrified me. I refuse to let my life be consumed by the negatives.

It was time to take action and be done with the self-pity. I went to my bedroom to get my Bible. I looked up the concordance at the back of my Bible to find out which book had the most references to joy. The Psalms. What a great book to use for a study; the poetry and rhythm of the Psalms, coupled with all the references to joy, would be the perfect answer to my current mood. I instantly felt my spirit lift.

PAUL

The salon has a lovely, relaxed vibe at the start of the week. I like that. Plus Si isn't blustering around moaning about appointment timings. Several of my regulars have realised that Monday and Tuesday appointments are longer, and, come with the bonus of no Chantelle.

My 11 o'clock appointment was Mrs Wilson, a well-to-do lady from the West End of the city. The West End is crammed full of its own hairdressers but a few years ago Mrs Wilson arrived at ByDesign in a panic, demanding an emergency styling before going on to a charity lunch she was hosting in the city. Ever since then she's been one of my regulars. I don't know much about her; she's been widowed for some time and doesn't have any children. Her life seems to revolve around her dog and her charity work. Set in her ways, she can be opinionated but, despite all that, I always enjoy our conversations. With Mrs Wilson I get a different perspective of the world. There are no 'so what you doing tonight?' discussions with her.

I'm always impressed that she comes to a salon that clearly isn't targeting her demographic. ByDesign is all about the young professional, not the more mature clientele. Every time she comes I wonder what she was like when she was younger. Did she always have the formidable side to her that she freely displays now? She is never sharp with me, but is happy to tell the juniors off if they don't follow her every command. She isn't shy about voicing her opinions either, some of which must offend those nearby.

However, today she was not her usual opinionated self. She was quiet and withdrawn.

"Are you okay Mrs Wilson?"

"It's my little Bailey. She passed away last week." Even as she spoke, tears came to her eyes as she mentioned her little dog's name. She dabbed at the corner of her eyes with her handkerchief.

"I'm sorry to hear that. What happened?"

"Heart failure. She seemed fine one day and the next she was gone."

"You must miss her."

"You cannot begin to understand how much. She was my everything, my companion."

"Will you get another dog?"

"There will never be another Bailey. She was irreplaceable. I do not know what I will do without her."

I'm not a pet person and couldn't understand why someone would be in tears over the death of a dog. But I appreciated that Mrs Wilson's grief was real. I had to bring down the usual tempo of conversation and ask the right questions that would give her space to talk.

"What is your favourite memory of Bailey?" I'd hit on the right question. From there she talked non-stop for twenty minutes about the happy times she'd had with her dog. Telling me all about Bailey's life from the puppy days until the last holiday they had been on.

When I switched on the hairdryer, the noise brought our conversation to a close. As I styled Mrs Wilson's hair, my mind drifted onto Matt's words about starting up my own salon. This appointment was strange, I don't get the whole pet drama, but I could see I had helped her, giving her the space to reminisce. The slower pace at the start of the week is more in keeping with who I am. I like to give clients the time they need. As I considered the past few weeks I realised that I was happier in the salon when schedules were slower, and I didn't have Si's little spy, Chantelle, constantly hovering around.

By the time Mrs Wilson's appointment came to an end, she was looking brighter and had more colour in her face. However, there were still a few tears lurking that had her dabbing the corners of her eyes as she left the salon.

"Paul!" Si hissed, rushing over as Mrs Wilson walked out the door. "What have you done? You can't have clients leaving the salon in tears. What kind of message does that convey? We want happy, satisfied faces leaving the salon, not grief stricken."

"Let it go, Si. She's lonely and needed a chat. Her dog just died, and she was upset."

"I don't care. You don't let clients leave the salon in tears."

I walked away from Si before I said, or did, something I would regret.

PAUL

Under normal circumstances I was more than capable of dealing with Si and letting his words roll off. But something about the way he'd spoken to me after Mrs Wilson's visit had me rattled. I refused to let my annoyance at Si control me. Ahead of me, I had an evening with Scott and Jennifer. I needed Scott's input on my career and the different options mulling around in my head. And it wouldn't hurt if I got time with Jennifer, to get some background on Kirsty.

As I was clearing up my station at the end of the day, Brian and Trish, two of the stylists, came over and asked if I would go for a drink with them. Brian had the look of someone with something pressing on his mind. I understood that burden.

We headed round the corner to Jack's Place. It was our regular for after-work drinks, and the starting place for nights out. At this time on a Monday night it was quiet.

"So what's going on guys?" I asked, keen to get this conversation dealt with so I could get to Scott's house.

"It's Si," said Brian, getting straight to the point. "He's driving us crazy. ByDesign used to be a great place to work, but he's taking all the fun out of it. It's always push push push with him. He never lets up. I don't know how much more I can take."

"Do you feel the same way, Trish?"

"Yep, he's on my case from the minute I get in the door. He's got his favourites, and I'm not one of them!"

"So, what's your thoughts?"

"We're pretty sure there's no point speaking to Si about it. He's not one to take any kind of criticism well, especially concerning his way of running things," said Brian.

"So, we were wondering if we should speak to Iain about it. Do you think he could sort out Si, or maybe even get us transferred to the Edinburgh salon?" said Trish.

"Management know what Si is like, but he's their 'golden boy' because he's turned the salon round, and profits are on the increase. You could speak to Iain and ask if there is the chance of a transfer. Maybe that would help get the point across that Si can't keep going the way he is."

Brian and Trish looked at each other. Was there something else they wanted to ask? I didn't have time to wait for them to pluck up the courage. "What? You've both got that look of wanting to say something else, but you're not sure how."

"Well…" said Brian, not rushing into further explanation.

"Just say it guys. It's me. You can talk to me."

"Well, we were wondering. Have you ever thought about starting up your own salon? And if you did would you think about letting us work with you?"

"Where has this come from?" Their question rocked me. Matt had planted the seed last week, and already here were two promising stylists willing to give up sought after styling positions to go into a business start-up with me.

"What makes you think I want to start my own salon?"

"Have you never thought about it? Everyone knows you're the best stylist at ByDesign. Even Si knows it, but his ego would never let him admit it. We know you're not happy there. So you must be considering moving or starting up for yourself. How can you want to keep working for Si?"

My mind was in overdrive. I didn't know whether to laugh or run away. I didn't want to manage other people. But then again, maybe it was time.

I had to be honest with them when they had taken this step of faith in confiding in me. "Your timing is perfect. I am restless at ByDesign. I'm weighing up my options, so I appreciate you coming to me about how you're feeling. But I need time to think this through."

"Take all the time you need," said Brian.

Trish nodded her agreement and added, "Paul, we don't want to be in a ByDesign that doesn't include you."

During the bus journey from the city centre to Scott's, my mind was going over and over the options before me. I needed to make sense of what was going on. Was it a coincidence that only weeks after the restlessness started I'd been offered a sought after promotion at ByDesign? Then there was the idea of starting up my own salon, the suggestion had caught me off guard. It had been so many years since I'd even considered the prospect, probably not since I'd been offered the apprenticeship at ByDesign. After all, with the kudos of being a senior stylist at ByDesign why would you leave, unless another top competitor head hunted you?

Was it crazy to consider starting my own place? The challenge of it excited me. But what did I know about running a business or being responsible for staff? Was it possible?

PAUL

As soon as I got into Scott's house I was tackled by three energetic girls. I had a big soft spot for these girls. They were fun; each of them enthusiastic for the play fights and tickle fights that always seemed to accompany my visits. I'd barely gotten the chance to say hello to Scott and Jennifer, before I was being pulled to the ground, tickled, bounced on and sat on. Anyone looking on would see nothing but a mass of arms and legs. I was convinced the pitch of the screaming and giggling would burst my eardrums.

With the high energy burst I felt revitalised. Who knew the perfect stress release was being attacked by three kids?

"Your home is the tonic I needed tonight," I said, as we moved through to the living room after dinner. I settled down into Scott and Jennifer's plush settee. For the first time in weeks I had a real sense of peace. "I could close my eyes and have a sleep right here."

"I don't think your fan club would let you away with that," said Jennifer, laughing at the prospect.

"Yep, in this house closed eyes are a sign of weakness, and just as you get settled and on the verge of sleep, three ninja sleep assassins will jump on you to ensure that sleep stays away," said Scott.

"Your girls are great, they're so much fun."

"So, why are you so tired?" asked Jennifer. "Was Scott's party too much for you?"

Paul laughed, "Yeah, keeping up with this old guy tires me out."

"Watch it," said Scott, more than capable of giving as good as he got.

"Work stuff is strange just now, Jennifer. I'm not sure what I want to do. And it's got me unsettled. But the weird thing is that since I've started feeling this way, several people have spoken to me about different options I should consider. So now I've got even more to think about."

"You're not thinking of giving up are you? I've loved my appointments with you, please say you're staying with hairdressing."

"I still enjoy the styling and meeting people. But it's not like I have anything to compare it to and I'm not qualified for anything else."

"Well, like I said, I think you're very talented. Which reminds me, before I make the coffee and deal with these crazy girls, can you cut my hair Friday morning?"

"I've not got my schedule with me, but I'll make that work. Text me in the morning and let me know what time you're thinking of and I'll see what I can do."

"Thanks, Paul, I appreciate that. Now, are you both wanting coffee?"

"That would be lovely, honey, thanks," said Scott.

"Thanks Jennifer," I said, forcing myself to sit more upright. This house is amazing, there is a cosiness about the place that lets you know you are always welcome. As I enjoyed a moment of silence, my thoughts returned to Saturday night, and the last time I'd sat on this settee. The place where I'd finally got the chance to speak to Kirsty, to wear down those defences and find the girl behind the mishaps. I smiled at the recollection.

PAUL

"Like I told Jennifer, I'm confused about work stuff," I said, by way of introducing the struggles I was walking through.

"Has anything else happened since we last spoke?" asked Scott.

I laughed. "You could say that! I got offered a post as the manager of the Edinburgh branch, which is a huge honour at ByDesign. But somehow I didn't jump at the chance. And I still can't decide what I think about the offer. Then Matt suggested I consider opening my own place. And, tonight as I was getting ready to leave the salon a couple of the junior stylists told me they wanted to talk. They asked if I was thinking about setting up my own place, and if that was the case would I hire them."

Scott laughed. "That is a lot to process in a short time. Have you ever considered opening your own place before?"

"In my enthusiastic early days I toyed with the idea of setting up on my own. The way you do before you realise the actual workings of the business; when you dream of greatness and being the next big name in hairdressing."

"These options, whilst posing more questions, may also provide part of the answer to your questions."

"I'm not aware of any answers here, only more questions."

"The last time we spoke you said you weren't sure whether to stay with hairdressing, or look at other options. But the fact that you've had a couple of different options presented to you from within the hairdressing industry, perhaps suggests that's the place you should stay. And if that's the case, part one of your question has been answered, and now the second part needs answered: what does that look like?"

I contemplated Scott's words. They seemed to make sense. Perhaps it was all down to changing the where.

"Can it be as straightforward as that?" I asked.

"I believe so. Things get complicated when we let them. You said before you were trying to determine if staying in hairdressing was a worthy enough job. But your job isn't the thing that makes you a better person. It's how you choose to live your life that determines who you are. You've got a gift for hairdressing, Jennifer is always singing your praises after her appointments. Use your gifts Paul, God made you who you are for a reason. Don't feel you need to fit into someone else's idea. The world wouldn't operate if everyone was an aid worker or church worker – we need hairdressers too."

Scott had cut through my questions and helped direct my thoughts. I wanted to get back to my flat, close myself in my room and read my Bible and pray. I only had till tomorrow to decide about the Edinburgh job.

As I let myself back into my flat, I realised I'd been so consumed by my conversation with Scott I'd forgotten to talk to Jennifer about Kirsty. Next time I'd make that the priority.

JENNIFER

The Psalms encouraged and inspired me. They were a prime example of looking at the world around me instead of becoming self-absorbed.

As I sat on my bed reading through a few Psalms, I noticed my journal leaning against my bedside table. I picked it up and leafed through it. I hadn't written anything since May. Perhaps it would be a good idea to write down some of my questions and feelings. It was amazing how often writing something down helped.

Where is my joy?
What brings me joy?
Why do I feel numb?
What are my dreams for the next season in life?
What should I do with my time?

A knock at the door interrupted my thoughts. It was the delivery of items for Chloe's room. As I tore into the package, I cast aside all my introspection at the excitement of the treasure trove in front of me. Chloe had selected a variety of items to finish her bedroom. There were canvas wall prints, cushions, fairy lights and wall stencils. I couldn't wait till three o'clock to get the girls from school and let Chloe finish her room.

"This picture should go here," said Chloe, as she buzzed around her room.

"Agreed. It's the perfect spot for it." I put the picture hook in place before she changed her mind again.

"Do you want to put the batteries in your fairy lights? It might make it easier to decide where to put them when they are lit up."

"Great idea, mum." She raced downstairs to get batteries. The break gave me a few minutes to catch my breath. Her exuberance was a little energy zapping. I looked round her room, pleased with the results of the new colours. It was fun giving Chloe responsibility in deciding where to put things.

With the fairy lights, and all the other new items, in place I stood back with Chloe admiring her room. "I love it all, mum. Thank you so much." She threw herself at me in a hug.

"Dad! Dad! Come and see my room." Scott came bounding up the stairs and scooped her into his arms.

"This can't be your room. It's far too grown up for a two-year-old."

Chloe giggled. "Dad! I'm five!"

"No way!" continued Scott. "How did that happen? Last time I looked you were two." Chloe's giggling continued at Scott's teasing.

"Do you love my room, dad? Do you? Do you?"

"It looks fabtastic."

"You're silly. That's not a real word. Mrs Simpson would give you into trouble for making up false words."

"Well, it's just as well she's not my teacher then, isn't it?" And with that Scott and Chloe were running around the house having a tickle fight. I laughed at their nonsense.

Chloe's room looked fantastic. I took photographs. Everything was fresh and in its rightful place. Who knew how long that would last?

I texted one of the photos to Kirsty. 'Chloe's room. All finished.'

'Wow! Looks amazing,' replied Kirsty. 'When are you starting mine?'

'Next week. Wednesday I'll do the prep work, then start painting on Thursday.'

'So excited.'

I couldn't wait to transform Kirsty's living room.

PAUL

I arrived at the restaurant early for my meeting with Iain. Nervous about how the conversation would unfold. Speaking with Scott last night, I had been so sure about things, and it all seemed straightforward. But the uncertainty had been creeping back in since then. Was I doing the right thing in turning down Iain's offer?

I took out my phone, and opened my Bible app: '*And the peace of God, which transcends all understanding, will guard your hearts and your minds in Christ Jesus.*'

The words were helpful. They reminded me that life didn't need to be complicated; I could trust God. As I thought over the verse, I knew I was making the right choice.

A few minutes later Iain came bustling into the restaurant. His mannerisms always shouted that he had somewhere else to be, there was another mission he was running late for, no time for small talk, unless it got him what he wanted. "So, have you thought about our offer?" asked Iain.

"I have. Thanks for the offer, Iain. I appreciate it, and a few months ago I would probably have jumped at it. It's been a dream for a while. But I've got a few personal issues I'm dealing with just now. So, while I appreciate the offer, I'm going to turn it down this time round."

"You realise there may not be a next time, don't you?"

"It's a risk I need to take."

"What could be more important than managing one of our salons? It's not like you've got a wife and kids to consider; lucky guy."

I appreciated that Iain was trying to make light of the situation, despite his obvious feelings of frustration towards me. I didn't want there to be any hard feelings between us. It wasn't my way of doing things.

"I appreciate the offer, but I'm going to stick with saying 'no thanks'. But there is something else I'd like to run past you."

"Okay, make it quick though, I need to be out of here in ten minutes." I realised the shortness of the appointment had been planned around the certainty I would say yes to the management position.

"There's a bit of unhappiness in the salon at the way Si is managing things. Quite a few of the stylists are feeling pressurised and unappreciated."

"There's always drama in salons, Paul, you know that. We can't be holding everyone's hands all the time. The stylists need to get over themselves. Si's turned the salon round and we're thrilled with the figures since he took over. He's done the job he was sent in there to do. The stylists need to do the job we pay them for. They should be grateful to be working for ByDesign, not grumbling because they need to work for it."

I was disappointed, but not surprised by Iain's comments. Management cared about the bottom line, and that was the area Si was gifted in. It was clear there would be no changes in relation to Si. They had the assurance of knowing they were one of the top salons and could always attract stylists. Mutterings amongst the workers were of no concern to them.

"You're a great stylist, Paul. Everyone knows that, top management included. We'd like to see you take over the management of one of our salons one day soon. When you're ready call me."

"Thanks Iain."

"But one parting word of advice," said Iain, as he stood to leave. "Don't rock the boat."

Iain's cheap shot annoyed me. This evening had helped confirm my position. I knew exactly what my next career step would be.

JENNIFER

"Jennifer! Great to see you," said Paul, as I arrived for my appointment at ByDesign. Once again I was pushing my timing to the limit. I had planned on leaving the house in plenty of time for my appointment. But my good intentions evaporated as soon as I switched on my computer. The beauty and creativity of the images on the home décor sites had me lost in time, my mind meandered around the different possibilities for finishing touches to Kirsty's living room. There were so many great options to choose from. I saw a design centring round a beautiful contemporary clock. I gazed at it dreamily before the hands on the image reminded me to check the hands on my watch. And once again I was rushing out the door, throwing on my raincoat and sunglasses.

"What can I do for you today?" asked Paul.

"Just a trim thanks. I'm loving this new style and want to stick with it."

"Glad you're enjoying it. It's still looking great."

"Chantelle, can you take Jennifer's through for her hair wash and head massage?"

"This way please," said Chantelle. By the time she got to the head massage, the part I adore, I felt relaxed. It was

211

exactly what I needed, a nice bit of calming pamper. I wasn't one for sitting about much, but sometimes it was needed.

"Thanks Chantelle, that was amazing!" I said to the junior as she led me back through to Paul's workstation.

"You're welcome, Jennifer. Can I get you a drink or a magazine or anything?"

"A cup of tea would be lovely, thanks. I don't need a magazine, I'm sure Paul will keep me entertained with his stories."

"You know something, Jennifer?" asked Paul, once Chantelle had walked over to the refreshment area. "You're the only person I ever see her being this nice to."

"I can't believe that. Look at her. She's so obliging."

"I'm not kidding! She never runs around after anyone else like that."

"I guess she knows how much I appreciate her amazing head massages. I love coming here. Maybe I'll stop dying my hair at home and get you to do my colour too. Would give me a great excuse to spend longer here."

"You're always welcome," said Paul. He laughed as I made myself more comfortable in the chair. "And how are those gorgeous girls of yours today?"

"They're all fine, thanks for asking. We've had a drama free week, and I can tell you, with three girls that's quite the accomplishment."

"Your girls are great, Jennifer. Lots of fun to be around."

"I hope they weren't too much for you on Monday night. They go by the opinion that anyone who comes to our house is only there to entertain them."

"Not a problem when they are so easily entertained. And what are you up to now the girls are at school?"

"Still trying to figure that out. I decorated Chloe's room the week she started school. And next week I'll be starting work on Kirsty's living room."

"Really? Funny you should mention Kirsty, I was hoping to talk to you about her."

"I noticed the two of you chatting for quite some time at Scott's party." With a lot of willpower I kept my voice level, trying not to get too excited. I was desperate to know how things had gone with Paul and Kirsty. I didn't get the opportunity to ask Paul on Monday night when he was at the house, Scott would have been annoyed with my 'interference'. But here was Paul opening up the conversation.

"Jennifer, you're as subtle as a sledgehammer!" said Paul, laughing at my reflection in the mirror. "We both knew what you were up to, getting us to sit together at the party."

"What can I say? I guessed right! You've already admitted you want to know more about Kirsty."

Paul laughed. "You've got me. Seriously though, I wanted to thank you for manoeuvring the two of us together." Ha! I was right. They would be good together.

"Did I see you with Kirsty and her friends after church on Sunday too?"

"Yep, we all went out together for lunch. They're a fun group. It's been nice hanging out with them."

"Any plans to see any of them again?"

"Jennifer! You're still doing it. Subtle as a sledgehammer. But yes, any time I've been with Kirsty, I want to get to know her more. She's not like any of the girls I've known before. Sometimes she seems so fragile, and other times she seems the most capable person around."

"You've not met her at her best. Her boyfriend broke up with her a few weeks ago, so she's in the relationship grieving process just now. But he was a bad match for her. She needs someone who will value her and look after her."

Paul responded with an uncomfortable laugh. I'd said enough. My instincts had been right up till now, I didn't need to push any further. The seeds were sown, now they needed time to grow.

KIRSTY

The next time I saw Gary was mid-morning Friday. I glanced over as he got out of the elevator and walked to his office. He spent a few minutes getting himself organised, then I got an instant message asking me to go to his office for an update meeting.

"Let's get these seating plans sorted out," he said, walking over to his meeting desk.

"I confirmed the menus with the hotel. And I phoned the companies you circled to get an update on replies. As you know there were two of them I forwarded on to you, but the rest were all 'yes'. In most cases the assistants had been delayed by checking or reorganising other appointments. I've now received the replies from all but one, but I've been told the official acceptance for that one will be in next week. From the rest of the list we've had another ten acceptances."

"Excellent. I have spoken to Jonathan and Richard and they have agreed to come, so we've got enough of a confirmation list to arrange the seating plan."

Despite how confusing it could be spending time with Gary at a personal level, professionally I was loving my new role. I was learning so much working with him. Not only in how he directed my time and attention but also observing his own working practices. Seeing how he prioritised and drove himself. I knew the possibilities went beyond the launch event; working with Gary could potentially lead to other projects or even a new job. I had witnessed other colleagues moving into promoted posts after working on high-profile projects.

"I need to make sure we optimise the seating plan, so that's our main focus this morning. By manipulating the tables we can maximise buy-in for our new structure. Plus, it will also help in procuring extra funding by putting competitive business leaders together."

"Do you know all these people?"

"Not everyone. But through my family connections I know of most of them. It's vital the event goes well. Seating plans can contribute a lot to that."

"In what way?"

"Take these two guests: Richard and Jonathan. If you sit them at different tables, they'll both pledge funding for the new initiative, they like to be seen to contribute, so they're both good for a donation. But if you sit them at the same table, they'll compete with each other. They will each want to be seen as the bigger benefactor to the city, and so we'll get more buy-in and extra funding. Their funding PR battle will also encourage others around the room to give, but it needs them to be close to each other to kick start it. It's these seemingly insignificant placement details which can make a huge difference."

I was enjoying the meeting. There was no tension. Gary was in good form, teaching me how to look at the bigger picture, imparting wisdom in the stories he was sharing. I needed this, not just the on-the-job learning, but constructive and safe time with Gary.

"I was at a big charity event with these two once. No one else in the room had a chance on the auction bids, they were going at it head to head. The event organisers must have been rubbing their hands. I thought they were going to end up fighting each other at one point, and all over a pair of women's earrings." His animated storytelling had us both laughing.

At that precise moment Irene entered the office. "The whole floor can hear the two of you laughing, it's very distracting."

Gary glanced up. "Irene. Do you need something?" The laughter was replaced with a level of disdain that even I picked up on.

I blushed, all too aware of how close Gary and I were sitting. Thoughts of Irene's warning about him were ringing in my head. Irene stood her ground for a further few seconds. It felt like an eternity. The tension in the office was palpable. Something was going on, but I had no idea what. Should I excuse myself and get on with some work, or should I leave it to Gary to direct what happened next?

"I came up to say not to keep Kirsty too much longer."

"We're working through the seating plans for the event. I'll be keeping her with me all morning. And, speaking of seating plans, I noticed that you haven't confirmed your attendance for the night."

"I won't be attending."

"Why not? For someone of your level it's mandatory to attend."

"There is nothing in my contract that says I need to attend such meaningless affairs."

"I'll be sure to mark that up in your next performance evaluation," said Gary. He stood up and walked over towards Irene, his tall stature towering over her short frame.

Irene wasn't intimidated. Instead of raising to Gary's baiting words, she repeated her initial comment. "Don't keep Kirsty too much longer. You can't commandeer all her time."

"And, as I told you, I need Kirsty for some time. I am well aware of departmental workloads. Kirsty is proving to be invaluable in her work to the department both in her normal tasks, and in assisting with the launch event."

"Kirsty, I need you to finish your report today," said Irene, ignoring Gary and looking to me. There was almost a hint of friendliness in her instruction.

Before I could answer, Gary replied for me, "Kirsty won't be able to work on any of her normal tasks for the rest of the day. Once we've finished up with this meeting, I'll be taking her out to lunch. And for the remainder of the day I need her following up on the points we've discussed this morning."

I didn't know where to look.

"Someone's in her usual cheerful mood," said Gary, as Irene finally walked back to her desk. Despite his joking words there was an edge to his voice. Irene had got to him. I didn't appreciate being caught in the middle of their issues. I wasn't laughing.

"Right," said Gary, his tone returning to the pre-Irene encounter. "Have you got enough information to have an initial go at compiling the seating plans?"

"I think so."

"Great. Draw it all together for our meeting on Tuesday morning. We'll give it the final check over and then you can get it over to the hotel for the place settings. Also, I would like you to put together the final timing plan for the evening, and anything else that you think still needs detailed out. And be thinking of potential problems that might need contingency plans for the night."

I scribbled down Gary's instructions.

"Have you got all that?" I nodded my confirmation. "Okay! Let's head out for lunch."

I walked back to my desk to leave my notes and pick up my bag and raincoat. By the time I had done that Gary was standing at my desk.

"Shall we go to our usual Friday lunchtime spot?" he said, in a voice loud enough for Irene to hear. The trouble was, if Irene heard, the rest of the section did too. The heat spreading up my face didn't help to downplay the situation. I dreaded the questions and the knowing glances that would be coming my way in the afternoon.

JENNIFER

After a lovely hour of relaxing and pampering with Paul, I met up with Scott for lunch. At least coming from my hair appointment ensured that I was on time to meet him this week rather than rushing in at the last moment.

"Your hair looks lovely," said Scott, as he greeted me with a kiss.

"Yes, Paul is a genius. I'm feeling very spoiled today between my haircut and now our nice lunch."

"How was Emma this morning? Did you see Kevin or Sarah at school?"

"No sign of either of them and Emma was fine. This week seems to have gone okay. I'm hoping things have settled down with Kevin. Time will deal with it. But it's hard to watch her go through this.

"How's your week been?" I asked.

"All good in the heady world of financial planning," said Scott, laughing at his witticism. His bad jokes always made me smile. I admired how much he still maintained his sense of humour even though he worked, in what I considered, a boring industry.

"Do you ever feel like we've lost the joy and the fun we had when we were younger?" I asked.

"Where's this coming from? What's wrong?"

"I don't know. I'm still trying to figure out what's next for me. Part of it also realising the joy in my life seems to have dwindled away somewhere. I don't know if I'm happy."

Scott was interrupted from answering by the ping of his phone lying on the table between us. He picked it up, read the text then proceeded to answer it.

"Scott!" I said, perhaps a little more forcibly than I intended. "I need you. I'm lost and I'm scared. I'm scared of this feeling of nothingness." I looked down at my glass and twirled it round in hands.

Scott put the phone down. He lifted my chin and looked into my eyes. "I'm sorry."

He put his phone into his pocket, finally giving me his full attention. "Jennifer, we'll get through this. Your joy is still here. Sometimes you can't see the sun for the clouds but it's still there. Even though you don't always see the sun, you're always prepared for it with your sunglasses. Every time you put on your sunglasses remember that your joy will shine out again, it's still there."

I sipped my water then smiled at Scott. I wanted to feel mad at him for bringing work to our lunches, for not giving me his full attention. But I knew the motivation behind his work ethic was to make a success of his company and provide for us.

Once again I missed those student days where dreaming and uninterrupted conversations were easier.

KIRSTY

It was Friday night ice-cream and chick flick time with Jo. As we made our way through a tub of our favourite Ben & Jerry's ice-cream, the hero and heroine met, had a series of misunderstandings, realised they'd been wrong about each other, kissed, happy ever after, the end.

"It's so easy in movies," I sighed.

"No you don't," said Jo. "You will not compare your love life with a rom-com."

"What's to compare? I have no love life."

"Maybe not in terms of dating. But you've got thoughts of Paul and Gary going round your head right now. Haven't you?"

It's so annoying when your friends know you too well. I dug down into the depths of the ice-cream tub, pretending my attention was focussed on the search for the last morsels of cookie dough.

"Why are you so determined to torture yourself?" asked Jo.

"In the movies the girl gets the guy. Whereas, I'm constantly getting dumped."

"Why do you think that is?"

"I don't know."

"Yes you do. You let these men walk all over you. Why do you need to have a boyfriend all the time?"

I fought back the tears that were threatening.

"I'm not trying to make you cry," said Jo, softening her tone. "I want to know what's at the root of all this."

Shrugging, I busied myself with my ice-cream tub again.

"I can stay here all night," said Jo. "I will keep asking till I get an answer."

She was silent for a few seconds before starting on another tact. "What age were you when you first dated?"

"Don't laugh. I was eighteen. It seems so young now, but it felt so old then."

"And who was this first date? Was he your first love?"

"No."

"So why did you go out with him?"

"Because he was the only boy to ask me out. My parents told me I wasn't allowed to date until I was seventeen. I was the only one at school not going out with someone."

"I doubt that was the case. It might have felt like it, but I doubt it was the reality."

"It felt real enough. Everyone in my year, if not the whole high school, knew about the seventeen age limit. Most people found it hilarious. And, as if that wasn't enough, having a policeman father and three brothers pretty much sealed my fate. To the boys at school I was a joke and not someone to view as a potential girlfriend. By the time I reached seventeen all the boys I liked were already dating. The boys like Paul and Gary were way out of my reach, never interested in me, but I liked them from afar. And now, Paul and Gary are in my life, spending time with me in a way that none of the popular boys at school ever did."

"You're not at school anymore. This is the grown-up world where men and women interact. Gary's your boss. Paul's your hairdresser."

"But they're not sticking to just those roles are they?"

"No, you're right. Real life is complicated and lines get blurred. Don't let yourself get carried away in some kind or Romantic Comedy script."

"Why is it so complicated, Jo?"

"I don't know," said Jo, as she pulled me into a hug. We sat side by side in silence.

"Jo?"

"Yes."

"I just want to be loved."

"We all do, Kirsty."

KIRSTY

I woke up crying. I was hot, clammy and gasping for breath. The last time I had attempted a ByDesign appointment I had dreamt about Gary too. But this dream brought out quite a different set of feelings. I looked around the room. In the partial light of early dawn I was able to make out the familiar shapes of the wardrobe and chest of drawers. I reached over to switch on the light, needing the reassurance of light to chase away the shadows of the dream.

There had been a boxing match between Gary and Paul. Paul was in the good corner fighting on my behalf, Gary was in the opposing corner, full of evil intent. Paul fought cleanly, Gary was using every dirty trick in the book, whatever it took to defeat Paul. With a knockout punch Gary had leapt out of the boxing ring and grabbed me. My legs wouldn't work, I couldn't get away from him. He dragged me away from the boxing ring; I cried to him to let me go.

I woke myself up as the tears started flowing.

I got out of bed and walked through to the kitchen to get a glass of water, switching on every light and hesitating at every doorway and corner as I went. The fear from my dream still dominating my senses.

Yesterday's strange public display by Gary in the office had embarrassed me, and, if the nightmare was anything to go by, had me more unsettled than I realised. I shivered as I thought back to our last morning meeting when I had felt a hint of fear at being alone with him. The memory of the meeting and the tension of the dream had me looking round the kitchen, reality and dream still trying to separate.

And then there was Paul. I was looking forward to seeing him. But, somehow, I couldn't see him clearly without images of Gary popping into my mind. What was wrong with me? I was making too much out of a dream. The dream had scared me that was all. No point trying to over-analyse it all, especially at this hour of the morning.

I persuaded myself it was safe to go back to bed; I picked up my Bible and read a few chapters from Matthew. The words soothed me and gave me the courage to switch off the lights and go back to sleep. Thankfully dream free.

With my appointment not until 4pm, I made good use of my free day and did some much-needed cleaning and tidying in the flat. Jennifer would start work on the living room during the coming week, so I needed to do something about the mess and clutter that had amassed on unit tops and corners. For the next hour I worked non-stop on de-cluttering the living room, a vacuum and polish finished it off. I smiled at the result, a room that looked presentable enough for Jennifer's clutter radar.

Now that the living room was taken care of I turned my attention to the bedroom. My bedroom is the neglected room, the last room to be tidied and even more of a dumping ground than the living room. The double wardrobe is full of clothes and shoes, and on top of it is a row of storage boxes containing yet more clutter. As I reached up to bring down the boxes, something fell out of one of them and clobbered me on my forehead.

"Ouch! That hurt!" I looked around to identify the object that had fallen on my head. There on the floor lay a snow globe of Glasgow, a cheesy gift that Steven had given me when we were on a day out, in the first flush of dating. I hadn't thought of Steven for a few days, but here was a painful memory of our time together. I picked up the snow globe and thought of Steven. When I started dating him I had been so sure he was the one. How quickly things had changed. I could now see the deterioration of our relationship, but at the time I had hidden myself from the truth.

"Move over Steven, I've got more interesting problems than you." I put the boxes back up on top of the wardrobe and threw the broken snow globe into the bin.

KIRSTY

When I walked into ByDesign Paul's assistant greeted me. As with the last time, Chantelle didn't seem keen to see me. She led me through to the sinks in silence and washed my hair. I tried not to think about the last time I had been at these sinks.

I'm fairly certain the hair washing and head massage experience is supposed to be a pleasant one. But between the attitude emitting from Chantelle, and the frequency with which her long scarlet false nails scratched along my scalp, I was thankful when the whole process came to an end. However, the pain wasn't at an end yet. Chantelle led me over to Paul's station and then proceeded to mercilessly comb through my hair, regardless of tugs. And that was when I noticed the large bruise on my forehead. That stupid snow globe! I put my fingers up to investigate; it was sore to the touch.

Paul walked over and leaned against the workstation. His easy confidence enhanced his physical attributes. "Kirsty! Great to see you again."

"You too."

"Glad to see you came out without your raincoat and sunglasses today."

"Well, that's where you're wrong. I took off my sunglasses as I came into the salon, it is nice and sunny outside you know."

"Lucky you getting to see that. I've been stuck in here all day. Sunglasses are passable, it's when they are teamed up with those boring coats that it all gets too samey."

I relaxed with the easy flowing chat and laughed at Paul's obsession with raincoats and sunglasses. But then the dreaded Chantelle cut into our fun chat. Making sure she drew Paul's attention to my bruise with her question of, "What happened to your forehead?"

"What have you done to yourself now?" asked Paul, as he took over from his assistant. He laughed as he combed through my hair and got ready to start the cut.

Between Paul's laughter and his assistant's cattiness my relaxed, happy mood evaporated. I didn't want to be here anymore. Instead of trying to make an effort to chat with Paul, I opted for sulky silence.

"So what are your plans for tonight?" said Paul. His question adding insult to injury. He wasn't even picking up on the fact I was annoyed with him. I replied to his question with silence.

Chantelle was once again by Paul's side. She put her hand on Paul's arm, ensuring she had his full attention. "Paul as you haven't started yet, could you take a call? One of your clients wants a quick word."

"I'll be back in just a few minutes Kirsty. Can we get you a tea or coffee while you wait?"

"No, I'm fine thanks."

The break gave me the chance to gather my thoughts and let go of my childish annoyance. I shouldn't be taking my frustrations out on Paul. It wasn't his fault I had bumped my head, or that his assistant was not the most sympathetic of people.

"Sorry about that," said Paul, as he returned. "So what shall we do with your hair today?"

"What would you suggest? It's probably been too long since I last had it cut."

"Do you trust me?"

"I know I should say yes, but I'm not sure. I don't know you that well."

"At least you're honest."

"As long as you promise not to do anything outrageous or wildly different, I'll let you go with what you think."

"Glad to see you're living on the wild side!"

Over the next half-hour Paul demonstrated his skill not only as a hairdresser, but as a purveyor of entertaining small talk. By the time he switched on the hairdryer I was laughing at his carefree chat. It looked as if Jo was right; he was a nice guy.

As Paul finished off the styling, I looked at my reflection in quiet appreciation. He certainly knew what he was doing. I loved my new haircut. While I was still admiring my reflection, Paul walked round checking the evenness of the length and the layers. He came around in front of me and crouched down slightly to check the side layers. As he ran his fingers through my hair, I became aware of how close we were to each other. The reflection of my new haircut no longer held my attention. That was all now fixed on Paul's eyes. The air between us charged with emotion and possibilities. My face was turning red as my mind anticipated the perfect scenario. Paul stopped running his fingers through my hair, but stayed where he was, gazing into my eyes.

"Excuse me, excuse me." The moment was broken by Chantelle's arrival to brush away the cut hair from around the chair.

Paul said nothing else as he completed his last few snips and held up the hand mirror to let me see my new hairstyle from various angles.

"That looks amazing. Thanks." I wanted to say so much more than a mere compliment on my perfect new hairstyle. But the words couldn't be found. Chantelle had ruined the magic.

"If you don't have any plans for tonight why don't you come out for dinner?"

"Really? I'd love too." The magic might have been broken, but there was still a glimmer of hope.

Bumped head withstanding, this was turning out to be a great day. All thoughts of checking potential boyfriends with my friends disappeared. Besides, they all loved Paul. They would approve. Life between dating had been as complicated as dating, so really this was by far the better option.

"Great, Matt will be here in ten minutes and then we can head out. You want to grab a seat at reception and I'll get finished up here."

What? So it wasn't a date then? Funny how he never mentioned Matt in his first question. Was he playing some game with me? I'd committed now, so it would seem petulant to change my answer. I don't understand men!

KIRSTY

We went to a nearby restaurant for burgers and beers. It was busy with Saturday shoppers, shopping bags surrounding their feet. With Paul and Matt sitting either side of me I decided not to pass judgement yet on how this evening could go.

"So, what are you going for, Kirsty?" asked Matt.

"I'm not sure yet. What would you recommend?"

"The mega burger."

"I'm thinking of one of the smaller options," I replied.

"Probably best, don't want you being sick on us again."

"Matt! I told you not to mention the S-word," said Paul. I wasn't sure if he was being serious or joking.

"Don't worry, Matt. I won't take offense at your jokes."

"See!" Matt said to Paul.

"Although, now you mention it, I would like to say a proper thank you for being there for me when I was ill. So dinner's on me."

"We can't let you pay, Kirsty. I was the one who invited you along," said Paul.

"I know. But it's the least I can do after all the trouble I caused. It's not up for discussion, I'm paying." I lifted my beer bottle up for a cheers, and the deal was done.

For the rest of dinner it was all banter and nonsense between the three of us. Every time I saw Paul I was dealing with some disaster or another, and yet he still seemed happy to spend time with me.

"I'm stuffed!" said Matt.

"That's because you always go for the Mega Burger. Stop being such a glutton!" said Paul, laughing at Matt's facial expression.

"I need a cinema trip to let me burger settle. Do either of you know what's on?"

I took out my phone and looked through the listings for the nearby cinema.

Paul and Matt both jumped at the movie that was all action and adventure.

"You up for it, Kirsty?" asked Paul.

"Count me in!" It was turning out to be the cliché guy night out, perhaps a break from girlie emotion was just what I needed. Maybe I should view this as more of a compliment than being asked out. I was one of the guys.

The movie was fast-paced but predictable. We came out of the cinema laughing about some of the crazy action scenes we had just witnessed.

"What's the best way for you to get home?" asked Paul.

"I can get a bus from here."

"We'll walk you to your bus stop and wait with you till you get your bus," said Paul.

As I got on the bus Paul and Matt waved me off. I smiled as I sat down. It had been an interesting evening, but I didn't have a clue how to process any of it. I needed help. I sent a text to the girls: 'lunch tomorrow?'

PAUL

"Mate, you've got to have a serious chat with that girl," said Matt.

"What are you talking about?" I replied.

"You know exactly what I'm talking about. You can read girls better than any guy I've ever met; so I know you know she's into you."

"Do you think?"

"Come off it. You know she is. That girl can't hide her emotions. It's obvious she's hoping for something to happen between the two of you. Don't confuse her. You need to tell her where you stand."

"I'm just being her friend. It wasn't a date. We had burgers, and you were there. What part of that says date? Can't I enjoy hanging out with a girl, without complications?"

"Other guys can, but I don't think that's an option for you. Until a few months ago you dated every girl you liked.

Do you know how to do friendship with a girl? You're fluctuating between your intense vibe and uncertainty. It's confusing the situation. You need to tell her where you're at. Be honest with her so you can decide what's best for both of you. Otherwise false expectations will ruin any chance of friendship."

"Thanks! I had a fun night hanging out and you need to complicate matters."

"I'm not the one complicating anything. I'm just telling it like I see it."

"It's infuriating that you're right!" I replied. "Normally by now I'd have taken what I wanted from Kirsty and moved on. There I've said it, I've admitted what I am."

"It's who you were. You're putting that behind you."

"But do I know how to? I was so up for the dating break, of being done with my cycle of non-stop dating, but Kirsty's got me so wound up I don't know what to do."

"We're here for you. Me, Scott and the rest of the guys. We're praying for you and we'll do whatever we can to help."

"I don't know why she's getting to me so much. It's nothing she's done or said. I'm just crazy attracted to her, and it's messing with my mind."

"It's hard. But you need to figure out where you're at and then tell her."

Despite forcing me to confront the situation, I appreciated Matt's words. I needed this friendship so much. Matt was right. I don't know how to be friends with a woman. And, with Kirsty I wanted more than just friendship. I was on a collision course and I had no idea how to avoid it.

KIRSTY

Paul wasn't at church the next day. I tried my best to concentrate during the service but my thoughts would insist on dwelling on the events of yesterday and trying to second guess what was going on. I had a vague awareness of Ben preaching from Romans, chapter five. He was talking about love, peace and joy, but I was unsure of the details of the sermon.

As soon as church was finished, we headed to the nearby café, our favourite haunt for a post-church lunch.

"So, tell all, what happened yesterday?" said Jo, "Loving your hair, by the way, it looks amazing. I take it this is Paul's handy work?"

"Yes, isn't it fab? We seemed to get on really well. And there was definitely a moment, or at least I thought there was."

My comments were met with 'oohs' and 'aahs' from my friends. They were clinging to my every word, desperate to hear of my latest antics.

"He invited me out for dinner once he finished cutting my hair. After I agreed he told me we were going to meet his flat mate, Matt. Then it was beer and burgers and action movie. What does that mean?"

"How was the chat? Did he flirt with you?" asked Jo.

"I don't know! I don't have a clue what's going on."

"Do you like him?" asked Lynn.

"It's me! Of course I do."

Despite my obvious pain and frustration my declaration was met with more giggles and knowing winks from my friends.

"What does it all mean?" I asked. "Help me!" But I had the distinct impression I would not get any help from this lot.

"One thing that did occur to me," I continued. "It was nice hanging out with Paul and Matt last night. Watching the interaction between the pair of them and being part of the carry-on. It makes me think there is wisdom in getting to know people first before dating. On the one hand, it was a learning experience, but on the other hand, I'm as confused as ever. I have no idea how I feel."

"Give it time," said Jo. "Sounds like you're already figuring it out."

"What do you mean? I've not figured anything out!"

"Kirsty, take a breath," said Carol. "Jo's right. You've just told us how much you enjoyed being part of Paul and Matt's night out, watching and learning. Stick with that for the time being."

I walked home on my own. I wasn't sure if the lunchtime chat had done me much good. My head was still full of questions

All I wanted was love. Why was it so difficult?

I thought Steven had loved me, but I had been wrong about him. And now I had two guys that were demanding my attention. But were they? Maybe, but not necessarily from a romantic notion. Gary was my boss and our closeness was all down to the launch event; just because I was attracted to him did not mean he felt the same way about me. Paul had expressed friendship, but was there anything more to it? It was all far too confusing. I felt overwhelmed; I was drowning in a sea of emotions with no idea how to save myself.

"GOD! Why is this so complicated? Even when I'm not dating, guys are still an issue. Why can't I find love? What is wrong with me?" As I cried out to God, the tears flowed. I'd never felt so alone.

PAUL

The world of hairdressing was looking more promising again. But until I made the final decision about my career, I was in limbo. Part of me still enjoyed coming into the salon each morning: the creativeness of the job; the time spent with clients; the buzz in the place. But for every positive there was a negative: the restlessness; Si; not knowing what atmosphere I was walking into.

When I got into the salon, I motioned to Brian and Trish that we needed to talk.

"So, have you made a decision?" asked Trish, her eyes gleaming with hope that I was about to become her liberator from this place of diminishing opportunity and fun.

"Have you?" said Brian. Who was doing a terrible job at not seeming too eager.

"I'm not there yet, guys. We need to discuss it in a lot more detail before we can decide the best way forward. But speaking here isn't a good idea. So let's get together later, I'll meet you in the pub again after work." As Brian and Trish walked away, I hoped I was making the right decision. The two of them were counting on me. I didn't want to give any false promises, nor did I feel capable of being responsible for anyone else's future. It was hard enough trying to navigate my own path.

For now, at least, I could set aside all those thoughts and concentrate on my clients. I looked through my day's schedule and had a quick glance at the other stylists' bookings. There were more gaps than usual in my day, and the rest of the schedules mirrored a similar picture. A day of lower client numbers did not bode well.

And, true to form, Si was stomping around the salon, nipping on about the slightest thing. By the afternoon he was even worse, and all the stylists kept their distance, focusing their full attention on the few clients who were there.

Trish was wandering around trying to look busy, tidying up her workstation and the pile of towels by the sinks.

"Trish!" Si shouted over to her, "I need to speak to you. Now!" I looked over to see what was happening. Trish walked towards Si with her head down. Everyone knew she was going to get a bawling out over something.

"I've been looking over your figures for last week. You had the least amount of repeat clients."

Trish responded with a shrug. Her response was the worst way to reply to Si, and the quickest way to send him over the edge. I knew Trish well enough to know she had done it to wind Si up.

"Do you not care that you're not contributing to this salon?" said Si, by this point screaming in her face. This would not end well. Si was out of line shouting at Trish, especially on the salon floor while there were still clients. Added to that Trish was at the end of her patience with Si and didn't care anymore. They were at boiling point. Only one of them could be victorious, and I knew which of the two it would be.

"You know how it goes, some weeks are better than others."

"What kind of answer is that?" said Si.

"Would you excuse me a minute?" I said to my client.

I walked over to Si and Trish, this conversation needed to be calmed down. "Si, why don't you and Trish go through to the staff room to finish this conversation, there are still clients in the salon," I whispered, trying to bring down the noise levels. But I was too late. There was no more room for compromise.

"Why don't I make it easy for you, Si," said Trish. "You don't want me here, you never have. Well you win, I'm out of here. You can stick your job and you can stick your snide little comments. I've had enough, I'm done." And with that she marched off to her workstation and cleared out her personal items.

"Speak to her before she walks out of here, and you lose a good stylist," I said to Si.

"You heard her. She wants to go."

I had been wrong. I thought Trish was the one pushing it. But it was the other way round. The look on Si's face told me he had won. Trish was hot headed and Si knew he could push her to this point. He had chosen his words carefully and achieved his desired outcome. He had reduced the headcount.

I walked over to Trish. "I'm sorry."

"It's not your fault, it's Si. I can't deal with him anymore. ByDesign may be one of the top salons but it's not one of the top places to work."

"You still want to get together after Brian and me are finished up here?"

"More than ever."

I watched Trish leave the salon. Despite her words of fight she was wiping the tears from her eyes as she left.

"You went too far this time, Si," I said, as I walked past him back to my workstation. A smirk was the only answer I received.

I was mad at Si, but I still refused to believe he was all out devious. He had to have some redeeming qualities. After all, he must have friends somewhere. Once I finished with my client, I wandered over to where Si was sitting looking over paperwork.

"Si, are you okay?"

"What concern is it of yours?"

"When you start an argument on the salon floor, you make it everyone's concern."

"There's nothing to discuss. Trish hadn't been pulling her weight in the salon for a while, it was time for her to go. Even she could see that."

"You know that's not true. Trish is a good stylist."

"She can't be that good if she doesn't get the repeat business other stylists get. The figures don't lie, Paul. And don't think I haven't noticed you whispering about with the other stylists. You hoping to get some bit of dirt on me to spread to your friends at head office so you can get my job? Don't think I don't know about your meeting with Iain."

"That has got nothing to do with this conversation."

"Hasn't it? I know you were offered the Edinburgh job, and that you turned it down. Is it my job you're after? Because let me tell you, you'll never get rid of me." I could hear the hatred in his voice as he spat out the words.

"Si, I don't want your job. And from what I gathered from Iain they're not likely to be looking for a replacement for you, they're happy with the results here."

"Don't think you can charm your way out of this. I know you're after my job. But you'll never get it, and I will make head office aware of what you're really like."

"That's your choice. But you've got this all wrong. I don't want your job."

"You do. I looked through your file and when you were interviewed for the job here, you said then you wanted to be salon manager one day. And I've seen you watching and learning from me in that time. You can't fool me. Everyone thinks you're the best. Well, you're not. I won't be driven out of my job by the likes of you."

"I've told you where I'm at. It's your choice not to listen and go with your own warped version of events." There was no point in arguing. Si obviously had his mind made up and nothing I said would change that. But how did Si know about Iain offering me the job and my refusal to take the Edinburgh position? Had Iain told Si? But why would he?

When Brian and I arrived at the pub, Trish was sitting drowning her sorrows in a glass of vodka, her mascara stained face testament to the tears she had shed while waiting for us to arrive. We needed to order food and let her talk.

Over food she apologised again and again for making things difficult. "Trish, you've not made anything difficult for us. We're here for you."

"Thank you. You're so nice. Why can't Si be nice? Why did he have to be so mean?"

"I don't know. It's not you that's at fault here, it's him. I think he pushed to get you to leave. "

"Really? Is that what he wanted me to do? Can't believe he got me to help him out with his precious profit-and-loss figures."

"You said you wanted to talk about future possibilities," said Brian. "Sounds like your timing is perfect."

"I do, but now's not the time," I replied. "Those conversations can wait for another night, when emotions aren't so frayed."

"Yep, there's always drama in salons," said Brian.

PAUL

The next day at the salon wasn't much better. Si was still in a stroppy, foul mood. To avoid contact with the rest of the staff, he was full-on attentive to his clients. I could never understand why Si got repeat clients, he was so grumpy and opinionated with them. Perhaps it was the title of Salon Director, or Si's own belief he was the top stylist, clients did ask for him time after time.

Once again, after work Brian, Trish and myself met in the pub. Trish still looked upset, she had probably cried today as she worked through the morning after headache and realisation of what she had done.

"Come on then Paul, you need to let us know what you're thinking. We're desperate for a change," said Brian

"Okay, but you also need to realise I'm still processing through recent events, and trying to decide the best way forward." The others nodded their agreement, desperate to hear what I was going to say next. "Iain met up with me a couple of weeks ago to ask if I wanted to take over the management of the Edinburgh salon."

"Wow, that's great," said Brian. "Would you be able to take us with you?"

"I turned it down."

"You did what?" gasped Trish. "We thought you wanted to manage your own salon."

"I thought I did too. And maybe I still do. But not a ByDesign salon. Si has sickened me of the whole thing, and head office have made it clear they like his results. I can't work for that kind of company anymore. I thought about giving up hairdressing. But I've decided I'm not ready to walk away from it yet."

"So, what are you going to do?" said Trish, a spark of hope in her eyes. "Are you going to open your own salon?"

"I must confess, until you guys broached the subject I hadn't considered that option for a long time. But now I'm wondering if it might work."

"Of course it would," said Brian. "You're the best stylist at ByDesign and I bet a lot of the clients would leave to follow you if you started up on your own."

"Yeah, get a list of all your clients and then you can tell them where your new place is, and steal them away from the evil Si."

"This isn't a vendetta for me. If I do this, I want to do it right and I don't want to start on a negative of stealing clients from anywhere else. If people find me on their own accord, I'll welcome them. But I'm not starting off with bad blood."

"You sure?" said Brian. "Don't you think it makes good business sense to start working on the clients you already have and get them prepped to move to your new place? Plus, with Si, there'll be bad feeling anyway, so may as well make the best of the situation."

"The hairdressing world is a small world. I want our salon to be a huge success. I don't want anyone to point the finger and say it was only a success because we stole our client list from ByDesign. This is crucial for me, I need to know you're on board with this before we take this conversation further."

"Okay if that's the way you want to go, I'll follow your lead," said Brian.

"Me too," said Trish. "Although it's not like I'm in the position to contact my client list now anyway."

"So, do we want to do this?" I asked. "Do we want to start our own salon?" The big smiles on the faces of the other two gave me their answer.

"It's a huge step guys, so we need to make sure it's the right thing. Let's look into it and see what the possibilities are. Brian, we're not going to throw in the towel at ByDesign just yet. And, Trish, let me talk to some of my mates in other salons and see if we can get you in somewhere else, at least a few days a week, to keep you earning."

As I got another round of drinks in, we spent time chatting and dreaming about what our own salon could look like. In the safety of the pub, dreaming of the perfect salon, it was easy to get carried away and give permission to the rising excitement and anticipation of starting our own creative space.

Trish volunteered to make use of her current free time to contact the local Business Development office and get us started on finding out what we needed. She would also check out commercial properties for rent in a few key streets in the south side of town rather than pay the high city centre costs. We agreed to get together the following week to discuss Trish's findings and decide our next steps.

Later that night I shared my dream of the new venture with the men's group. As the discussion focussed on the pros and cons of striking out on business on your own, a peace settled over me. This was crazy, I was on the verge of walking away from the security of a paid job. I was going to risk it all to become my own boss, being responsible for balance sheets and top lines. What if it turned me into a Si? Constantly worrying about where the next client was coming from? Worrying about how I would pay any staff? The questions suggested it wasn't the most sensible option, but the peace told me it was. And even though the questions continued to circle round, they found no place to rest. For the first time in weeks, peace conquered the questions and doubts.

'And the peace of God, which transcends all understanding, will guard your hearts and your minds in Christ Jesus.' The words were turning from aspirational to real, so real I could almost touch the peace they promised.

JENNIFER

If I like housework, then I love decorating. The smell and sight of fresh paint fills my senses with anticipation. My favourite part is when the first touch of paint marks the beginning of the transformation. Like these boring walls, I needed colour in my life. I longed for that first dab of colour to signal that something new was coming.

But today was not a day for melancholy. I had a job to do. And it was one of my favourite jobs.

My love of decorating started with our first flat. Painting our little flat changed it from being the previous owners to ours. And that same thrill continued with each move, decorating our terraced house and then our current home. Within that there was the changing décor for the girls as they grew from babies, to pre-school to primary school. Next year I would update Amy's room as she moved from primary to high school. How unbelievable that I had a daughter on the verge of high school. We would soon be attending the high school visits and preparing for her to finish primary school. It was captivating watching the emotions playing through Amy; she pretended to be so grown up, but there were still glimpses of the little girl.

By the time I finished painting the ceiling my neck was stiff from the continual upward focus. I rolled my neck and glanced at my watch, aware that when you have a project, the school day is no longer as long as you think. I had enough time to start the gloss work.

As I shuffled along the floor painting the skirting board, I thought of some of the accessories I would like to get for Kirsty's living room. Last night, at small group, we had veered away from the recommended topic again and looked at First Corinthians chapter Thirteen. As a passage that focusses on love and the attributes of love, it is often used in weddings, but beyond the 'nice words for a wedding ceremony', it contains so much wisdom and truth. My intention was to keep the small group within those verses for the next few weeks. We needed to focus Kirsty on the security of the love that was there for her with Jesus. I made a mental note to check out gift company websites, perhaps I could find a cushion with some verses from the passage. It would be good for her to have a constant reminder of what real love stood for.

I was thankful for Jo, Carol and Lynn. Kirsty had good friends; friends who were there to laugh through the good times and surround her for the bad times.

I prayed that the next few weeks would bring a fresh start for more than just her living room!

KIRSTY

After all the turmoil of the weekend, life calmed down for a few days. It gave me the chance to get a clearer perspective and enjoy the day-to-day routine. Work had been enjoyable. With Gary out of the office all week, I could deal with my regular duties and the final planning for the launch event. I couldn't believe how much fun work could be with an enjoyable task to delve into. The previous day I had taken over one of the meeting rooms to make use of the large boardroom tables. I spread out the event seating plans. With chart paper, different coloured highlighters and my notes, I had been lost in the afternoon hours pulling together the complicated seating plans. It was so refreshing to leave work with a sense of accomplishment and a smile on my face.

Irene had even been relatively pleasant to me and didn't give me a hard time about the hours I was putting in to the event organising. Part of the enjoyment was the temporary nature of the project, another few weeks and it would be all over, no time to get bored or frustrated with it.

By the time I got to my Friday lunchtime treat at Chocolate & Vanilla I was feeling good about my work and, more importantly, about myself. I sat down with my latte and muffin and opened the Bible app on my phone. Jennifer had changed our small group focus on Wednesday night and had started a study on First Corinthians Chapter Thirteen. I read the words of verse eight over and over again "love never fails". It was a beautiful phrase. We hadn't got as far as this verse on Wednesday night and I wasn't sure I understood what it meant. My experience suggested quite the opposite. As far as I was concerned, love always failed. What would it look like to experience that kind of love?

Sitting back in the chair, I closed her eyes, hugged my latte and thought about love.

"Are you sleeping?" And, just like that, Gary shattered my thoughts into a thousand fragments as once again he became part of my Friday lunch retreat.

"No, just enjoying a few minutes to myself." Would he take the hint?

"I need to go over some seating plans with you. I had hoped to be in the office during the week, but it didn't happen, and I've got back-to-back meetings all afternoon."

"It's my lunch break, I don't have any work notes with me."

"That's fine. I've got a few things I want you to incorporate into the final plans when you go back to the office this afternoon."

There were no innuendos or camaraderie to his voice as he issued his instructions. It was all work and coldness. On the bright side, at least I wasn't lost in any romantic notions for him. I was too mad at him for invading my Friday oasis, demanding my time for work on the one lunchtime he knew I protected for alone time.

As I watched him stride away from my lunch break, work actions noted and to do list updated, I decided it was time to stop being besotted with Gary. My nightmare had upset me, and there had been a few times when we'd been working together where I'd felt on my guard with him. I was certain the words I had just been reading would be lost on him. Did Gary understand the concept that love never fails? Did he know what love was? It occurred to me that he probably wasn't even looking for love. I didn't want to be with a guy like that, in fact I didn't even want to waste my time thinking about someone like that. I was getting fed up with his assumptions. Never knowing which Gary I was going to be speaking to; the all work and cold Gary, or the overly attentive one.

There was no middle ground with Gary, it was all or nothing. I chose nothing!

JENNIFER

"I've got a couple of things to talk to you about before we head out to church this morning," said Scott, as he joined me at the breakfast bar for coffee and toast. He slid an envelope along the counter towards me.

"What's this?" I asked.

"If you open it, you'll find out."

Opening the envelope revealed a booking for our favourite hotel for the following weekend. "I've spoken to your mum and dad and they are happy to take the girls for the weekend."

"Wow, Scott! Thank you. This is amazing!" I hugged him and smiled at the thought of a weekend away together.

"What's the occasion?"

"An apology. It's been a strange few weeks between the girls getting back to school routine, my work levels and my birthday party. So time for us, no kids and most of all, no housework for you!"

"Thanks, I love it. I'm already looking forward to it."

"And now the smaller apology. Sorry, I forgot to tell you I've invited Paul to have lunch with us today after church."

"You've done what?" I asked.

"I know I should have told you sooner, but I thought you'd be okay with it."

"Of course I'm okay with Paul coming over. It's just that I've invited Kirsty over for lunch. Guess we both had similar ideas."

"They're going to think we're setting them up," said Scott.

"Yep, there's no point explaining ourselves. They'll never believe us."

"Oh well, this will be interesting."

As we sat round the dining table enjoying Sunday lunch and discussing a variety of topics, from Kirsty's work project to Paul's potential new venture, Kirsty seemed a little on edge. In contrast, Paul was his usual laid back self, leaning back in his chair talking over the ideas for his new salon. Had something happened between Paul and Kirsty already?

"Paul, if you do set up your own salon, I'll move with you. You're the only reason I go to ByDesign," I said.

"I'm trying to decide how to deal with my current client list. I don't want to poach them, but it would be good to have some of them move to my new place. It's easy with you because we know each other out with the salon."

"I'm sure word will get out and you'll have a group of your regulars who will stick with you."

As we discussed Paul's dreams, Kirsty was holding back. She sat quietly, chewing on her lip. It would have been the perfect opportunity for her to align herself with Paul's new salon. It took all my willpower not to invite her to be part of Paul's moving-clientele. I was so proud of myself!

"If everyone's finished with lunch, why don't we go to the park," said Scott. "The girls can run off some energy while we enjoy a walk beside the river."

It was a beautiful late summer Sunday afternoon, and the park was bustling with families and groups enjoying the fresh air. I often brought the girls to the park, it was almost a second garden for us. As we entered the play park each of the girls ran off to their favourite play thing, all of them shouting their 'hellos' to their fellow playground users.

Scott and Paul had walked on ahead while I made sure the girls were okay. As I came out of the play park, I linked arms with Kirsty. "What's going on Kirsty?"

"What do you mean?"

"You were quiet and guarded through lunch."

"Was it so obvious?"

"It was to me. But I know you more than certain other people who were at the table."

"I'm so confused. My thoughts are all over the place. I'm trying not to let my emotions overtake me and not be desperate for the next boyfriend. But I've no idea where I stand with Paul, or what he's thinking. I've no idea if he's interested in me that way, or just wants to be friends. I like him, but I don't know where I stand."

"And what if it is just friendship for this season? Why does it need to be more?"

"I guess you're right."

"Give things time. Don't let your insecurities dictate the outcome. You are stronger than that. Enjoy friendship."

Paul and Scott walked over to us. "Jennifer, come and see these flowers, I think this is the kind of thing you said you wanted for our garden." Scott took my hand and led me over to the flower bed in question.

"And you say I'm the obvious one!" I said, laughing at Scott's ploy.

"Okay, you've got me. Your matchmaking thing must be rubbing off. I see what you mean about those two. There's a connection there, but they both seem so uncertain."

I looked round and smiled as I watched Paul and Kirsty walking together along the banks of the river. Though I couldn't hear the conversation, they looked relaxed in each other's company.

"Friendship, Kirsty, friendship," I whispered towards my friend. The words would not reach her, but I prayed the sentiment would rest on Kirsty's thoughts.

KIRSTY

Scott was getting as bad as Jennifer with his not-so-subtle people manoeuvring. I walked over to the side of the river, not quite ready to engage in conversation.

What if it was just friendship with Paul? Would that be so bad? In some ways it made so much sense. As I considered the idea, I realised there was a freedom about it all. Changing focus would give me permission to enjoy the moment and stop with all the striving.

"What are you thinking about?" asked Paul, as I stood gazing at the swans.

Turning round, I smiled at him. "Just little thoughts about learning to enjoy the moment."

"You should always enjoy the moment," said Paul. We walked on together for several minutes, enjoying the peacefulness and beauty of the riverside.

"I'm very impressed," said Paul.

"With what?"

"The last two times I've seen you you've ventured out without your raincoat."

"Wow, you do obsess about things!" I laughed at the expression Paul made.

"If you promise not to wear it on Thursday night would you come out to dinner with me?"

I held my breath. A date with Paul!

"Well, I can't promise the raincoat won't be joining us, but that would be lovely."

Feeling confused on a Sunday night was becoming a habit. I had been so proud of myself earlier with my resolve to consider Paul as just a friend, to stop complicating life by always looking for the perfect relationship. And then just as I had persuaded myself that friendship was the way to go, he asked me out on a date. Okay, so strictly speaking he hadn't said it was a date, but the two of us going out to dinner could only mean one thing. Especially with his insistence about the dress code.

As I lay in bed, my thoughts skipped along my encounters with Paul. The first day at his salon was best forgotten about. Our second meeting, Scott's party, where he'd guided me from embarrassment to laughing at his easy going chat, to ingratiating himself with my friends. Then last Saturday when I finally made it for my haircut. We'd had that *moment* during the haircut, and the fun of hanging out together at night. And today. I was sure Jennifer and Scott were mixing things by 'accidentally' inviting us for lunch on the same day. Lunch had been awkward, but I knew that was my issue.

And then, as we walked together in the park, I had felt so comfortable walking beside him. My mind stayed in the park, dreamily contemplating our walk along the river bank.

In my imaginings the path didn't take us back to the play park, instead my dream-world walk took us further away from other people, to a romantic pond where Paul held me in his arms and kissed me.

Surely this time I had it right. The timing was perfect. I had cast Gary from my mind on Friday. I was done with the adolescent fantasy about my boss. My attention was fully on the man who could give me the commitment I longed for.

Thursday night was going to be perfect. I fell asleep thinking about what to wear.

PAUL

As I opened the door to the pub, I couldn't wait to find out what Trish had learned over the course of the week. Would the conversation still excite us, or would cold reality defeat our optimism?

"Have you had the chance to get much information since last week?" I asked.

Trish pulled out a folder full of notes from her bag. "Yep, had a really constructive week. I've got information from Business Development and I've got property portfolios to show you. But first we want to run something past you."

"Okay, what's that?"

"The two of us have been chatting. We all know you're the guy who has the main draw for this new venture. The whole thing is a risk and we don't want to add to that burden. One of the things we've been talking about is the option of us renting our workstations from you."

Before I had the chance to raise any objections to the idea, Brian continued. "You are the senior stylist, and you've got more experience than the two of us combined. We know you haven't managed your own place before, but we're also sure you'll have a better idea of what to do than we will. We can get it drawn up legally, but we'd still like to be involved in the set-up of the salon."

"Wow! Thanks for your encouragement and faith in me. I've got to say I like your suggestion from the purely selfish reason that I wouldn't be responsible for your salaries. But I would value all the help and input you can give in setting things up. I'm not saying we'll definitely go down this route, but it does looks attractive. Give me some time to think about it."

Trish had picked up lots of information from the Business Development office. More than we had time to read through or process. "If we want further help or advice, we can sign up to some of their business start-up courses and we can book ourselves in for our own meeting with one of their advisors."

"That all sounds great. Let's look at the courses on offer and see what we can get along to," I said.

"I'll have a look and email you. I think the key thing is to set up an appointment with one of their business advisors."

"Agreed. There's far too much information here for us to process on our own. Why don't you see if you can get us an appointment after work one day, so the three of us can all get along?"

"Will do. And I've also got these retail unit schedules for us to have a look at. There are a few places available on the South Side. If we go look at them, it will give us an idea of the size and condition we can get for our budget."

At the mention of budgets we got a bit quieter. Going it alone would be a stretch. We would all need to pick up new business tasks and planning, the kind of things that didn't come naturally to any of us.

Trish was the first to voice her concerns. "There is so much to consider. How do we know how much to budget? How are we going to pay for things up front before we even earn anything?"

Despite the business and finance questions, there was still a peace. "We need to break it all down into manageable steps. Let's not get bogged down and scared by the big picture. Let's take it one step, one task, at a time."

"Sounds easy when you say it like that," said Brian.

"Trish, can you phone the letting agents and get us some viewing times for these commercial properties? Brian, can you get in touch with a few of the supply companies to get catalogues and price lists? It will help us understand how much we'll need to spend to get the basics in the salon."

Finishing up the meeting, I was still optimistic about the new salon. But Brian and Trish were getting more fidgety and uncertain as we discussed the business side of things. Their initial enthusiasm and dreams were being tempered by reality. I would see how they were doing next week after we had further investigated the various aspects of running a salon. If they were still as unsure, maybe this wasn't the way to move forward.

I walked home from the meeting. As I walked, I thanked God that I was in the position to consider this as an option. I spent the rest of the walk home talking to God about my hopes and dreams for the new salon. I was excited about hairdressing again!

JENNIFER

I had been planning on spending the day at Kirsty's flat to get the second coat of paint completed. However, those plans looked to be in jeopardy when Emma arrived at the breakfast table crying and clutching her stomach. "Mum, my tummy's really sore today, I don't want to go to school. Please let me stay here with you."

The sore tummy thing is the worst! You're never quite sure if it's an attempt to get out of school or if there is a problem. Once I'd sent Amy to school when she was complaining of a sore stomach, only to get a call from school half an hour later to say she needed collected because she had been sick all over her table. When a child told you they were ill, it always required parental second guessing, and you had to hope you got it right.

"Try having some cereal and see how your tummy feels after that," I suggested, hoping it wasn't another bug about to do its rounds through the house.

Emma sat staring at her bowl, pushing the floating rings of cereal around, not even attempting to eat anything. This was worrying. I put my hand on Emma's forehead to check her temperature, but it seemed fine.

"Emma, what's wrong?" My question was met with tears. Why did these things happen in the morning? Even on a regular morning I wanted to give myself a gold star if I got the kids to school on time. As I sat holding Emma, Chloe and Amy came racing into the kitchen.

"Mum, tell Amy to give me my teddy back."

"I don't have your teddy."

"Yes you do, I saw you take it."

"Why would I want your smelly old teddy?"

"He's not smelly! MUM!!!"

"Girls! Get upstairs, get dressed and brush your teeth." The tone of my voice sent the girls racing back out of the kitchen.

"Emma, you need to talk to me now while your sisters are upstairs. They'll be back down in no time."

"It's Kevin," said Emma, struggling to talk through her sobbing tears.

"What's happened now?" This situation was exacerbating.

"He told everyone I still sleep with my dummy. And everyone believed him. And now they're all calling me baby."

"I'm so sorry, Emma. But I can't keep you off school for that."

"No! I can't go back!"

"It's okay, sweetheart, I'll come in with you and speak to the head teacher about this."

With even less time than normal to get ready for the school run, I flung on whatever clothes were at hand, and applied mascara. I would still be relying on my sunglasses, but I couldn't keep them on when I was talking to the head teacher. I threw on my raincoat and issued orders to each of the girls to finish off the school preparation.

Once again the walk to school involved a clinging Emma. She had brightened when I told her I'd be going to see the head teacher but, even with that reassurance, her only comfort was holding on to me.

As I waited to be admitted into Mrs Evans' office, several classes of children walked past me on their way to their rooms. Many of the children waved to me as they walked past, used to seeing me in and around the school. At least as head of the PTA it wouldn't seem untoward to be waiting outside the head teacher's office.

"Come in Mrs Thompson, how can I help you this morning?"

"Thanks so much for being able to speak to me on such short notice." I like Mrs Evans. She has a good awareness of the intricacies of the school. And, she knows each of the children by name, which amazes me, I can't even get my own children's names correct at times.

"It's about Emma," I said. "She's having some problems with Kevin this year. It's a little awkward as I'm friends with his mum, but as the issues are happening at school, I thought it best to discuss it with you rather than Sarah."

"Quite right. I've seen more parents fall out over children's arguments than children. I'll speak to the class teacher and ask her to monitor the situation. We'll see what can be done in terms of moving children around in the class, etc."

"Thanks, I appreciate that. Emma seemed better this morning just knowing I was coming to talk to you."

"We don't want any of our pupils to be unhappy. Please keep me informed on the situation. If it gets worse, we'll take further steps."

I appreciated the sentiment and hoped the school would be able to help. There was still the potential for problems at lunch and play times. But at least now that I had spoken to Mrs Evans about it, the school would help resolve the conflict for Emma.

It was a beautiful sunny day, but I couldn't wait to be indoors and treating Kirsty's living room to its second coat of paint. I needed the creative distraction of decorating to relieve the parenting pressures.

As I applied the second coat of emulsion to Kirsty's living room walls, the stress faded away. Between the creative task and the upbeat tracks provided by Scott Nicol through my playlist something resembling joy took over my soul. I sang along with the familiar words as I finished the painting. With the last roll of paint I let out a contented sigh. I stood back and admired my handiwork. The colours were fresh and beautiful.

I sent Kirsty a text: 'Painting all done.'

Almost immediately my phoned pinged with her reply: 'You can't just tell me, send me a pic.'

'There's no point, the paint's still drying. You need to wait till you get home.'

'You're such a tease. I'll see you later at small group. Thanks.'

I smiled as I put my phone back down. Now the painting was finished it was time to turn my attention to the accessories. I had acquired various bits and pieces, but wanted to wait until I had finished the painting before I made my final decision about blinds, curtains, rugs and what occasional furniture would be needed.

Looking around the room I was satisfied with my handiwork, but more importantly I had glimpsed a hint of joy. Was joy almost within my grasp again?

JENNIFER

When I went to collect the girls from school, I felt a bit apprehensive. The fun of my carefree day replaced with the uncertainty of wondering how Emma was. But a child's mood can transform through the course of a school day, as demonstrated by the smiling Emma that ran to greet me.

"Mum, Mrs Evans took me out of class today. She told me I was doing well and if I had any problems with anyone I was to tell her immediately."

"That's great, sweetheart. And were there any Kevin issues today?"

"No. He got moved to a table at the other side of the class from me, and then at lunchtime he got assigned a special duty that kept him inside."

I smiled to myself. Thankful for the swift and careful handling of the situation by Mrs Evans. As far as Emma was concerned the ultimate voice of authority in the school was now in charge of her situation, thereby resolving her issues. The reassurances of that had Emma smiling again, and I was happy to see that it also heralded the return of her appetite. A happy Emma led to a stress free evening.

With Kirsty's flat still in transformation mode, I once again hosted small group. Kirsty came bounding in, first to arrive. "Jennifer! My living room looks amazing. Thank you so much. I love the colours."

"I'm so glad you like it."

"Have you ordered the blinds and new cushions yet?"

"Yes, I did that this afternoon."

"How much do I owe you for those?"

"Nothing. This is my treat to you."

"But you're already giving up your time to paint, you can't pay for things too."

"I want to do this for you. I'm giving you your new-look living room as a turning point in your life. Don't wait around for life to happen, live it now – in colour. Plus, it's giving me something fun to do with my time."

"Thank you, Jennifer. You don't know how much this means."

The rest of the group arrived, and we settled down to our Bible discussion over tea, coffee and cake. We continued looking at First Corinthians chapter Thirteen.

"Tonight, I'd like us to look at verse eight. In fact, just the first three words of the verse. 'Love never fails'.

"Last week we looked through the list of what love is and isn't: *Love is patient, love is kind. It does not envy, it does not boast, it is not proud. It is not rude, it is not self-seeking, it is not easily angered, it keeps no record of wrongs. Love does not delight in evil but rejoices with the truth. It always protects, always trusts, always hopes, always perseveres.*

"I'd like us to keep thinking of these attributes of love through the coming week. Most of all I want us to consider: 'love never fails'. People fail. But love doesn't. Human love fails but God's love never fails.

"I'm not going to say anything else about it tonight. Love is a subject we could do a lot of talking around.

However, rather than talk about it anymore tonight, I'd like us all to keep thinking about God's love this week. Reflect on it. Read through this chapter some more. And then let's talk about it next week."

"I read this verse last week," said Kirsty. "And I have to say, I don't really get it. So I'm looking forward to hearing what everyone has to say about it next week."

"What don't you get?" I asked.

"Love always seems to fail."

"Where are you looking for love? Think about family, friends, relationships. And then also have a look at what Jesus said about love. Give yourself time this week to think about it, and see how you get on."

I would be praying for each of them this week, especially Kirsty. She, more than most, needed to realise what true love was.

PAUL

Completely out with our comfort zone, we walked into the suited enclave of the Business Development office. Despite my worries that the meeting would be full of unfamiliar terms and jargon, it went well.

"What's the success rate of new salons?" I asked.

"We see both success and failure here," said the advisor. "The more you plan and prepare, the better your chances of success. As a sector, it's a relatively easy place to dip your toes into a business start-up: you don't need a lot of capital to launch; there are various options of how to get started, from opening a salon, to working from your home, or being mobile and going to clients' homes."

"As it's for the three of us, we want to have a salon," said Trish.

"Are you going in as equal partners? Will one person be the senior partner? Will one person be the owner with the other two renting workspace at the premises?"

"To be honest, we're still trying to work this out, we aren't sure what business model to go for," I said. "But we're swaying more towards me being the owner or lead partner, with Brian and Trish renting their workspaces from me."

"We've seen that work well for several businesses. We're here to help you work your way through this maze, so don't hesitate to ask any questions you have along the way. Why don't we meet up again next week once you've had the chance to discuss your options and we can drill down into some of the practicalities?"

"Thanks for your time. You've helped us understand the next steps we need to consider." I was enthusiastic. Formulating things in my mind, considering what our next steps would be. It was exciting to take control of our plans.

And, on the personal front, I was taking Kirsty out for dinner tomorrow night. I was excited about life and looking forward to this next phase. I sighed in satisfaction at the peace filling my soul.

KIRSTY

The restaurant was beautiful. It was a small, intimate hideaway, decorated in subtle shades of grey, black and red, the mood lighting working the colours to a perfect level of ambiance. Treating myself to a new dress for tonight had definitely been the right decision. This was no jeans and t-shirt, beer and burger kind of place. This was a 'first date' restaurant!

Monday night had been a fun shopping experience with Jo. Best friends always know when you need a shopping advisor. I tried on an array of dresses in a couple of department stores. Jo was a worthy dress shopping companion, steering me away from the safe, boring options and persuading me to go for the chic, flattering dresses instead. We had chosen a black dress for the work event, and a gorgeous grey dress for tonight. In my new dress and sparkly high heel shoes I was ready to take on the world. I felt a boldness to engage in the evening. I was taking control of my life and excited about the possibilities of a relationship with Paul.

However, that confidence was almost eroded as soon as I stepped into the restaurant. The shiny floor tiles and my new high heels did not play well together, and as soon as I stepped onto the first tile my right heel skidded away from me. I regained partial control by grabbing onto the reception counter.

"Hi, I'm meeting my friend here. He has a table reserved under the name of Smith." Between the embarrassment of my skid and the irony of a date reservation placed under the name of Smith, I had to work hard at not dissolving into a fit of giggles. As the head waiter led me to the table I took slow, careful steps to keep my feet from sliding away from me. How could other women look so confident and graceful in heels while I always resembled Bambi learning to walk!

Paul was already waiting. Gentleman that he was, he stood as I approached the table and gave me a kiss on the cheek. He looked amazing in his smart shirt and trousers. The cut of his clothes enhances his toned physique.

"The raincoat? Really?" said Paul.

"What can I say? I know how fascinated you are with them." Under normal circumstances I wouldn't have worn my raincoat for a night out, but part of me couldn't resist teasing Paul.

Paul laughed as he sat back down. "What do you think of the restaurant?"

"It looks amazing. I can't wait to taste the food."

The food lived up to expectations. The décor wasn't the only thing that was gorgeous about this restaurant. Yes, I liked this place a lot. This would be our special occasion restaurant.

Tonight it was just the two of us, no friends, no hairdressing assistants, no parties, no group outing. Now that Gary was no longer invading my dreams or my imagination, I was ready to give Paul my full attention, no other men lurking about in the shadows of my mind.

"Your friends seem like a great group," said Paul.

"Yes, they are. They always know what to say and do to cheer me up."

"It looks like you and Jo are especially close."

"Oh yes! We're best friends. We do lots together: we eat ice-cream; I tell her everything; we go shoe shopping, she's the one who introduced me to high heels; and watch chick-flicks together."

"That's like me and Matt – only without the shoe shopping, chick-flicks and ice-cream. With us it's more beer, burgers, action movies and no talking."

"We're both such clichés," I said, laughing. I was enjoying the ease of conversation with Paul. This was all looking very promising.

"All joking aside though, Jo was the one who helped me adjust to life in Glasgow. We moved here at the same time, and, even though she also moved from a village, she seemed to manage the transition much better than I did. Jo's confident and outgoing. I think I need that in a best friend."

"What was life like growing up in a village?" asked Paul, as he continued to ask the getting-to-know-you questions.

"Well, I can't compare it to anything else, but I loved it, especially as a child. I loved the space and freedom of being out in the country. And, in a village there is the whole community aspect. Parts of that are negative, like everyone knowing everything about you, and the restrictions that can bring. As a teenager I was sensitive to people knowing too much about me, but as a child it was a wonderfully safe place to be.

"Safe? That's an unusual description. Don't you feel safe here?"

"Sometimes. It's just different."

"I hope you feel safe right now." In some conversations Paul's words would have been nothing more than a throwaway comment floating off into space. But here, in this timeless moment, his words sparkled and took life, hanging between us full of promise.

"And what about you?" I asked. "Where did you grow up?"

"Glasgow, born and raised for me. From the age of six it was just me, my mum and my sister."

I wasn't sure if I should ask him about his dad, but the way he rushed out his answer suggested he wanted it left at that.

"What family do you have?" he asked.

"My mum and dad and three brothers, Andrew, James and Craig."

"Three brothers? Wow. So back home in Argyll did three brothers help or hinder the dating?"

I tried to ignore the blush spreading over my face and answer as nonchalantly as possible. "Big hinder! My dad was one of the local policeman. Two of my brothers were older, both of them big guys. Andrew wanted to follow in my dad's footsteps and become a policeman and James wanted to get into forestry work. So between the three of them no boy my age would dare come near the house even if he wanted to."

"I wouldn't have let them scare me off." The sparkle in his eyes confused me, was he teasing me?

"I can guarantee you would have been nowhere near my door."

As the waiter brought our coffees over at the end of the meal, Paul leaned over. Butterflies of anticipation fluttered around my stomach as I wondered what Paul was about to share with me. Was this the point when he would make his feelings clear and explain that this was a date? I wanted to play it down, but my fair complexion gave away my true feelings, my cheeks flushed with hope.

"I wanted to talk to you about what happened the last time you were at the salon."

This was it. There had been a connection. This was the moment he was about to say he felt it too that we were made for each other.

"Just as I was finishing your haircut there was a moment between us. I'm sure you felt it too."

I nodded in reply. The butterflies were multiplying, and I was forming the words to tell Paul I'd love to be his girlfriend.

"I'm sorry I allowed that to happen. I'm sorry that I didn't keep my feelings in check."

What? What was he talking about?

"Kirsty, before I became a Christian I was with a lot of women. Someone different every week. I have to confess at the time I loved that lifestyle. But over the last few months I've realised it wasn't a good way to live. It was destructive for me and the women I was with. I used so many people. And now I'm working at breaking that cycle."

I struggled to take in his words. It was as if I was in a dream state and the words were floating around, out with my grasp. What was he telling me?

"So, hopefully you see I can't pursue a relationship with you now. I'm on a break from dating. I need to learn who I am. When I date again I need to make sure it's for the right reasons.

"Kirsty, I hope you can tell…" I didn't wait to hear anymore. There was no way another guy was going to dump me, especially before we'd even started dating. I stood up, grabbed my raincoat and bag and walked away from the table. I walked out the restaurant to the nearest taxi rank, desperate to get away from Paul as quickly as I could.

In the safety of my flat I cried. I cried in mourning for my false expectations. I cried for the wasted hours of dreaming about Paul. I cried for myself. I cried for love; it was all I ever wanted, but it was the one thing that continually eluded me. Love always failed.

PAUL

What had just happened? Didn't she realise how confused I was right now? For the last few weeks I had been going back and forwards on whether to ask Kirsty out or not. When she had come to the salon the previous weekend, I'd been so aware of the chemistry between us. I had been so close to asking her out, but bottled it at the last moment and included Matt in our plans. We'd had a great night. It had been fun testing out the friendship thing and, for the first time in my life, I considered friendship with a girl I was attracted to as a viable proposition.

But now as I sat alone in the restaurant, nursing my empty coffee cup, I felt defeated. I hadn't expected Kirsty to walk away and leave me like this. I had expected a reply, not silence. I had expected appreciation for sharing my honesty and confusion. I wasn't the bad guy here; I had been the bad guy in the past, but now I was trying to make good.

In the past I had always known how to speak to women, known how to smooth things over. Even when I broke up with someone we seemed to end on good terms, leaving me free to move on to the next conquest with no baggage. Although, looking back, I wasn't so sure that had been the case every time. What kind of guy had I been to continually date different women, to tell them I wasn't looking for anything more than a few dates?

And now here was Kirsty. An enigma I couldn't solve. In the past I had known exactly what I wanted and almost always got it. But with Kirsty, I wasn't sure what I wanted. I was attracted to her but, with everything else going on in my life I wasn't sure whether to pursue a relationship with her or just be friends. My uncertainty had me rattled. I'd never handled relationship issues this badly before. We hadn't even dated, and she was storming off as if we had just broken up from a long-term relationship. Where did she get off being so high and mighty? Who was she to judge? Couldn't she understand how far I'd come? She must be one of those high maintenance girls. The worst kind of high maintenance. She hid it till you got too close to escape. Then wham! And somehow you were the bad guy when she was the one who had been walking along the path of wrong expectations. She was hard work. Maybe it was best not to take this any further.

And yet, as I walked home I couldn't stop thinking about her. She drew me in like no one else ever had. She was tall and beautiful and yet she seemed completely unaware of the effect she had on the men around her. At times, she could seem so capable, while other times she cried out to be looked after. The more she tried to play things cool the more she got herself into crazy situations. Life with Kirsty would never be boring. But, after tonight, I would never get to experience that first-hand.

JENNIFER

Emma was a much happier girl for the rest of the week. The authority of teachers had neutralised the fear of what Kevin might do. Happy children equalled happy me, especially on the brink of a lovely weekend away. But the week wasn't over yet. When I rushed into the school playground on Friday morning, Sarah was waiting for me.

"We need to talk," said Sarah, in such a forceful tone that it took me by surprise.

"Okay, do you want to come to mine for a cuppa?" Under the circumstances, my Friday housework would need to wait. It was best to deal with whatever the issue was in private, not in the school playground for all to see. I had a feeling of dread as we walked back to my house in silence. Was Sarah about to lambast both Emma and myself?

As soon as we entered the kitchen Sarah got straight to her grievances. "I don't know what's going on in Kevin and Emma's class this year, but for some reason my poor boy is being blamed for causing issues in the class. I'm not having it."

I took a deep breath. Much as I would love to tell Sarah what I thought of her precious little Kevin, I was also aware that no parent ever knows the whole story. Pushing back at Sarah all guns blazing would not resolve anything. "What's been happening?" I asked. Deciding that the best policy was to assume nothing and let Sarah air her grievances.

"I had a phone call from Mrs Evans the other day telling me they had concerns about Kevin this year, and that he was displaying anger towards some of the other children in the class. I'm sure they must be provoking him."

With a lot of effort on my part, I maintained a passive expression. My thoughts weren't important. Sarah needed to talk, and I needed to give her the space to do just that. I tried a different line of questioning, "How is he at home? Is he showing signs of upset, or anything because of school issues?"

"He's fine," said Sarah. There was a defensive tone covering the words. But at least, so far, Sarah hadn't accused me of anything, or mentioned Emma, so it looked like I was in the clear.

"Is he able to do all his school work okay?"

"Of course he is. He's such a bright child." I fought the urge to roll my eyes.

"How are things with your work?"

"Why are you asking about my work? It's Kevin that I'm concerned about."

"I'm just wondering. If you're under pressure at work, it's the kind of thing Kevin could pick up on."

"No, no of course not. Everything's fine." But her voice broke a little, and the strong façade started to show some chinks.

"Sarah, what's wrong?"

"This is silly," said Sarah, as she tried to compose herself.

"Tell me. Something's bothering you."

"It's no one else's business. I'm not telling my personal issues to have them gossiped about in the school playground."

"Sarah, you know I don't do that. If you've got a problem, please let me help you. If something is making you unhappy, you need to talk to someone. You're obviously worried about things. Let me help you."

"If anyone else hears about this, I'll know you were the one who told."

"I won't say anything to anyone else, not even Scott, if you don't want me to." My concern for the woman sitting in front of me overrode all other emotions. I could see something was bothering her, but would she open up to me? I watched as she battled her emotions. After a while Sarah let out a sigh and looked at me.

"Fine. It's my marriage, I think it might be over. We keep arguing all the time, and I think Kevin is picking up on it. When things started going wrong, we were careful to keep it away from him, but over time we've let that slip and Kevin has been all too aware of our arguing and the severity of the situation. I'm just waiting to see which of us throws out the idea of divorce first."

"Oh, Sarah, I'm so sorry. Is there any way you can work this out?"

"I don't know, and more to the point I'm not even sure if either of us wants to. How's that for a terrible admission?"

"How long have you been struggling with this?"

"I don't even know anymore. It's become such a part of our lives I can't remember when we last spoke without it leading to an argument."

"Would it help to speak to someone together, like a relationship counsellor?"

"Who sees a marriage counsellor?"

"Lots of people do, Sarah. Have a think about it. This isn't just about you and James, you need to consider Kevin too. Have you spoken to Kevin about what's happening?"

"It's not the kind of thing you talk to a child about."

"Perhaps not. But he's picking up on it and it's affecting him. You need to help him understand what's happening, and let him know his security is still there, whether you and James stay together or split."

"What a mess," said Sarah. "I don't even understand it myself or know what I want, so how can I explain things to Kevin?"

"Sarah, you're all miserable with things as they stand at the moment. You need to find a way to make the real conversations happen rather than the non-stop fighting."

"I don't know if we're even able to have a conversation anymore."

"Have a think about it, try to talk over the weekend. Scott and I are available if you don't want to go to a counsellor. We'll help if we can."

I waved Sarah off, not knowing if I'd helped or not. She had entered the house all guns blazing, but left a lost, forlorn character. I felt genuine sympathy for her as I watched her walk down the garden path. In one conversation, I had gone from being annoyed at Sarah and Kevin to being sorry for them, wondering if I could do to anything to help. It was a sad situation, and no glib remarks or magic wands could solve this one. Context changes things.

KIRSTY

A blotchy face wasn't the look I had been hoping for. But last night's tears had left their mark. This required some careful makeup application. As I left the flat I put all thoughts of Paul behind me. It was time to be professional Kirsty and concentrate on work. It was time to banish all my silly romantic notions and day dreams. Love was only for fairy tales. I was done with it!

I pulled my raincoat tightly around myself and put on my sunglasses. At least for the commute I could look every inch the professional.

There was a real buzz about the office. Everyone seemed to be anticipating the approaching event. Although all the work had been done, I still felt the ripple of nerves, hoping all arrangements would go according to plan. I spent the morning enclosed in an empty meeting room going over all the last-minute arrangements, more for peace of mind than anything else.

More than ever, I needed my Chocolate & Vanilla lunchtime break. Even the walk from the office to the coffee shop helped. It was a beautiful, sunny autumnal day. People always thought it only rained in Glasgow, including Glaswegians, and it was true we did experience more than our fair share of rain, but there were also many days of glorious sunshine. I enjoyed the heat of the sun on my face, my sunglasses shielding my eyes from the glare off the office block windows. The streets were bustling as city centre workers, who would often stay confined within their offices, ventured out to enjoy the beauty of a bright, warm day.

Despite the sunshine, I made my way to my usual mezzanine level spot, rather than taking my order to go as many of the lunchtime consumers were doing. I snuggled up in the chair ready to enjoy a peaceful hour with my lunch and novel.

"I'm surprised to see you here today," said a familiar voice. Looking up from my book I smiled at Gary. I hadn't seen much of him over the last few days, he had barely been in the office. It was nice to see him again. Space had given me perspective.

"You look nice and peaceful sitting here, maybe I'll stay for ten minutes and see if your calmness rubs off on me." He settled into the chair opposite sitting his take-away cup on the table between us.

"You think I look calm?" I said. "I'm a bundle of excited nerves for tonight."

"Well, you don't look it." There was an edge to Gary's voice. Was he nervous? He was always the poster boy for assured confidence, it never occurred to me that he, like anyone, could have his moments of doubt and uncertainty.

"You okay?" I asked.

"I'm fine, thanks for asking," he said, as he fidgeted with a napkin. How many people were given the chance to see the real Gary? My resolve to stop thinking of him as a potential boyfriend unravelled a little bit.

"I've put a lot of weight on this event for moving my career forward."

I was honoured that he was sharing such personal thoughts with me. Maybe he wasn't as calculating as his reputation suggested, maybe I was someone he could be real with. My resolve unravelled further.

He reached over and took my hands in his. "Thanks again for all your help with the event, Kirsty. It's going to be a success, and a large part of that is down to you."

"Thanks," I said. Blushing at his compliment.

"Hopefully, we can sneak away for a drink together at some point tonight." And with his words of promise floating around me he walked away. The butterflies were back in my stomach, not nerves for the event arrangements this time, but thoughts of alone time with Gary.

My resolve went down another notch. Soon I would have no resistance left. I realised there was a danger that surrounded Gary. He was a hot, confident guy who knew exactly what to say to get what he wanted. The combination of the sound of his voice, the touch of his hand and the depth of his gaze had the power to melt my heart in a moment. His spell would captivate me while I was in his presence. Only after he departed did the spell break and sense return, only then was I able to see his charm for what it was. And yet, no matter how clear my thoughts might be in the aftermath, in the heat of the moment I was under his power.

KIRSTY

By mid-afternoon it was time to transform into event Kirsty. I had considered getting ready at the hotel, in far nicer surroundings than the draughty office toilets. However, getting changed at the office meant I could leave my work things at my desk, rather than needing to stash a bag somewhere at the hotel.

I unzipped my suit carrier bag and took out my gorgeous new dress. Compared to my usual shopping budget it was expensive, but there was no denying the increase in style that came with the higher price tag. It was a sophisticated dress, the kind I would be able to wear again, assuming I was ever at another event that required such formal attire. The black sparkly shoes I'd worn the previous evening, complemented the dress perfectly. The height of the heels probably wasn't the most sensible choice. As last night demonstrated, I wasn't the most capable in heels and added to that I would have to do a lot of walking and standing about as I oversaw the event. But I loved my new shoes.

Walking back to my desk, I had an Irene encounter. I prepared myself for some sarcastic remark about me being all dressed up. But instead she almost whispered, "Be careful tonight," as she looked over to Gary's office.

I struggled to think of a reply. What could I say in response?

"Work events and alcohol don't always go well together. Be careful."

As if knowing something was happening, Gary appeared at his office door and shouted me over.

I walked over to him with uncertain steps, glancing back at Irene, trying to understand why she had whispered her warning.

"Well, you do scrub up well."

"Thanks. I think," I replied. Was 'scrub up well' really a compliment?

"No, I mean it. I approve." Gary's eyes shone with approval, in case I was in any doubts as to the sincerity of his words. "Now, just try not to spill anything down such a beautiful dress, or twist your ankles on those impressive heels. I need my right-hand girl tonight."

I suppressed the desire to giggle like a schoolgirl. He had succeeded in turning my emotions round from Irene's warning. And, once again, he had me in the palm of his hand. My resolve to ignore him was almost completely gone.

"Are you going to the hotel now?"

"Yes, I just need to collect my folder and I'm ready to go."

"Okay, see you soon."

As I walked towards the lift, I looked over to Irene. There was concern in her eyes.

JENNIFER

The drive to the hotel was beautiful. Even though we hadn't left Glasgow until six o'clock, there was still enough late September sunshine to get us to our destination in beautiful daylight. The earliest tinge of autumnal colours made the drive even more spectacular. I relaxed into my seat, resting my head against the headrest, drinking in the beauty. The tensions of the last few weeks drifting away as the distance from Glasgow sped past.

"How was work today?" I asked.

"Surprisingly good for a Friday. Some meetings got cancelled, so I was able to clear my desk of paperwork that had been hanging around for longer than I care to admit. Good timing too, helped me get that Friday feeling in time for my wanton weekend!" I laughed at the crazy face he made as he spoke. Yes, I was looking forward to this weekend.

"What did you get up to today?" asked Scott.

"Housework and packing, obviously. But before that, an unexpected talk with Sarah. She was waiting for me in the school playground and demanded we talk, the way she does. I wasn't sure what to expect, she started off talking about

Kevin's issues at school and then she opened up to the fact that things weren't great at home. I had no idea."

"Really? I guess that explains a lot."

"I told her we're available if she and James ever want to chat things through, but she didn't seem too keen on the idea of outside help."

"Give her time and see what happens."

"Poor Kevin, though. I've gone from being annoyed at him to feeling sorry for him. Feel kind of bad at being so judgemental about him."

"No point in beating yourself up on that one, honey. Now you know what's happening you're better equipped to deal with the situation."

"I suppose so." I thought about what Scott had said. He always had the ability to compartmentalise things so clearly. I couldn't help but let emotion steer my thoughts.

"But enough of all that," I said. "Let's enjoy our time away!"

"Absolutely," agreed Scott.

Walking into the hotel reception area, we tried our hardest not to laugh out loud. The twee setting of tartan carpet, wood-panelled walls, old ancestral portraits and large fireplace looked so old-fashioned compared to the décor of the rest of the hotel. It was to wow the tourists, but we couldn't help laughing at the look the hotel was trying to achieve. Past the reception area the hotel was beautiful and tasteful, a wide sweeping staircase led us to the first floor and the corridor our room was on. On this floor the carpets were plain, and the walls painted in subtle shades of creams and browns, modern Scottish artwork adorning the walls.

Our room was gorgeous. A large four-poster bed initially commanded attention, but then your gaze was drawn to the view. The large oriel window framed a stunning view of loch and hills. The September sunshine was showing off the loch in all its breath-taking beauty.

I sat down in a chair next to the window, a two-seater settee and coffee table completing the seating area of the room. "This is amazing, Scott. Thanks for organising this." I gazed out of the window, enjoying the view over the loch. Scotland on a sunny day: you couldn't beat it. I sighed and looked forward to the weekend ahead of us.

KIRSTY

The event was in full swing before I got a minute to myself. From the time I got to the hotel it had been nonstop; questions from the event planner and hotel staff, delegates to help and direct. As I looked around the function suite, I was pleased to see lots of smiling faces. Conversations and laughter filled the room. The food, and drink, seemed to be going down well.

I sat down at my allocated place, close enough to the head table if I was needed, but far enough to the side to avoid detection. My feet were killing me, I had made the wrong choice with my shoes. I desperately wanted to kick them off, but that would be fatal; my feet would never agree to go back into my shoes once they were freed. I would simply need to grin and bear it. The waiting staff put down a plate of food in front of me. Only when the smell of the food reached my nostrils, did I realise how ravenous I was.

"What a great night," said the man to my left.

"I'm glad you're enjoying it," I replied.

"I've seen you around the office. You work in Gary's section, don't you?"

"Yes, that's right. I've been helping out a bit with organising tonight."

"You've done a great job. This is a brilliant night." As he spoke he filled my glass with wine. I didn't bother to tell him I wasn't drinking, as far as I was concerned I was still working, no wine for me. He seemed tiddly, so I suspected he probably wouldn't even notice that my wine glass remained untouched.

The more he drank the chattier he got and the more he encroached my space. My defences were rising but my still grumbling stomach told me I needed to stay where I was and eat more of the delicious dinner before I dared go elsewhere. There was nothing else for me to do at the moment, so best so stay and wait for my favourite course, dessert.

I tried to engage some of the other guests at the table in conversation, but my drunken neighbour kept talking over everyone to keep the conversation with him. I could see from the looks around the table that everyone was getting fed up with his behaviour.

He leaned in even closer and slurred, "I can't wait for the dancing to start, Kirsty. And, when it does, you will be my partner for the night. I bet you're a great mover."

Time to make a sharp exit. "Thanks, but I'm really not that great a dancer. And besides I'm working, I need to be available for the hotel staff all night."

"I'm not going to take no for an answer," his voice increased in volume with the forcefulness of his request. "You'll be my partner for the first dance."

I needed to get away from this table. As the waitresses cleared away the dessert dishes, I made my apologies to the rest of the table and explained that I was needed by the entertainment group. I moved away quickly before the drunken guest could make any objections.

I didn't need to check on the entertainment group, but it was a good excuse to get away from the function room. The group were ready to take to the stage. After their act Gary and some other managers would give their speeches, then it was over to the band to get everyone dancing until midnight.

The cabaret were so-so, probably a taste thing rather than a performance thing. The speeches all went well and people were polite enough to quietly sit through them, laugh at the right moments and clap at the end. Gary delivered the best speech of the night. From my vantage point in the hall I could tell it had gone down well. The introduction of the band was my cue to escape before the drunk man could find me. I dreaded to think what his dancing style would be like. My work for the night was done, but I had promised Gary I would stay until the end.

I had the perfect spot to disappear to. The coffee lounge to the side of the bar beckoned me. With their own bar area at the function suite, I was confident none of the delegates would venture to any of the other hotel bars.

The coffee lounge was even more perfect than I remembered. Here was my event oasis. My place of calm to hide from the noise and boisterousness of the party. The aroma of freshly filtered coffee delighted my senses. The coffee served in the function suit was bland compared to here.

I gave in to the cries of my feet and kicked off my heels, flexing my toes in relief at being freed from their prison. As the waiter brought me a latte, I curled my legs up under me and let out a sigh of contentment. I couldn't believe my luck at being able to find such a quiet spot on a function night, and as if that weren't reward enough I realised I couldn't be seen from the doorway of the bar. This was the perfect place to hide from drunken guests, and, from Gary. I had been thrilled when Gary suggested we might have some time alone at the event, but now that my senses were back to normal I knew it was good to keep a distance. Hopefully, he would be so busy working the room and pursuing funding he would forget all about me. My plan was to hide in this spot then go back to the function suite for the last half-hour, giving me ample time to ensure the evening finished well and everything was in order. In peaceful silence I enjoyed the warmth of the coffee and the mesmerising dancing of the flames from the fire.

"Should have known you'd be where the coffee is." The appearance of Gary shattered my peace; he had a knack of intruding on my alone time.

"Gary, what are you doing here?"

"I'm at the launch event, remember, silly." He was obviously happy with how the night was going, I wasn't sure if it was relief or wine responsible for his flippant remarks.

"Skoosh up and let me in." I uncurled myself and made space for Gary beside me.

Between my exhaustion, the romantic fireside ambience, his insanely intoxicating aftershave and his ability to melt my resolve I was on dangerous ground. 'God, help me,' I silently prayed. I needed all my strength for dealing with Gary tonight. He was on a drink, or work, high. Who knew what he would view as acceptable in this situation.

He squeezed in beside me. "You've put on a great event, Kirst." With his face inches away from mine I was all too aware of the wine on his breath. "Management is very pleased with the night, hailing it one of the best launch events ever. Well done, you."

"It wasn't only me, though," I said, keen not to be the centre of attention. "You were the one with the ideas and the vision for it."

"Waiter! I'll have a coffee," Gary shouted over to the poor waiter at the bar. As he got his coffee, he raised his cup, "Here's to us, we make a great team."

I was relieved to see him drink his coffee, hopefully it would sober him up. Who knew what drunk Gary might come out with?

A few mouthfuls of coffee and he seemed to relax and quieten down. He stretched himself out and made a relaxed sigh. As he adjusted his position in the chair, he put his arm around me.

"What are we going to work on next Kirst?"

"I don't know. I guess I'm back to regular duties after this."

"Nonsense! You're far too talented to be kept under the constraints of stuffy old Irene. I want you on my team all the time."

"Thanks." But how could I take his words seriously? Did I want to work for a boss who thought it was acceptable to have his arm around me? I was regretting my choice of seat, we were hidden in our own little corner and I couldn't see any way of escape.

"I gave a great speech tonight, didn't I, Kirst?"

What was it with his shortening my name all of a sudden, as if we had become more chummy or intimate? Another warning flag shot up.

"You did. I could see people were really listening to you and enjoying what you had to say."

"And what about you? Did you enjoy my speech? People love me, Kirst. Especially women. Well, apart from stuffy old Irene! People love me. After tonight, and my management of the whole rebranding, I'll be heading up the next rung of my career ladder. Come with me Kirst, be my next PA."

I laughed, as much as anything to try to dispel my nervousness. "Let's just take it one step at a time. Tonight's going well. Let's not consider 'what might be' yet."

"So, we're just lost in the moment of tonight are we?" said Gary, with so much innuendo attached to his question that even I was left with no doubts as to his meaning.

"You better head back to the function suite," I said, desperate to stop this conversation. "There will be business leaders up there wanting to talk to you. You've finished your coffee, now go."

"Yes, miss," he said, giving a mock salute. "I'll see you at the end." But, as he moved to get up, he stumbled and fell onto my lap, I wasn't sure whether by accident or design. Before I could react, he put his hands on my cheeks and moved in for a kiss. There was nothing gentle in his kiss, only demanding and taking. With my back against the chair, I had no way of escape. Thankfully, his intention was only to grab a quick kiss before he went back to the ballroom.

I wiped my hand over my mouth and ordered another coffee in an attempt to erase the kiss. I curled back up in the chair. Tears welling up in my eyes, but I would not give them the satisfaction of coming to fruition. I couldn't believe I had ever felt any level of attraction to Gary. There was no way I was going back to the function suite until midnight. My tranquil oasis was no longer my own. Gary had once again tainted my safe place.

JENNIFER

After a delicious sampler dinner, we made our way through to the hotel bar with our coffees. The large room was a warm, inviting place; the bar itself was part of the décor of the room, a beautifully crafted wooden affair taking up one corner. Behind the bar a bright glass wall reflected rows of bottles of spirits and whisky. Across the room from the bar a wall of windows provided a full vista to the loch and hills in front of the hotel. And best of all, to ward off the slight chill of a Scottish September evening, a fire roared in the ornate fireplace. Its wooden surround matched the design of the bar and, in front of the fire, leather settees beckoned us in. We made a bee-line for one of the settees. I kicked off my shoes and made myself at home, putting my feet up on Scott's lap.

"Mmm, that's lovely," I said, as Scott stroked my ankles.

"I could get used to nights like this," said Scott.

"Put your feet up, and I'll give them a rub too."

"Oh yeah! May as well make ourselves well and truly at home." I laughed as he swung his feet up beside me.

We sat in companionable silence for some time, enjoying the intimacy of the setting, the warmth of the fire and the ambience of the room.

"Would you like something from the bar?" asked a waitress who came over to clear away our coffee cups.

"I'll take a beer, thanks," said Scott.

"I'd love a glass of red wine," I said.

"Look at you sitting back, relaxing and letting people get things for you," said Scott.

"Only because I don't have anyone demanding from me. For tonight, at least, I'm going to enjoy being lost in the moment of the night."

"That sounds like game on," said Scott, giving me an exaggerated wink that made me laugh out loud. "Which also reminds me, there's a little something for you to change into in our room."

"Is there now? And I didn't get you anything."

"Oh, but you did," replied Scott as he sat up. He reached over and smoothed my hair behind my ears. Stroking my face, he closed the rest of the distance between us and kissed me. The intensity of his kiss promising a special weekend. Healthy marriages needed moments like these.

KIRSTY

Just before midnight I squeezed my poor aching feet into my towering heels and made my way back to the ballroom. The band was striking up their closing song for the night. Those still in the ballroom made their way onto the dance floor. I felt obliged to join in. Kicking off my shoes I stood beside people I didn't know. I kept my gaze on the floor and didn't pay too much attention to who else was swaying around the dance floor. As the drunken revellers sang and bounced about to the familiar song I longed for it to draw to its conclusion so I could finish up and head home. But as the final notes of the song played out the band immediately went on to 'Loch Lomond'. Their last-ditch attempt to keep people on the dance floor. I was done.

As the last of the glasses were drained, the band packed up, and I went in search of Samantha, the hotel event planner. We both agreed the night had been a success and, with no issues outstanding, I made my way back to the function suite for one final look around before heading home.

The only people left were a group of investors and Gary. With back patting and handshakes all round, Gary thanked them and made arrangements for a game of golf the following week.

"Kirsty, Kirsty! Gentlemen, this is my right-hand girl. She organised tonight." The investors all shook my hand before making their way to the door.

"Kirst, tonight has been amazing. But one thing is wrong with it." I couldn't think of anything that hadn't gone to plan. I was sure I had done everything right.

"We never got to dance." He took out his phone and put on some slow music and drew me into his arms. The smell of his expensive aftershave, the warmth of his body and the smell of wine on his breath all overwhelmed me and once again I was incapable of resisting him. It was easier to give in and dance. Thankfully, he didn't seem inclined to talk, but was happy to hold me and dance his drunken shuffle.

As the song ended, he stepped back and looked into my eyes. Time stood still as his gaze intensified and he moved closer. Before any words could be spoken his lips were on mine. Soft and slow to begin with; then he pressed harder and his arms pulled me so close I could hardly breath. I tried to push him back, but he was too strong. I wriggled and pushed, desperate to get away from him.

He was the one to stop the kiss. "It's taken me a while to get you alone in a hotel room, Kirst. My first attempt was thwarted when I had to pull out of the menu-tasting at the last minute. I couldn't believe you were so focussed on those samplers. Didn't you realise we didn't need to go through that? It was only a ruse to get you here, alone. Finally, it's time to get it right. Let's take this party to my room." Even drunk,

Gary knew what he wanted, and nothing would stop him getting it.

Terrified, I backed away from him. He laughed and reached out his hand to grab hold of me. I ran! Grabbing my bag from the nearby table I didn't stop running till I was outside the hotel. I was grateful for the taxis in the hotel taxi rank. As the taxi drove away, I realised I had forgotten my raincoat and shoes.

But this was no Cinderella story, and it was no Prince Charming I was running away from. As the tears flowed the spell was well and truly broken. Gary would never wield power over me again.

JENNIFER

Waking up next to Scott still gave me a thrill. Especially on mornings like this when we had the luxury of waking up gradually; snuggling, enjoying the warmth and comfort of the duvet and each other, legs entwined, wanting to be as close as possible. These moments were precious and neither of us wanted to break the quiet and the closeness. But grumbling stomachs and the luxury of child free activities persuaded us to get up and take full advantage of the day.

The hotel breakfast was delicious and filling. After a large cooked breakfast there was only one thing to do: take to the heather-clad hills to walk off our meal and enjoy the bracing fresh air. We arrived back at the hotel mid-afternoon to enjoy coffee and cream scones. After an hour of reading the weekend newspapers, we headed to the spa for a relaxing dip, sauna and massage. Dinner was, again, a beautifully presented sampler menu, showcasing local delicacies and highlighting the chef's culinary expertise.

By the time we made our way through to the bar to enjoy our coffees, we were completely relaxed and fulfilled by our day together. Again, we claimed one of the settees in front of the fireplace.

"I don't want to ruin your relaxed vibe, but I wanted part of this weekend to include talking about where you are at and your thoughts on what's next for you," said Scott.

"That's okay. It's good to keep processing. Especially with you.

"In some ways I don't feel much further forward. I see some of my 'mum friends' moving forward with their careers, either increasing work hours or going after those promotions they've been shying away from for the last few years. They're moving on and I'm still in the same place."

"Yes, but they are continuing, while you are looking to something new."

"I guess you're right. It all feels so vague right now. More questions than answers."

"When you're brave enough to ask questions you open up space for the answers to come."

"I like that idea! To be honest, I'm still trying to define the questions."

"Sometimes that can be the toughest part."

"And then there's the other side to it. I want to experience joy in the day-to-day aspects of life. To not just survive parenthood and the daily routine but to thrive in it. I love the girls, and everything about them, but I don't think I've stopped to enjoy parenthood, to laugh enough as a family, appreciating all that we have."

"I know what you mean. You've got me thinking about joy too. Since you mentioned it the other week, I've realised that I'm living in a default setting where the demands of work take up so much of my time, as if I'm living on auto-pilot."

"The other day I read this great nugget in the Psalms: *You make known to me the path of life; you will fill me with joy in your presence*'. Seems as if there is a connection between how we spend our time and joy."

"I like that."

"It makes so much sense. But I don't even know if I'm on a path. And if I can't work that out then how can I possibly feel joy? There are glimpses of joy. You and the girls. The first PTA meeting was promising. Painting Kirsty's flat. Leading the small group. But I want more than just glimpses of joy. Am I expecting too much?

"No, you're not. I can't believe how bogged down we've become in our routines. Perhaps we should have checks in place to help us stay focussed on the important things," suggested Scott.

"Checks? Like this weekend away?"

"What a great idea. Let's make this an annual occurrence."

I leaned over to kiss him. "Why not twice a year?" I laughed at Scott's eager expression. I always wanted to experience moments of joy with this incredible man. If I couldn't be grateful for the blessings I already had, I would never be able to experience joy in anything.

JENNIFER

"Jennifer? Hi, it's Jo, I'm worried about Kirsty."

"What's happened?"

"I don't know. She won't even tell me. She didn't turn up for church, and when I phoned her she didn't answer. So I sent her text messages, and she didn't reply. I just tried to call her again and she sent me a text back, saying she couldn't bear to leave the house and she would talk to me when she could."

"Oh no! That sounds bad. We're leaving the hotel now, so we should be back in Glasgow in a few hours. Once we've collected the girls and I've got everyone settled, I'll go and see her. I'll send her a text too."

"Sorry, I know you're on your weekend away, but I didn't know who else to talk to."

"Don't worry, it's fine. As I said, we're checking out of the hotel now. We'll be back soon. I'm glad you called."

The weekend had been wonderful. It was sheer luxury to have time together like this. But now it was back to normal life. Back to thinking about others.

"What's happened?" asked Scott. I filled him in as we made our way out to the car.

"I'd like to go over to see her tonight after dinner."

"Sounds as if she needs time with you."

Thinking about Kirsty also brought back my concerns for Sarah and Kevin. But my weekend away wasn't quite over yet and I was going to enjoy the drive back to Glasgow. With Scott driving, I reclined my seat and gazed out of the window, enjoying the warmth of the sun on my face as I watched the rugged landscape rushing past.

As we got closer to Glasgow, I looked over at Scott. The talk with Sarah on Friday and the weekend we'd spent together reminded me of how lucky I was. It was easy to get frustrated at each other. To get annoyed at his work getting in the way of our time together. But I was thankful for Scott and, in that thankfulness, there was another spark of joy.

And somewhere in the back of my mind a new plan, a new dream, was forming. A new direction for life that would provide the creative challenge I needed. I couldn't articulate it quite yet, but it was simmering somewhere inside of me. *You make known to me the path of life; you will fill me with joy in your presence'*

I smiled as the joy of those words captured my imagination; life wasn't a drudge, there was joy in the day to day. There was joy in my future.

PAUL

On Sunday afternoon I got together with Trish and Brian for another catch up. We had read through the information the business advisor had supplied. Our goal was to decide which business model to go for.

"Let's thrash out the positives and negatives of the various options," I said.

"I'll start with the obvious ones," said Brian. "The main positives are getting away from Si and doing this for ourselves. The negative is having the risk of a business start-up hanging over us."

"Do we have enough credibility to start up on our own?" said Trish. "You do Paul, but what about me and Brian?"

"This is an unknown for all of us," I replied. "Yes, my schedule is busy at ByDesign, but does that carry over to our own place? Am I the attraction, or ByDesign, or most likely a combination of both?"

Brian and Trish both looked thoughtful, and perhaps a bit less enthusiastic than when we started our meeting.

"At the end of the day, this is something we want to try. Like the Business Development officer said, this is a business with a relatively low cost of entry. Let's do this. If we don't try, we'll always regret it."

"You're right," said Trish.

"So, what do we do next?" asked Brian.

"First of all, let's agree on the business model."

"I still think we should go with it being your salon and the two of us rent from you," said Trish.

"Me too," agreed Brian.

"Okay. Let's talk to the advisor about all the implications of that at our next meeting. Next up, Trish, do you have the schedules of the premises with you?" Trish brought them out of her bag and spread them on the table.

"When suits to view them? Even if none of them are suitable, it gives us an idea of budgets and space."

"What about late afternoon on Wednesday?" said Brian. "I'll finish up early at work, and then meet the two of you at whichever property we go to first, say about half four?" We both nodded our heads in agreement.

"How are you doing Trish?" I asked. "Have you been able to pick up any work anywhere?"

"Not really. I know we can't rush this new salon too much, but I need work as soon as possible. I've got one day a week through one of your contacts, but I need more."

"I'll ask around some other salons in town again and see if there are any short-term slots."

"That would be great, thanks. I appreciate any help you can give."

I already felt responsible for Trish and Brian even with our agreed upon model. Their success, or otherwise, was down to me. The peace was still there, but being responsible was a concern. Was this all part of maturing and taking that next step?

JENNIFER

When Kirsty answered the door, I knew something was seriously wrong. I had been there for many of Kirsty's traumas: boyfriend breakups; misery over missing her parents and rural home; work problems. But this was different. Her face was blotchy and red, and yet deathly pale underneath. Her body language spoke of defeat and exhaustion.

"Kirsty, what happened?"

Kirsty fell into my arms in floods of tears. I led her over to the settee. It would be some time before she could talk. Right now it was about being there with her and giving her the space to talk when she was ready.

After a lot of tears, I made us both a coffee. As we sat hugging the warm, comforting mugs, Kirsty's tears began to subside. She looked so lost and unsure of herself. She chewed on her lips and glanced up at me.

"Jennifer, I've been such an idiot. I don't know if I've been gullible or knew exactly what was going on."

"Tell me what's happened."

Kirsty told me all about Gary, the lifts to work, the Friday lunches and then the dramas of the launch event.

My heart broke for Kirsty. She *was* gullible. It sounded like she had been attracted to this Gary, or at least mesmerised by him. And now here she was, the distraught one, whereas he was probably out somewhere enjoying himself, not giving Kirsty, or the mess he'd caused, a second thought. It would take time to get through this. She was a bruised and battered soul.

"Aww, Kirsty. I'm so sorry you experienced all that. But don't go blaming yourself, you got yourself out of there as quickly as you could. You're safe, that's the thing to focus on for now. Try to keep yourself from going down the path of self-recrimination or what-ifs. What's happened has happened, but you're safe."

"Why am I such an idiot with guys? What's the point of hoping for a relationship when they are all twisted and wrong?"

"I can see why you would think that, but not all of them are." I almost felt guilty for having had a wonderful weekend with Scott while my friend had been going through a terrible time. "Yes, there are a lot of men out there who will try it on and see what they can get away with. But Kirsty, there are also lots of great guys too. Don't let yourself get bitter. Good is out there. You've just had a few bad experiences."

"A few bad experiences?" said Kirsty, her voice rising in panic at my words. "A few bad experiences? More like an ongoing pattern of disasters. I don't think I've ever been in a good relationship. In fact, I know I haven't. Look at me. I'm single!"

"Now is not the time for the big discussions. For the next few days, it's only about getting over the shock of this weekend. Look at me, Kirsty. You're safe."

My soul grieved at the look of resignation that haunted Kirsty's eyes.

"Let's deal with the first practical thing; are you working tomorrow?"

"No. I'd already requested some days off to get over the extra work of the last few weeks."

"Good, that gives us a few days before you even need to see Gary again." At the mention of Gary's name Kirsty started crying again. Sitting in silence once more I held her close and prayed for her.

I didn't want to run out on her if she was still upset, but it was getting late. "I'm sorry, but I need to go now to get the girls ready for the week ahead. Do you want to come and stay at ours tonight?"

"No, I'll be fine here. Don't want to cast my gloom over the girls." I ignored the sense of self-pity emanating from Kirsty. I couldn't really find fault with her for feeling that way, but neither would I say anything to encourage her in it.

"You're going to be okay, Kirsty." The look I received conveyed just how much Kirsty doubted me.

I took a CD out of my bag and put it on the settee next to her. "I've been listening to this CD all week, you know me, always love finding a new artist to listen to. It's by Ellyn Oliver. I'm going to leave it with you. Have a listen to it. The song I really want you to listen to is 'Arms Wide Open'." Kirsty picked the CD up and looked it over before placing it down on the table.

"I'll pop in and see you again tomorrow. Try to get some sleep." I bent down and gave Kirsty a hug, whispering in her ear, "We're all praying for you."

JENNIFER

Monday afternoon was spent preparing a lasagne. It wasn't something I made often, yummy as it was, it took far too long to prepare and cook in my opinion. But I had a plan for this lasagne. I would leave Scott and the girls with their portions and then take the rest to Kirsty's for the two of us to share.

In between all the cooking stress I had the joy of organising all the accessories I had acquired for Kirsty's living room. There were new cushions, picture frames, candle holders, and blinds. My favourite new additions were two prints I had found by a local artist. One was of the Glasgow skyline, the other was of the Argyll coast, near to Kirsty's home village. How perfect to give her paintings of her old home and new. Hopefully completing the living room would cheer her up.

A red-eyed Kirsty answered the door. It looked like there had been more tears today. But she was standing taller, no longer slouching over, facing the world with a bit more confidence.

"I've brought our dinner," I said, holding up the lasagne container.

"Thanks, I don't know if I'll manage much."

"Give it a try and see how you get on. You must be hungry by now. I've also brought some of the finishing touches for your living room. Did you get any deliveries today?"

"Yeah, there are a couple of table things in the living room."

It was time to get this flat, and its owner, brightened up.

As we ate, I engaged Kirsty in mindless chit-chat, hoping to focus her attention on the outside world. The conversation, however, was very much one-sided, with Kirsty floating in and out of engagement. Despite her lack of enthusiasm for the conversation I was relieved to see her clear her plate. "Thank you, Jennifer that was great."

"Glad you enjoyed it. You feeling any better?"

"A bit better than yesterday. Now, I just feel embarrassed. Like I allowed it to happen. I let myself get carried away with the flattery of Gary's attention."

"Oh Kirsty! Don't let yourself think that way. I don't know this Gary, but I've come across his type before. He's only using, not giving. Don't mistake looks for character."

"I know! See, that's how pathetic I am." And, as Kirsty spoke, the tears made a fresh appearance.

"I'm not having a go at you when I say that. I want you to see for yourself that you have nothing to be ashamed of. He was the reason for the incident, not you. Yes, he might be attractive and have some magnetic pull, but he's probably only out for his own ego. He doesn't care how you're feeling today. I bet he's not been in touch with you since Friday night?"

"No."

"I suspect he was using your naivety to get what he wanted. Don't let your insecurities define your choices. And, don't take the blame for something that's not your fault."

"So, do you think he knew I liked him?"

"I'm sure he did. Men like that expect every woman to be infatuated with them. Even if you hadn't liked him, he would probably have assumed you did. Unfortunately, a lot of men think they can say and act however they please towards younger women. We've all been there, the recipient of the inappropriate words. But words, never mind actions, have consequences. There's a fine line between flirt and predator. The guilt and the blame is not on you, Kirsty, it's on him. But I doubt he'll own any of that."

"How can I go back to work on Wednesday?"

"See how you're feeling tomorrow. If you're still not up to it phone in and say you want to extend your days off till the end of the week."

"I suppose I could."

"I also think you should consider talking to someone in your HR department about what happened on Friday night."

"I don't know that I could do that."

"Well, have a think about it," I said, giving Kirsty a hug. "You don't even need to put in a formal report, just get help and input from those qualified to know how to deal with such situations.

"Now let's have fun finishing off your living room. Time to crank up the volume on some great music and decide where to put everything."

"Thanks so much, Jennifer. I really do appreciate all this time you've put into decorating my living room."

"It's my pleasure. Plus, it's selfish on my part, I needed something to do with the girls at school."

I unwrapped the two prints, eager to cheer my friend up with the lovely artwork. "What do you think of these paintings? I love them. It was a close call whether they'd make it to your flat or I would keep them for myself."

"They're amazing! How on earth did you manage to find an artist who had paintings of Glasgow and Argyll?"

"Well, it's not as if they are a million miles apart! Where will we hang them?"

After an hour of placing and moving, reorganising, hanging pictures, fitting the blinds, rolling out the new rug, putting up the new ceiling light shade, placing the matching table lamps on the end tables, puffing up cushions and lighting candles Kirsty's living room was perfect.

Best of all, was seeing Kirsty engage with her new setting. As she took in the ambience of her little living room, with its new freshness and brightness, a smile spread across her face. The new colours had woven their magic through the room.

Yes, it was good for her to have a fresh start.

However, there was an element of the bitter-sweet about it all for me. It was fulfilling to see Kirsty's reaction to the new décor, and to see the completion of my work, but my sense of achievement mingled with a sense of loss as I wondered what was next. During the weekend there had been the hint of future dreams, almost within my grasp, but were those dreams for a far off future or for next week?

PAUL

After work I went to see Scott and Jennifer. This time it was Jennifer I wanted to talk to. I needed to get some insight about the best way to approach Kirsty. I should have spoken to Jennifer in the first place rather than running with Matt's advice of telling Kirsty I wasn't looking for a girlfriend. Maybe if I'd talked it through with Jennifer, the fateful dinner would have ended in friendship and laughter, instead of me walking home alone, confident in the knowledge that Kirsty would be sitting in her flat crying. She had cried enough recently, I didn't want to be the cause of any more tears.

"Hi Paul. Come in," said Scott, as he ushered me into their living room. "How are things?"

"Okay, I guess, but I've kind of messed up on some stuff, and it's actually Jennifer I need talk to."

"Sorry, she's not here. She's round at Kirsty's. Seems she had some big drama over the weekend, and Jennifer's went round to help her out."

A drama? Surely it wasn't about Thursday night. Had I upset her that much? I sat down, the weight of the world on my shoulders. "Scott, I've screwed things up. I didn't mean to upset her at all, let alone hear that she's still upset."

"What are you talking about? I'm not sure about what's going on, but I don't think it was anything to do with you. I think something happened at a work event she was at on Friday night. Why would you think it was something to do with you?"

I looked down at the floor. "I was out with her on Thursday night and told her I wasn't looking for a relationship, I guess she thought we were moving in that direction. She didn't say anything, just walked out of the restaurant and left me there alone."

Scott's laughter was not the response I had been expecting. "Sorry," said Scott. "I shouldn't laugh, I know you are trying to do the right thing."

"I can't laugh about causing Kirsty misery."

"I'm sure this thing with Kirsty, whatever it is, isn't down to Thursday night. Why don't you wait for Jennifer to come home? She made a huge lasagne. We've already had ours but there is still some left. Have dinner, hang out with us and wait for Jennifer to get back."

"Thanks that would be great." I smiled. I couldn't get mad at Scott even if he had laughed at me… again. There was wisdom in his words. Too often recently I had been out of my depth between trying to work out the whole running my own salon thing and trying to figure out what my feelings were for Kirsty. Scott spoke sense and kept me grounded. I knew I had to speak to Kirsty and smooth over this misunderstanding. I wanted - no I needed - her friendship in my life.

We cleared away the dinner dishes and settled the girls with bedtime stories before Jennifer got home.

"How's Kirsty?" I asked, as soon as Jennifer walked through the door. "What's happened?"

"Hey guys," said Jennifer, as she walked over and kissed Scott. "Sorry, Paul, I can't say too much about it. She's had a tough time and is pretty upset."

"Was it because of what I said to her on Thursday night?"

"No, it's something else, a work thing. But I'm not able to tell you any more than that."

My immediate relief at being let off the hook was short lived. Whether it was me, or someone else, who was the culprit, Kirsty was still upset.

"What can I do to help her?" I asked.

"Why don't you pop in and see her on your day off."

"Thanks, I'll do that. I can shuffle things round on Wednesday to make time for her."

"She is despondent after what happened at the weekend, and her opinion of men is quite low. So don't expect a red carpet welcome, but bear with her. She needs friends, especially those who will be there for her."

"I don't know if that description fits me right now," I said. My initial excitement at the thought of going to see her and making her feel better was quickly disappearing. The only image of Kirsty I could conjure up was the look on her face as she walked out on me at the restaurant.

"She told me about Thursday night," said Jennifer softly. "Go slowly with her, Paul. Time will heal. But, like I said, you may not get an enthusiastic welcome this time round."

KIRSTY

On Wednesday morning I called HR to let them know I
would be taking the rest of the week off. I was feeling better,
but the thought of going back to work filled me with dread.
Once I was through with the phone calls to work, I would
decide on a constructive way to spend my day. I'd done
enough brooding. After speaking to HR, I called my
department to update them.

"Kirsty, where are you?" gasped Sally. "You're missing
all the big news."

"What big news?"

"Gary. He's engaged!"

"Are you sure?" As if there could be any doubt over
such a statement.

"What a funny thing to say! He came in Monday
morning and announced that he popped the question on
Saturday night – it was cakes all round. You missed out on a

real treat. He said because the event had gone so well on Friday and then with his engagement we all deserved a treat. The cakes were amazing, from a little coffee place called Chocolate & Vanilla."

"That's nice," I said. Not feeling the least bit gracious about the news, or the fact that Gary had bought cakes from my coffee shop to celebrate his news. "Listen, I'm still run down after the event and everything, so I've called HR to let them know I'm taking the rest of the week off as holiday. Can you let Irene know? I can't bear the thought of speaking to her."

"Of course. Kirsty, you really don't sound too good, take care."

As I hung up the phone I felt numb. What on earth was going on? Gary had been so obvious with me on Friday night, there was no mistaking his intentions. Any ambiguity had been stripped away by the kiss and the enticement to his room. Even I knew exactly where I stood after that. But then to hear he'd gotten engaged the next day, when he'd conveniently never even mentioned that he had a girlfriend! What was he playing at?

I thought I was all cried out, but from somewhere a whole new wave of tears came crashing over me. Could you get dehydrated from crying too much? All my resolve to do something with my day vanished. Despondent, I shuffled back to my bedroom. I closed the bedroom blinds, put my phone on silent and hid under the duvet. A mere raincoat was no longer enough to protect me.

PAUL

Wednesday morning was the follow-up appointment with the business advisor. He agreed with the business model we were opting for and gave us further things to consider in setting up the salon. Informing us that he couldn't recommend a particular lawyer or accountant, but he could provide us with a list of offices providing the services we required. I took the list of lawyers, I would ask Scott if he would take care of our accounting needs. He stressed that all ownership details must be documented from the outset with no ambiguous issues left outstanding.

After the meeting I bought sandwiches and cakes and made my way to Kirsty's flat. It had only been a few days since I had last seen her, and even though things hadn't gone well at the restaurant, I was excited at the prospect of explaining myself and putting the misunderstanding behind us. I imagined myself as the good guy showing up on her doorstep to swoop in and make everything right between us. And, as a bonus, saving her from whatever anguish she had been through at the weekend.

But when she opened the door, I knew things were worse than I'd imagined, and Jennifer's words of warning came back with alarming clarity. The look she gave me told me I was not forgiven for my words of rebuff. As if the look of hurt at seeing me wasn't enough, I was shocked by how pale and lacklustre she looked. There was no welcome here. I had no right to offer her any comfort.

"What are you doing here?"

"I saw Jennifer on Monday night. She said you'd had a hard time. I wanted to see if you were okay."

"Jennifer shouldn't have said anything, especially to you. All you men must be laughing at me right now. Is there some kind of 'be mean to Kirsty' club out there?"

"Jennifer didn't tell me anything, except that something was wrong."

"So, what? You've come over to get the gossip first hand? Do you want every juicy detail? Do you want to feel sorry for poor little Kirsty? Or maybe even vindicated for Thursday night?"

The tears were streaming down her face. I wanted to interrupt her. I wanted to stop the pain, but she wouldn't let me get a word in.

"Poor, stupid Kirsty. She hasn't got a clue about men. Text dumped by one, told by another he's not interested, even though he is! And then to top it all she has the boss who thinks it's totally acceptable to kiss and grope his assistant. That's right Paul. I'm a complete loser when it comes to men. So I'm done with you all. I'm done."

"Kirsty, please."

She started to close the door. I couldn't let it end here. I needed to let her know how much I cared. I needed to let her know not all guys were out to make her feel used. I couldn't walk away from a girl who could barely speak for crying.

"Kirsty!" I stepped forward and drew her into a hug. She didn't pull back, but nor did she engage in it. I released her from my arms and looked into her eyes. They told me nothing. Those beautiful eyes were lifeless. A bolt of sadness pierced my heart. And in that instant I saw myself through her eyes. I was part of the reason she was crushed and broken. She was lost and confused and for the first time in my life I had no idea what to say to a woman. I had nothing to offer.

"I'm sorry," I whispered.

As she closed the door on me, my resolve strengthened. I would not give up. Despite what she said, she needed me. And, I needed her too.

KIRSTY

I closed the door on Paul. I didn't even care I had caused that look of dejection on his face. Maybe it was time for me to be the one dishing it out. That wasn't the kind of person I was but, for today I didn't care.

I was fed up with men. Guys like Paul and Gary were ten-a-penny. But then again that wasn't true. They were still in the minority with their cloaked words and their stealth touches, compassionate gazes that promised you the world, but were empty on delivery. If they really were ten-a-penny their effect would not be wielded with such superhuman power.

How did they manage it with merely the slightest touch, their captivating smile and their delicate words? They made you feel so special, but it was all just a façade for their ego.

Today wasn't supposed to be about pity, it was supposed to be about getting over everything. But the news of Gary's engagement had rocked me.

The only place I wanted to be was in bed, hiding under my duvet. But I wouldn't go back to sleep, the nightmares were following me from real life to the dream world, twisting events and creating even more chilling tales.

As I crawled back into bed, my phone pinged with a new text. It was from Jo. 'How are you today? Read this earlier and thought of you: 1John4:18: *Perfect love drives out fear.*'

Fear and love. Love and fear. The two emotions were completely intertwined in my life. According to John, they couldn't co-exist. But wasn't this pairing the crux of my problem? I was so fearful of never feeling love that whatever shred of love came my way I clung onto it. And then fear would cast its shadow. Fear it wouldn't last. Fear I wasn't good enough. Fear it would all end. And it always did.

What would it be like to experience love without fear?

PAUL

I walked over to the nearby park. The clarity of the colours, from the blues of the sky to the hint of changing leaf colours, were in stark contrast to Kirsty. The paleness of her face haunted my thoughts. I should have asked her to come out for a walk, but she could barely look at me, never mind spend time with me.

I was mad at Gary. I didn't know him, but I was mad at him. Mad because I guessed the angle he had been playing on Kirsty. I knew what Gary was up to because I'd done the same thing a thousand times myself. It was the old word and touch routine. Identifying the vulnerable prey. Knowing the right words to say, words that seemed comforting to the unsuspecting, but words that were all about getting her under your spell. The touch that made the connection. It was all about making her believe the guy standing before her really was there for her, had her best interests at heart, and most importantly understood her. But he wasn't. That guy was all about self-gratification.

I was angry at myself. When I chose to take a break from dating, I thought it was to break the habit – but it was showing up the dark side to my old life. I didn't want to look at it. It was vulgar. Seeing Kirsty's pain made me realise that my past behaviour had hurt so many 'Kirstys'. Of course they hadn't all been fine with 'moving on'. I hated myself for all that pain I'd caused. Perhaps, in helping Kirsty, I could redeem myself.

I called Jennifer and told her of my encounter with Kirsty.

"I'm sorry Paul. She is hurting right now. I don't know how she's going to come out of this. But, whether or not she acknowledges it, she needs her friends. And I believe that includes you."

"But she looked awful, Jennifer. She wouldn't even look at me."

"Give her time. And let her know you're there for her. Why don't you phone Jo and arrange to go to Kirsty's with them?"

"Good idea, thanks Jennifer."

I needed to do something, anything that would solve this problem. "Hi, Jo, it's Paul. I was wondering when you're next going to Kirsty's?"

"We're heading round tomorrow night for movies and pizza. Do you want to join us?"

"That would be great, I'll bring Matt along too. And Jo, don't mention to Kirsty we're coming. I messed things up with her last week and I'm not sure how much she wants to see me, but I need to see her."

"No worries. I won't say anything."

"Thanks. I appreciate it."

"Paul, I know what happened last week at the restaurant. You really upset her, but I also realise that wasn't your intention."

"Of course it wasn't. I need to tell her that."

"You need to let that go for now. Getting together tomorrow night is not about you, it's about Kirsty. It's not about relationships, it's about friendship. It's helping her understand that people get love wrong at times, but overall love never fails."

PAUL

Later that afternoon I met up with Brian and Trish to view potential salon premises. However, my thoughts were still so centred on Kirsty I found it hard to concentrate and think about what we should be looking for. Thankfully, I wasn't doing this alone!

Trish came into her own, seeing the potential and pitfalls of each property. It was exciting to see the possibilities for our new venture but, at the same time it drew attention to the various aspects that would need to be paid for up front; such as salon signage, refit of the properties for sinks and workstations.

"When you dream of your own salon, you don't consider the costs of joiners, plumbers and paint," I said. "You only think of hairstyling."

"I know what you mean," said Brian. "How are we going to pay for all this?"

"I'll give the business advisor a call and ask his advice on loans. Depending on the costs, it might even be a case of maxing out credit cards on 0% loans. He did say ours is a market with low cost of entry. But I guess that's a relative term," said Trish.

"Good idea," I said. "Why don't we head to that pub over there? It would be good for each of us to rank the properties on location, space, potential, price and gut feel."

After a beer and some consideration we all picked the same unit as our number one choice.

"Let's hope all our decisions are this easy," I said.

"What next?" said Brian.

"Trish, can you call the agent and see if there is any other interest in the property? I'd like to meet the business advisor again before we take things any further. We need to determine what needs to be done to get us up and running, including advertising the new place and handing in our notices."

As the decision to set up on our own loomed nearer, and the practicalities began to take shape, I waited for a feeling of fear, but still peace remained. I thought again of the verse Scott had shared a few weeks ago.

'And the peace of God, which transcends all understanding, will guard your hearts and your minds in Christ Jesus.'

JENNIFER

On Wednesday night I took dinner over to Kirsty's again. I wanted to have time alone with her before the others arrived for small group. I had been praying for her throughout the day.

As we ate dinner together, Kirsty told me about Paul coming to see her that afternoon. "I guess I should apologise to him for being so rude, but at the moment I feel no remorse whatsoever."

"Kirsty, you've had a rough time over the past few weeks. Paul told me how bad he feels about what happened at the restaurant, so I'm sure he's harbouring no ill will towards you for your reaction today."

Kirsty averted her eyes and put all her attention to pushing the remains of her dinner around her plate.

"But don't put Paul in the same camp as Steven and Gary. He's trying to do the right thing. He's had a bit of a past and he needs time to get that sorted out. In taking this break he's protecting his girlfriend/wife of the future. I see how it might feel like a negative directed at you but, you never know, maybe it's a positive."

"I doubt that. And right now I don't care. I'm done with guys."

"You're hurt and vulnerable right now, but don't hold on to those thoughts. Bitterness won't help you get through this. Learn what you need to from the situation, identify the cues that will help you in the future. Don't rush it or force it, and you'll come out the other side stronger and more aware of who you are and what you want."

"You make it sound so every day, like this happens to everyone."

"Different situations happen to different people all the time, but it's how you deal with it that defines you, not the thing that actually happened."

"What if I'm not strong enough to deal with it well?"

"You're stronger than you think, Kirsty. And you don't have to go through this alone, you've got me, and you've got your lovely group of friends. But most of all, you've got God, and He'll give you the strength you need to do this. God's plan for love is for it to heal and make whole, not something that leaves you bruised and battered."

I watched Kirsty as she went back to concentrating on her half-eaten dinner. This wasn't a one-off conversation, it was a conversation to be continued over the days and weeks ahead, bite-size pieces for Kirsty to process and deal with.

"Why don't I clear up these things and you can set up for the girls arriving?" I said.

As Jo, Lynn and Carol arrived, I was delighted by all the *ooh*, *aah* and *wows* they were making at Kirsty's new look living room.

"Jennifer! You need to go into business as an interior designer," said Jo. "The room looks amazing!"

"Thanks Jo, that's so encouraging." Jo's praise provided a further nudge to my future plans.

As everyone settled down with their tea and coffee, I introduced my plans for the evening. "Last week I said we would spend time talking about 'Love never fails', but as it's been an emotional week I want to change tact. I've lined up several worship songs, specifically about love. Rather than talking, let's just spend the time in prayer and listening to the songs."

For the next half hour we sat in silence, listening to the songs. As the music came to an end, I watched the interaction within the group. Jo, Lynn and Carol prayed over their friend with love and hope. Kirsty would get through this.

KIRSTY

I flopped into bed, exhausted. What a day. Another day of roller-coaster emotions. From feeling better at the start of the day, to finding out about Gary when I phoned the office. Then Paul turning up. I was thankful for small-group, time to be with my closest friends, the girls who had my back and cared for me more than anyone else. Despite the upswing at the end of the day, I was nervous about going to sleep. The nightmares of this morning still haunted me.

I switched on the TV, hoping for some mindless, funny programme that would distract me and take me to the edge of sleep, but all I seemed to land on were adverts.

I looked around the living room for inspiration. Jennifer had done an amazing job on the living room revamp. Maybe I could persuade her to tackle my bedroom too. As I looked around, I noticed the Ellyn Oliver CD lying on the lamp table. Switching on the laptop I put the CD in the appropriate drive and selected the song Jennifer had noted, "Arms Wide Open".

As I listened tears streamed down my face. But these tears were different. They were cleansing, washing away the rubbish that had been in my life over the last few weeks. I put the song on repeat and let the words sink in.

'They're you're standing
With arms wide open
There's nothing I can do
To make you love me
To make you love me more'

I walked through to bed, the words of the song still playing in my mind. I picked up my Bible and read the story of the woman who sat at Jesus' feet. Her tears of sorrow washed his feet, which she then dried with her hair, before pouring perfume over them. It had been one of my favourite Bible stories when I was a teenager, but I had forgotten about it. I'd forgotten to sit at Jesus' feet and just be with him. It was time to let the words sink deep into my soul, no longer just head knowledge, but heart knowledge. Knowing that Jesus really did love me, not just because I'd heard it all my life in Sunday School and youth groups, but because I finally realised that love was meant for me. Perhaps this was where all true love sprang from.

"Jesus let me sit at your feet tonight as I sleep," I prayed as I switched off the light. "And let me have a dreamless sleep."

JENNIFER

The next morning I decided to do something about the situation with Sarah and Kevin. I sent Sarah a text: 'Would Kevin like to come and play with Emma after school and stay for dinner?' I wasn't sure how pleased Emma would be with this plan, but I would wait for Sarah's reply before I said anything. My phone pinged a few minutes later with Sarah's text to say Kevin would love to.

As I expected, Emma wasn't overly pleased with the prospect of having Kevin over after school. I didn't go into any details with her, but I told her that Kevin needed a good friend right now. Hopefully, the play date would help the two of them get over the fall outs of recent weeks, as well as give Sarah some space.

As we walked back home from school that afternoon, Kevin seemed a lot calmer than he had been the last time I had seen him.

"How was school today everyone?" I should have known better than to ask a question without directing it at one of the children. I was met with three answers all at the same time.

"One at a time," I said, laughing at their enthusiasm. "Chloe, you're the youngest, you go first."

"Today was brilliant. We got to paint this afternoon."

"And what were you painting?"

"The castle for our Princesses and Pirates topic."

"And what about you Kevin?"

"Okay, just maths and language. But gym was pretty cool. We got to do touch rugby; that was fun."

"That does sound fun, and what about you Emma?"

"I didn't like the rugby so much, but I did like language today because we got to start The Lion, The Witch And The Wardrobe. I'm going to read it over the weekend."

"Well, it sounds like you all had things you liked in your day, which is excellent. So, I think you'll all be ready for the hot chocolate and brownies that are waiting for you back at the house."

They all cheered and became extra excited at getting home.

Kevin and Emma played well. At dinner Kevin was polite and well mannered. And it wasn't just Kevin who was making the effort, Emma selected games and activities she knew Kevin liked. It seemed as if things were repairing. Hopefully, the time spent together now would also help them get along better in school.

After dinner I took Kevin home. I was hoping to chat with Sarah but, as she opened the door, she was talking on her phone. I waved over to her and drove off. In the morning I would invite her round for coffee.

Kirsty

By Thursday night I was desperate to have fun with my friends. I had spent far too much time wallowing; it was time to get over this mess and face life again. Jo came into my flat carrying a stack of pizza boxes. My stomach rumbled at the smell of hot, cheesy pizzas. I hadn't eaten much over the last few days, and I was now ravenous. Although, she seemed to have brought a lot of pizzas for just the four of us!

In terms of movie choices, I insisted on a break from our usual chick flicks. Stories of romance were the last thing I needed. I took my cue from my night out with Paul and Matt and opted for car chases and fugitives. Tonight was all about fun and laughter, friendship and pizza.

We settled down with our pizza and beer, the first movie ready to go. "Don't any of you get pizza stains anywhere, or you'll have Jennifer to answer to," I said.

"She's done a fantastic job in here, you'd hardly recognise the place," said Jo.

"It's great isn't it? I'm loving it. I'm thinking of asking her if she'll make over my bedroom next."

"You should," encouraged Jo.

"How come you brought so many pizzas?" I asked, helping myself to another slice.

"There may be other people joining us," said Lynn, with a mysterious look on her face. I decided to play along with her game and not probe any further. Jennifer hadn't said anything about coming over tonight. But who else could it be?

As the opening scene started, the doorbell rang. Jo got up to answer it. She returned to the living room followed by Paul and Matt.

"Hi, hope you don't mind the intrusion. We heard you were having beer and pizza tonight and it sounded like a great idea," said Paul.

I wasn't sure how to react to Paul. My initial instinct was to smile at him, it was good to see him, but I felt awkward about how things were between us after yesterday's encounter. "Beer and pizza is on the table, help yourself, and grab a space where you can." When all else fails, you can still be hospitable! Matt's presence helped lessen the stress.

Paul seemed to enjoy being part of my group of friends, now it was up to me to accept it for what it was. Friendship. I smiled, it was nice to express a positive emotion again.

The combination of people, easy going movies and food seemed to lighten everyone's mood and gave us plenty of excuses to laugh together. As the second movie came to its conclusion, Jo looked round at me. "So, we've all been chatting and have decided that we're going to tag team over the weekend to ensure that you have a fun-packed time, hopefully without sprained ankles or bruises."

"You don't need to, but thanks. I'd love that."

"We know we don't have to do it, but we want to," said Paul.

"On Saturday we're going sledging at the indoor snow slope. Then it's coffee and cake, some retail therapy, all finished off with dinner. I believe Cinderella needs to go shopping for a new raincoat and heels," said Jo, and winked at the group.

"Yes, ha ha. Let's not go down the route of Cinderella references please, that would assume a wonderful Prince Charming."

"Then Sunday is mystery day. After church, me, Jo and Matt are taking you on a surprise outing. All I'm saying is wear jeans and t-shirt. And please, leave the raincoat and sunglasses at home," said Paul.

"Aw, thanks all of you, I really appreciate it." And as I looked round the room I did appreciate this group of friends. Was there potential friendship with Paul and Matt? I still wasn't sure, but I was willing to give it a go. I liked the idea of having some new guy friends around. Perhaps it would be good to take a break from dating, to stop letting my imagination and daydreams get the better of me. Putting my hope in fairy tales had only led to disappointments, it was time to be real.

I said a quiet prayer of thanks for good friends. Who knew beer and pizza were an answer to prayer!

PAUL

Walking into the salon the following morning, I felt at peace. I was excited and nervous about the new hairdressing venture. It had been what I wanted for a long time, but I'd pushed those thoughts aside, going with the more sensible, or perhaps easier option, of being given a salary.

I was sure Si guessed change was in the air. He was blowing hot and cold between giving me a hard time and being nice to me. Part of me was looking forward to handing in my notice. And, I confess the thought of Si getting two resignations in the one day appealed to my sense of humour.

As Si made signals I was taking too long with a client, I immersed myself in the thoughts of handing in that resignation letter.

My next client was on my 'why do they keep asking for me' list. Emily was a beautiful girl in her twenties. Whenever I cut her hair, she ignored me and spent all her time on her smart phone. Normally I was frustrated by clients who didn't engage in some level of conversation, but today I was glad for the silent appointment. It gave me time to let my mind wander through the new business options. I thought about the property we had picked. The place was perfect, or at least had potential, it needed some cosmetic work to bring it into line as a smart hair salon. Last night I'd been amazed at the difference in Kirsty's living room. I would ask Jennifer if she would be willing to take on a commercial project. No harm in asking.

It was exciting to think of these aspects of the business, it wouldn't all be spreadsheets and paperwork. The thought of fun business decisions was encouraging. I knew the hairdressing side of things would be much better. It would be good to have decent appointment times. People told their hairdressers things, and I wanted them to have time to do that. Scott was right it wasn't about making yourself into somebody else, it was about doing the thing you were created to do.

And it wasn't just work that looked promising. Last night had worked out well too. Although Kirsty hadn't welcomed me with open arms, she allowed me into her home. It probably helped having Matt with me. By the end of the evening the tension had eased. I was looking forward to spending Sunday with her.

In amongst the unknowns that lay ahead, there was peace.

'And the peace of God, which transcends all understanding, will guard your hearts and your minds in Christ Jesus.'

JENNIFER

"Thanks for having Kevin over last night, he really enjoyed it," said Sarah, when we met in the school playground.

"He was no bother at all. Do you want to come back to mine for a cuppa just now?"

"Just for a quick one. I'm at the hairdressers later this morning."

"How have things been this week?" I asked, as we sat at my kitchen table enjoying coffee and biscuits. Sarah looked tired. She wasn't the easiest person to be friends with, but sometimes you had to persevere; everyone needs friends.

"Okay, I guess. Things haven't been as bad this week. I took your advice and suggested to James that we might want to speak to a counsellor."

"And what did he think of that?"

"I can't repeat his initial reaction. But then he came round and said he'd think about it."

"That's positive."

"Part of me isn't even sure if I want it to work." Sarah looked unsure of herself, like a lost little girl.

"What's going on?"

"We've been drifting apart for years. James' job takes him on business trips all over Europe. At first it was a great adventure. Before Kevin started school, he'd sometimes arrange for us to fly to wherever he was, and we'd make a weekend away out of it. It was so much fun going to lots of different European destinations, almost on a whim. But then Kevin started school, and that essentially ended the trips. I got fed up being the one having to deal with all the childcare issues for Kevin and working and taking care of the house. I began to suspect James was seeing other women on his trips. So… I decided to play the same game."

"You mean…"

"Yes. I'm not proud of it, but I wouldn't undo it."

"Oh, Sarah." I walked over to her and gave her a hug.

Sarah pulled back. "I thought you would judge me, like everyone else does."

"There are plenty of people to judge."

"And I thought you would be one of them. You are always so perfectly put together with your raincoat and sunglasses, living in your perfect house with your perfect family."

"Oh Sarah. Do you really think that? Do you know why I'm always in my raincoat and sunglasses? It's because underneath I'm a mess; I've been so busy getting the girls organised and tidying up after breakfast that I'm wearing some uncoordinated outfit and no makeup. The raincoat and sunglasses hide all that!"

We both laughed.

"I guess things aren't always what they seem."

"No, they are not. And, regards to you and James, only the two of you can decide what to do next."

"I don't think we know how to speak to each other without fighting. Has it gone too far to be salvaged?"

"I don't know Sarah. Why not spend time together this weekend? I could take Kevin Sunday afternoon, give the two of you some space."

"You would do that for us?"

"Of course I would. You're not going to resolve anything in one afternoon, but right now you need to figure out what your options are and what you're willing to try. And that's not a conversation you want to start with Kevin about."

"I'm not sure James will agree, but I'll say to him and let you know."

This time Sarah was the one to hug me.

JENNIFER

After Sarah left, I zoomed round the house for its Friday morning clean. I needed the therapy of housework to process the conversation I had just had with Sarah. All I could do now was pray. As I cleaned I prayed. I prayed for Sarah. I prayed for James and I prayed for Kevin. Golden beams of sunshine warmed the kitchen as the clouds of the morning began to clear, a reassurance that God was close, that he saw and he knew.

As I switched off the vacuum, the telephone rang. "Jennifer? Hi, it's Paul."

"Hey Paul, how are you?"

"Doing well, thanks. I've been mulling over some thoughts regarding the new salon. We saw some properties on Wednesday and I think we may have found our new place."

"That's exciting!"

"Yeah. We're all buzzing. The reason for my call is that I was at Kirsty's last night and saw her stylish new living room, and I wanted to ask if you would be interested in a commercial project?"

"Wow! I'd love to. Do you know you are an answer to prayer? With Kirsty's living room completed I wasn't sure what I was going to do next. So yes, I'm totally up for helping you with your salon."

"That's brilliant Jennifer. It will look great with you in charge of design. Although I need to caution you that we don't have a big budget to work on."

"Don't worry about that, we can even loan you the money for the supplies, and you can pay us back interest free once you're up and running."

"You would take that risk on us?"

"Of course. This hasn't been a rash decision on your part. You've thought about it and you're getting the proper advice to get things going. I know first-hand what an amazing stylist you are. You'll be a success. I'm no expert in design, so doing the salon is as much for me as it is for you."

"Wow, Jennifer. I'm actually lost for words. Thanks."

Hanging up the phone, I let out a contented sigh. Yes! A new path was opening up to me. And it was exciting. *'You make known to me the path of life; you will fill me with joy in your presence.'*

Once again, time-keeping beat me. I just had time to grab my raincoat and sunglasses before dashing out the door to meet up with Scott for lunch.

"Wow, you look so much more like your old self today," said Scott. "You're glowing."

"That's probably the sweat from having to rush to get here." As I glanced at the table, I was glad I had made the effort to arrive on time - there was no phone between us today.

I told Scott about my conversation with Sarah.

"Go you," said Scott. "Sounds like you've got this well covered."

"I don't have a clue if I'm helping or not. I'm trying to, but what if I'm making it worse?"

"You're there for her, honey. How can there be anything wrong in that?"

"I hope you're right.

"How was your morning?"

"Good. I handed over another client to Peter today. And, I'm going to make sure that any time I take on a new client some of my existing workload gets passed to other people in the office."

"That's brilliant. I suspect you might get a call soon from a prospective client."

"Really? Who?"

"Paul. He phoned this morning to ask if I would design their new salon."

"That's great. I take it you said yes."

"Absolutely! I need a new project now that Kirsty's living room is done. He's a bit tight on cash with the start-up costs, so I told him we'd give him an interest free loan. Is that okay?"

"I wouldn't make a habit of offering loans to every new business, but I agree it's a good decision for Paul. So is he looking for an accountant too?"

"Yes. I think he's hoping to talk to you about it soon."

"I'm so pleased for him. And, I'm intrigued to see where this will lead for you too."

"As we were driving home last weekend I was wondering if interior design might be the thing for me to explore."

"That's so exciting!"

I smiled at Scott's words of affirmation. With the anticipation of a new challenge, joy soared too.

JENNIFER

Saturday was declared as a family fun day. I realised it had been a while since we'd been out together as a family. Various options were discussed and their merits weighed against each other. The winning activity was 10-pin bowling, followed by dinner at our favourite restaurant.

The competition was fierce. Each one driven to win the family bowling competition. Emma and Chloe were allowed to have the lane guards up and use the bowling frame, the rest of us were working on pure technique. I was in the lead by a few points as we entered the final round. Now was the time to break the competitiveness and make everyone laugh.

I wiggled and waddled up to the line to take my turn. I stood with my back to the pins and rolled the ball between my legs. As I turned round, I watched all ten pins fall down. Strike! I did a celebration moon walk dance right there at the end of the lane, not caring about anyone else, only caring about the gorgeous family in front of me. Even Amy forgot her pre-teen self-consciousness long enough to laugh and jump about.

"I declare milk shakes all round," I said, as we arrived at the restaurant.

The girls all cheered and decided on their preferred concoctions. Fuelled by milk shakes and burgers we continued the celebrations, making a competition out of who could come up with the craziest selfie pose. Looking round my family I smiled.

Joy was still in my life. It had never left me. I had just got stuck in the ordinary for too long. It was time to step out of the ordinary and discover my next adventure.

KIRSTY

Saturday was a perfect day of laughter. A day of friendship and fun. Sledging proved to be a great way to start a day out. We giggled and laughed like schoolgirls. In fact, the kid's party sledging next to us were much more serious. I was convinced the instructor thought we were drunk!

After sledging we went upstairs to the bar and indulged in hot chocolate and cake. A table with a view of the ski-slope provided extra entertainment, even if it did mean laughing at the poor beginners on the slope who were trying their best to master the complexity of snowploughs and turns.

We split the day up with a quick stopover at my flat to get showered and changed before heading out for the second part of our girls-day-out. During the shopping stage we all bought new killer heels, which we then wore to dinner. Dinner was at a stylish new restaurant in the centre of town.

The kind of place that was good to treat yourself to every once in a while.

Jo invited herself back to my flat for the night. I wasn't ready for the night to end yet. After too much time spent alone in the flat this week, I realised how much I needed these wonderful friends in my life.

"It's been so good seeing you laugh again," said Jo. "Are you feeling the benefit of our crazy day?"

"Absolutely, it's been exactly what I needed."

"And you've still got tomorrow's surprise to look forward to."

"Do you know what the boys have got planned?"

"No, they wouldn't tell me in case I let slip where they were taking us."

"I'm not sure whether or not to take that as a good sign."

"So, what are your thoughts on Paul after Thursday night?"

"One good night doesn't make up for the bad night. But, I'm willing to give him the benefit of the doubt if he can make me feel half as good as this tomorrow."

"I do think he's one of the good guys, Kirsty."

"So everyone keeps telling me. I'd like to believe it, but for the moment I'm happy to go for friendship."

"And then…"

"And then nothing. He made it very clear it's only about friendship."

"Keep an open mind. I've got a good feeling about this one."

"Of course you do!"

As we settled down to sleep, I hoped Jo was right.

KIRSTY

For the first Sunday in ages, I was able to engage and concentrate at church. I was looking forward to the mystery afternoon with Jo, Paul and Matt, but the thought of spending time with Paul wasn't consuming me. I felt at peace.

Ben, the pastor, introduced the sermon for the day. He wanted to go back to Romans chapter 5, and explore the concepts of love, joy and peace in more detail. I wanted to laugh out loud. Really? It seemed like a lot of Bible discussions and texts were coming my way about love. For the next half-hour I listened to what Ben had to say on the subject and considered how that love compared to my recent troubles.

I was beginning to understand that love could look very different depending on where it came from. At times I had thought of Paul and Gary as similar in their attitude to women. But I could see now how different they were.

Gary was all out for his own gratification, a world where women were conquests or trophies. Who had he proposed to? Did she know what he was? Did she assume she would change him?

Paul wasn't perfect, he'd hurt me with his explanation at the restaurant the previous week, but he was trying to change. Was the friendship worth pursuing? Was it all too complicated to deal with?

The next twenty-four hours were critical. This afternoon with Paul would show whether friendship was even possible for us. And tomorrow morning would be my first encounter with Gary since the launch event. I shivered at the prospect of seeing him again. How would he react? How should I react? I thought back to the text Jo had sent: *'Perfect love drives out fear'*.

'God, I'm scared for tomorrow. Please let your love drive out that fear. Teach me how this works.'

PAUL

When Jo and I had conspired earlier in the week to give Kirsty a weekend of fun, I had immediately decided on karting. A challenge that combined skill and adrenalin in equal measures. Including Matt and Jo in the afternoon was my way of letting Kirsty know it was purely about friendship.

As Matt parked at the karting centre, the look on Kirsty's face was priceless. "Surprised?" I asked.

"Yes and no," she replied. "It seems fitting for the two of you. I bet you guys come here all the time and are master racers."

"Something like that," said Matt.

I opened the door for Kirsty and Jo, welcoming them into the world of racing and kart suits. I noticed Kirsty's hesitation; the challenge of a new place and a new experience, not quite sure what to do or where to go. As the ones familiar with the centre, it was up to Matt and I to direct Kirsty and Jo and instruct them on what they were about to do.

As Kirsty got into her kart suit and helmet, I noticed with satisfaction, that after the initial uncertainty, she was ready for a bit of fun and a challenge. With Kirsty there was no girlieness about ruining her hair or getting dirty, she was up for what lay ahead. As the instructor ran through the rules and instructions I kept glancing over at her to see how she was reacting. There was a smile on her face and a building enthusiasm for trying something new.

"Take it easy for the first few laps, get used to it, then we can go for it," I said.

"Great, let's get racing," said Kirsty, as she prepared to get into her kart.

As suggested, we took the first few laps slowly, letting Kirsty and Jo get used to the controls. After the second circuit I nodded, the signal it was time to go. I let Kirsty take the lead. After just a couple of laps she was going pretty fast. No wonder she was accident prone, she went full pelt on new challenges. She was a mystery. She could seem so vulnerable and yet give her a challenge and she threw herself at it. I was liking her more and more.

On the next lap round, Matt was struggling to overtake Kirsty, so he bumped into the back of her kart and sent her into the tyre barriers. She was stuck and had to wait for one of the centre workers to come and push her back. After another couple of laps, the four of us came in for a break.

"Who pushed me into the barrier?" said Kirsty.

"Too slow," said Matt. "Stay out of my way or you're at the side."

"Oh, don't you worry about me going too slow this time round, Matt. On the next lap, I'll be the one ramming you into the barriers!"

"I'm not sure which one of you to feel sorry for," I said. "Could it be you've both met your match?"

"Yeah, watch out Matt," said Jo. "This one takes no prisoners. If you challenge her be prepared for the consequences."

Back on the track Kirsty was true to her word and took off before the rest of us were even settled into our karts. We all laughed. This was turning out better than I imagined. Kirsty had taken to karting and was giving herself fully to the enjoyment of it. As distractions went, this was going better than expected.

"That was amazing," said Kirsty, as we went back to the locker room to change.

"You still drive like a girl though," said Matt.

"Like a girl who will beat you next time!"

I laughed as Kirsty rose to Matt's bait. This girl was ticking boxes I didn't even know I had!

"How about beer and burgers to celebrate?" I suggested.

"Of course," said Matt.

"I'm in," said Kirsty. "And I think Matt should pay!"

"Sounds like a great idea," said Jo. "But I need to get back home to do class prep for tomorrow."

"Can't you stay out a bit longer?" said Kirsty. "You need to eat."

"Well, here's a turn up for the books, you trying to persuade me to stay out later. Sorry, I really do need to get back home."

Jo and Kirsty hugged their goodbyes before we headed on for dinner. Kirsty's enthusiasm dipped with Jo's departure. I wasn't sure if it was down to saying goodbye to her friend, or the reminder that she was edging ever closer to Monday morning.

JENNIFER

On Sunday Kevin joined us for lunch. I was ashamed of my earlier thoughts about this child. No wonder he had been kicking off. His entire world had been plunged into uncertainty.

When Sarah came to collect him after dinner, sunglasses hid her eyes. But as she spoke her thanks, I could tell there had been tears that afternoon. Her tone was softer than usual. Hopefully, it meant they were going to work at their marriage, but with children running round our legs, now wasn't the time to ask questions. That would need to wait for another time.

After Sarah left with Kevin, I tried to call Kirsty to find out how she was, especially with the prospect of going back to work tomorrow. But there was no answer on her house phone or mobile. I took it as a good sign that she was still out having fun with Paul and Matt.

As I put the phone back down, Scott brought me a mug of tea. "Thanks," I said as I took it from him.

"Look at that big smile on your face," said Scott.

"I guess the last few weeks have reminded me not to lose sight of who I am. I'm mum to three amazing girls, and wife to one sexy guy, but there's also more than that, there's faith and purpose too."

Scott leaned over and kissed me. "Exciting times."

"It's good to be looking forward again."

"So, what's next?"

"It will be another week or two before Paul needs my input. As soon as they decide what they are doing and get a date for taking over the premises I'll be in there. But, until then I'll make myself available for Sarah, and Kevin."

"Why not also use this time to think a bit more about interior design? Maybe even check if there are any courses you could take."

"Good idea. It's exciting, and scary, to think of starting something new."

My phone pinged with a text. It was from Kirsty. 'Sorry I missed your calls. I was out with Paul and Matt. Everything great, we're taking it slowly.'

I was desperate for more details. But for the moment a text back to say, 'Great. Hope all goes well tomorrow, will be praying for you,' was all that was needed.

"Who was that?" asked Scott.

"Kirsty. She was letting me know she's had fun with Paul and Matt."

"So… the girls are in bed. All is well with the world. How about we head upstairs and celebrate?"

I leant over and kissed Scott. "Sounds like a great idea. Why don't you head up and check on the girls, I just need to do something first."

I walked over to the photograph of Scott and myself on his motorbike. This new stage of life wasn't empty, but as full of potential as every other new beginning. And with every new beginning there was the promise of endless joy.

'You make known to me the path of life; you will fill me with joy in your presence.'

KIRSTY

"You want to come back to mine for coffee? I can't face the Sunday evening dread yet?" Our day had passed too quickly. After my initial concerns about karting I had loved it. It was an activity I could see myself getting addicted to it. Paul and Matt knew what they were doing when they made the day about adrenaline fun.

"That sounds like a great idea," said Paul.

"Count me in, too," said Matt.

Back at my flat the banter flowed over coffee. During a lull in the conversation, Paul picked up the two carrier bags he had brought into the flat. "This seems like the appropriate time to give you these. This one first," he said, as he handed me the larger of the two bags.

I pulled out the raincoat and shoes I had left at the hotel on Friday night. "We went to the hotel yesterday to retrieve them for you," said Matt.

"Wow! Thank you!"

"And now, your present for tomorrow," said Paul, handing over the second bag.

I pulled out a dusky pink raincoat.

"If you must wear a raincoat, then at least make it fun and bright rather than those boring beige ones. Use the pink to give you confidence tomorrow," said Paul.

"It's beautiful. Thank you," I said, as tears once again threatened. I couldn't fight off the sadness any longer. Work was only a few hours away. I had enjoyed a brilliant time with Paul and Matt. The guys had proven themselves as great friends, people I could relax with. Perhaps they were here now to help me deal with my emotions.

"I need your help," I said.

"Anything," the both answered.

"Gary, my boss, kissed me at the launch event last Friday." I let the words hang in the air, waiting to hear if they would judge me for letting it happen. The girls had told me I had done nothing wrong, but there was still a guilt hanging over me, refusing to release its cruel grip.

"At the end of the event I went into the function room for one final check. We were the only two people there. Gary said we needed to dance. He was really drunk by this point. He put a slow tune on his phone and took my hand and started to dance. Then he kissed me. He also invited me to go up to his room with him."

Paul and Matt looked at each other. Were they judging me? Blaming me for allowing the kiss to happen?

"How can I face work in the morning?"

"Why are you questioning yourself?" said Paul. "You didn't do anything wrong. If anything, you could report him for harassment."

"Who would believe me? I think it's easier if I forget about it and move on. But I don't know how I'm going to face him."

"You need to report him to HR. He's the one at fault in this," joined in Matt. "Does anyone at your work know what happened?"

"I don't think so. But on Friday my manager, Irene, called me. She said she wanted to check that I was okay. Which is really strange because until a few weeks ago she was always a bit sharp with me."

"Do you think she's guessed something happened?" asked Paul.

"I don't know. Maybe?"

"I wonder if Gary has been on edge this week and she's picked up on something," said Matt.

"Whatever. I still feel I'm the one that's done something wrong? I know I'm going to be the self-conscious one tomorrow. I'm dreading it."

"Kirsty, look at me," said Paul. He got down on his knees in front of me, taking my hands in his. "You didn't do anything wrong. He's the one in the wrong. And do you know what?" I shook my head. "He'll know it too. So don't go in there tomorrow as one defeated. He doesn't know if you're going to speak to HR about a sexual harassment suit or not. Go in with confidence."

"I don't think I can," I said, the tears brimming up in my eyes. Paul got up and sat beside me on the settee, pulling me into a hug. As he sat there and hugged me, Matt bent his head in prayer. I was touched by their response. This was exactly what I needed. The dread and fear were still there, but I was able to offer up a prayer of thanks; thankful for these new friends in my life. I had been besotted by the romance of fairy tale love, but here was something far more precious than anything I had discovered through my string of dating disasters. Friendship. True friendship. Guys who actually listened and were here for me. Maybe, when the dating thing was taken out of the equation, true friendships could begin.

"I really think you should speak to your HR department," said Paul. "Don't even see it as making a complaint if that is too much stress. Why not look at it as talking to them about it and getting their advice?"

"I don't know if I can."

"Of course you can. If you can drive as crazy as that your first time karting, then you can do this," said Matt.

"If it seems too daunting to do it on your own, why not ask someone to go with you?" said Paul. "Why not call Irene now? Tell her about what's happened and ask her if she'll go to HR with you in the morning?"

I felt a surge of fear and panic, but with Paul and Matt beside me I also felt enabled. Wasn't the media full of stories about women taking power and control of their situations? Stories of women saying 'enough'. Maybe this was my time to say enough. I reached for my phone and called Irene.

PAUL

I was so proud of Kirsty for making the phone call. I really wanted to kiss her, but for now it was about being here for her and giving us both the space we needed.

"Well, no going back now," said Kirsty, as she hung up on Irene. "I really am glad you've been around for me this week. You've been great friends and helped me more than you'll ever know."

"Kirsty, it's been great hanging out with you too," said Matt. "Now remember. You didn't do anything wrong. You can do this. And, if things get a bit heavy, just text me and we'll set up our re-match at the karting centre."

Matt hugged Kirsty goodbye, leaving me to my own goodbye with her.

"I messed up with you last week at dinner," I said. "I didn't explain things properly. A lot of things are changing for me. Learning about faith, setting up the new salon, the next few months will be crazy, and I think I need more time to break my old dating cycle. I'm not able to commit to a relationship just now. I need to figure out who I am and where I'm going."

"It's fine, really," she said, a beautiful smile lighting up her face. "Turns out you were right. I think I also need a break from dating. Plus, I don't know what's going to come from this mess at work."

"But, having said all that, and not wanting to skip out on what I need to learn, I would like to add that I am completely captivated by you, Kirsty Price. And I wouldn't be at all surprised if part of that is because of all the accidents, misunderstandings and everything else we've been through. I've got so much to learn, but I'm hoping you will be part of it all with me."

"I like the sound of all that. I'm glad we're friends, and who knows maybe it will become something else in the future. But right now it's lovely having you here as a great friend who gives the best hugs." As she spoke, she stepped forwards and initiated a hug.

That one action was all I needed to confirm there was hope for our future.

Eventually I let go of Kirsty, kissed her on her forehead and smiled goodbye. I joined Matt downstairs, grinning like a Cheshire cat.

"Something you want to share?" asked Matt.

The smile didn't leave my face.

"What's with that big stupid grin? What have you done?"

"Nothing! Just looking forward to a lifetime with the future Mrs Smith."

Matt laughed. "Only you could find the woman of your dreams in a non-dating stage of life!"

"Yeah, funny that."

"And have you made your feelings known to the woman in question?"

"Kind of. But, for now, it's all about friendship. I still need a bit of time but, more importantly, so does she. She needs all the support we can give her as she deals with the Gary situation." As I talked to Matt, I realised how much I had changed over the last few months. Was this the first time I'd been aware of how the girl felt and what she needed? It probably was, and it felt good.

The next few weeks would be busy with setting up the new salon. There would be long hours working at ByDesign during the day and preparing the new salon in the evenings. This wasn't the time to pursue an important relationship. But over these next few weeks I would be spending time with Kirsty. Enjoying the process of becoming friends. And covering it all was a pervading sense of peace. *'And the peace of God, which transcends all understanding, will guard your hearts and your minds in Christ Jesus.'*

The next morning as I walked to work I prayed for Kirsty. Today would be a difficult day for her, but I knew she could do it. I smiled at all the office workers wearing their raincoats and sunglasses. In the sea of beige there would be a beautiful woman standing out from the crowd in her pink raincoat. Raincoats and sunglasses didn't need to be boring.

Kirsty

Monday morning dawned a beautiful bright, sunny day, with a hint of a red sky. It was the perfect day to wear my gorgeous new pink raincoat. There was still a shadow of dread in the unknown before me. I wasn't sure if HR would believe me or take Gary's side. Irene had been incredibly supportive when I spoke to her last night, it was strange to be walking into a work situation with Irene on my side. She even suggested we meet at the office reception so I wouldn't need to walk into the department and face Gary on my own. I had no idea what lay ahead of me for today, but faith and friendship gave me the strength to take each step.

My phone pinged to signal a new text message: "Be courageous in pink!" Paul really did know how to cheer me on.

I said a prayer of thanks for Paul, and for God's perfect plan. A plan that looked so much better than anything

I could have dreamt up. Today would not be easy but I had faith on my side, and the love of an amazing group of friends.

My thought returned to the verse: '*Love never fails*', I was beginning to understand it now. Over the weekend I had experienced that kind of love through the words of my Bible and the actions of my friends. I would cling to those words today. Love was no longer some elusive emotion that only caused fear. It was a thing of beauty that I could be confident in.

I buttoned up my new pink raincoat and put on my sunglasses. I was nervous, but ready...

The End

Bible Verses:

Love never fails
1Corinithians 13:8 NIV

Perfect love drives out fear
1John 4:18 NIV

You make known to me the path of life; you will fill me with joy in your presence.
Psalm 16:11 NIV

And the peace of God, which transcends all understanding, will guard your hearts and your minds in Christ Jesus.
Phillipians 4:7 NIV

Acknowledgements

"It takes a village to raise a child" is an African proverb. It's one that I feel also relates to writing a book!

I am so incredibly grateful to everyone who has contributed to the completion of Raincoats & Sunglasses.

Innes for non-stop encouragement. Calum, Cameron and Cara for having no hesitation in calling me a writer! And for Calum's work on author graphics.

The team of lovely first readers who waded through all my mistakes to help craft a professional offering: Fran, David, Ian, Lorna, Eleanor, Mark, Innes and Tara. Thank you so much.

My musical friends Scott and Ellyn. Thanks for being part of this project and for the amazing music. Why not find out more about these two great artists?

www.scottnicol.us

www.ellynoliver.com

Tanya Rochat for the beautiful cover. I've known for years you were the artist for the task.

www.tanyarochat.com

And thank you to you the reader for buying this book and encouraging an aspiring author.

Keep In Touch

Check out my website for further information and my online shop. Why not sign up to receive regular newsletters?

www.carolinejohnston.co.uk

Follow me on Facebook or Twitter for updates and news:

www.facebook.com/carolinejohnstonauthor

www.twitter.com/author_caroline